A Streetful of People

A Streetful of People

by

Winston M. Estes

J. B. LIPPINCOTT COMPANY

Philadelphia / New York

F
Es

U. S. Library of Congress Cataloging in Publication Data

Estes, Winston M   birth date
  A streetful of people.

  I. Title.
PZ4.E794St   [PS3555.S8]   813'.5'4   71-38307
ISBN-0-397-00768-X

Diu 3.81

For Bryan Hawley Estes

Contents

Take any streetful of people buying clothes and groceries, cheering a hero or throwing confetti. . . .

CARL SANDBURG

A Streetful of People

1.

~~

Judge Crawford and His Friends, Including the Governor

To call Judge Crawford a drunkard wouldn't be fair, for he got drunk only on special occasions, and those occasions were relatively few. Christmas, Armistice Day, Thanksgiving, the Fourth of July and Texas Independence Day just about accounted for the regular stops on his happiness schedule—if you didn't count the first Tuesday in November every fourth year when he celebrated his re-election to the bench, although he had not been opposed at the polls in over thirty-five years. All other special occasions were one-shot affairs: his children's weddings, his grandchildren's baptisms, his wife's hysterectomy, and Sam Abernathy's tragic hole in one when he was playing the course alone without another living creature in sight. In other words, the Judge didn't drink just to be drinking; he drank only when there was something to drink about.

Yet, no one thought to predict that on the day the Governor of the State of Texas came to town, the Official Greeter, His Honor himself, Everett Philander Crawford, County Judge, would go on the granddaddy of all binges. According to reliable estimates, his glorious toot on that day set the temperance movement back ten years, maybe twenty. The occasion turned out to be so special that certain of his friends have been commemorating it each year ever since.

Had the Official Greeter been anyone else, the situation might have been tidied up by substituting a less prominent and more sober citizen. That, however, is as iffy as speculating on the number of fish you might catch in Pease River if it had any water in it. The Judge and the Governor had enjoyed a close and personal friendship that went back to their college roommate days, and the Governor had agreed to a twenty-minute stop-off on his campaign trip only for old times' sake and as a favor to the Judge. Under the circumstances, then, it was unthinkable that the town's official greetings could be extended by a pinch hitter.

But there was yet another consideration. No one but the Judge could hope to get away with the program he had arranged for the Governor's brief visit. As planned, the high-school band would open the ceremony with two choruses of "The Eyes of Texas," followed by the high-school glee club's arrangement of "Beautiful, Beautiful Texas." The sixteen-year-old Ida Bell Clifton then would present a bouquet of American Beauty roses to the Governor's lady. After that, Judge Crawford would deliver the Official Welcome in a carefully timed four-minute speech. With that out of the way, he would be joined on the platform by delegates from the local civic clubs, who would present a ceremonial scroll to the Governor. This would leave exactly five minutes for the Governor to say whatever was in his heart and on his mind, a built-in limitation to keep him from talking the entire twenty minutes the train was in the station. Only the Judge could keep that kind of show on the track and on schedule, for the distinguished guest of honor was surely the windiest chief executive ever to guide the affairs of the Lone Star State.

The day was a scorcher—110 degrees at one o'clock—without a cloud in the sky. The squat, square huddle of houses and buildings that made up the town cooked in the sun, a bump on the flat landscape, a speck against the immense sky. A parching wind blew in off the prairie, gathering up whirlwinds here and laying down heat mirages there as it crossed the flatlands unimpeded. It whipped the brick and cinder-block structures along Main Street with determination, hot enough to blister your face in the shade and wither the petunias on the windowsills. Whether you were outdoors or in, there was no escaping it. Nevertheless, the town put on its holiday clothes and gave itself up to a festive spirit. Holiday flags lined the curbs, and a gigantic streamer welcoming the Governor flapped in the wind across Main Street down by the depot.

From the four corners of the county and from towns twenty and thirty miles away, men, women and children came to see the Governor. They wore their Sunday clothes, brought their picnic lunches, carried parasols and Kodaks and left their worries at home. By noon, all the parking spaces around Court House Square had been filled. The people milled about on the sidewalks, moving up and down looking in store windows, dropping in to finger the merchandise, use the telephone and go to the bathroom. They visited happily with one another on the curbs and swatted at their children, who chased one another around lampposts, jumped off car fenders, pestered their parents for money and all but wore out the plumbing in the City Hall and courthouse rest rooms.

Had it not been for the flags and the welcoming streamer, the day could have been like a busy, prosperous Saturday, except for the unfortunate circumstance that nobody bought anything. They had come to see the Governor, not to shop. So they strolled back and forth, up and down, in and out, waiting for the train to come in. Mr. Hudgins at the City

Drug Store claimed that if everyone to whom he gave a drink of water had bought a five-cent Coke instead, he could have retired by sundown. Callie Davis at Delsey Jacobs' Drygoods Store said she didn't know when she had ever enjoyed a workday so much. All she did was lean on the glove counter at the front of the store, watch people go by, and visit with those who stopped in to get out of the heat or to pass the time of day. White's Auto Store advertised a "Governor's Day Special" on rearview mirrors, but nobody paid any attention to it. Ennis Grissom at the Eatmore Bakery filled his window with Texas-shaped sugar cookies, but his price was too high, and he had to put them on Special the next day. Mr. Akers, alone among the merchants, turned the occasion to his own financial ends; he rolled his popcorn machine out onto the sidewalk in front of his Variety Store and sold popcorn as fast as he could sack it. Mr. Hudgins blamed Mr. Akers' popcorn rather than the 110-degree temperature for the gush of free water from his soda fountain.

At a few minutes after twelve, Marvin Cross returned from dinner and took up his customary station at the bottom of the stairs that led to his real-estate office at the top. It was an enclosed stairwell that separated Akers' Variety Store from the City Drug Store. Marvin transacted more business on the sidewalk at the foot of those stairs than he did in his office above. Or so it seemed. If his stenographer, Geneva Caldwell, needed him, or if someone wanted to speak to him on the telephone, she yelled down the stairwell at him. Sometimes he responded; sometimes he did not. It depended on how engrossed he might be with the comings and goings of his fellow townsmen along the dusty two blocks that was downtown Main Street.

On this particular day, he was standing idly, picking his teeth, watching people go by and wondering why Jean Harlow's husband shot himself, when his attention was nailed by a barrel-shaped stomach followed by a blue seersucker suit and topped by a wide-brimmed straw hat coming around the corner by the City Drug Store. It was Judge Crawford, five feet, five inches tall, affable as a used-car salesman and friendly as a lapdog. That in itself was nothing unusual, but the fact that he could not navigate the corner without bumping into it was.

With suspicions growing, Marvin watched the Judge push against the brick wall to shove himself back on course and make his unsteady way head on into a cluster of teen-aged girls. Giggling and chattering, they broke ranks to let him through. With a politician's smile, he tipped his hat chivalrously and bowed as deeply as his short, pudgy body would permit.

The Judge was stewed.

"Why, hello there, Marv!" he shouted as he came to within focusing distance. "You got on a clean shirt to meet the Governor? Haw-haw-haw!"

Marvin didn't reply. He stared at the tubby figure weaving toward him, unwilling to believe what he now knew to be true. In panic, he glanced at his watch. It was twelve-fifteen. The Governor's train was due in at two-thirty. He studied the Judge and sized up his condition with alarm. He figured that if the Judge were to spend the next two hours under a cold shower drinking hot coffee, he'd still be seeing double when the train rolled in. The situation had all the potentials of a disaster. The Governor of the State . . . the influential officials accompanying him . . . the crowds . . . the photographers . . . the reporters . . . the raised platform and unobstructed view . . . the Official Greeter who couldn't hit the ground with his hat. . . .

Marvin was no politician, and he had no political stake in the Governor's visit, but he was a responsible citizen with civic pride—lots of it—and his immediate concern was for the

County Judge's personal reputation and the town's public image. His duty, as he saw it, was to protect both. After all, the Judge was an honorable, respected public servant who, if the truth were known, toppled from grace no more frequently than many of his neighbors. It was just that his falls had a way of making more noise and attracting more attention than most. Those who did not understand this might be less than sympathetic to the Judge's unfortunate and misguided desire to relax on this, of all days.

Marvin tried to think his way through the messy problem that had careened its way into his presence. He shuddered. The Judge yelled across the street at someone he thought he recognized and took in after him. Marvin chased him down, grabbed him by the arm and pulled him back onto the curb and across the sidewalk to the foot of the stairs.

"Had your dinner yet, Judge?" he asked, exaggerating his concern and stalling until he could figure out what to do.

"Had my dinner yet? Haw-haw-haw!" The Judge had lost interest in whoever it was across the street. "You know what I had for dinner, Marv?" he asked. "Just take a guess. Come on, Marv—see if you can guess." He tapped Marvin on the chest. "Well—I'll tell you—'cause you'll never guess it. I had a Nehi Grape and one of those little packages of peanut butter and crackers that comes in those machines. You put a nickel in the slot and push the little valve down and the—and the—music goes round and round HO-HO-OH-OHHHHH-HHHHHHH–AND IT COMES OUT HERE!"

Marvin clapped a hand over the Judge's mouth.

"Watch it, Judge!" he hissed nervously. "You want everybody in town to see you like this?" He grabbed his arm and turned him away from an approaching group of citizens whose eyes had already begun to widen.

The Judge was unconcerned. "You know what, Marv? I had to borrow a nickel from big, fat Marcella Overton. She was coming down the hall—that goddam machine won't take a dollar bill. Did you know that? Well, it is most certainly the truth. I stuffed and I stuffed and that dollar bill wouldn't go in. I tore up a whole dollar bill—one hundred cents—tore it all to hell in that machine—big, fat Marcella had to take one of her big, fat bobby pins and fish out the pieces. . . ."

Marvin wasn't listening. He was keeping an anxious eye on the passing people, too many of whom were more than casually interested in the happy little scene being played at the foot of the stairs.

"Why don't we just sit down here on the stairs a minute, Judge?" he suggested kindly. "It's too hot to be standing around on the sidewalk. Come on, let's get out of this heat and up where it's cool."

Judge Crawford thought that was a splendid idea, and he was grateful for it. Lovingly and tearfully, he was grateful. He smiled at Marvin through misty, bloodshot eyes and clasped his hand with feeling.

"Now you know, Marv, that's right kind of you to think about me like that," he said, a catch in his voice. "Right kind, indeed it is. Yes it is, indeed. Lena made me wear my coat today—she said I had to wear it to meet the Governor. I told her I'd just carry it along and put it on before train time, and do you know what she said? She said, 'No, you wear it all day, or you'll go off and leave it somewhere and won't have it when the train comes in.' As a matter of fact, I was on my way somewhere to sit down and take off this coat and cool off—that's where I was going when that goddam drug store jumped out at me . . . I think I'll speak to Frank Hudgins about that brick wall. I'll bet it violates every building code in town by sticking out too far. Wanna bet?"

"Everybody in town runs into that wall all the time," Marvin said helpfully. "Now why don't we—"

"AND IT COMES OUT HERE! HO-HO-OH-OHHH-

HHHHHHHHH-oh!"

Marvin had spun the Judge around and aimed him at the stairs.

"What th—"

"Upsy-daisy, your Honor!" said Marvin. He shoved him up into the stairwell onto the first step.

"But Marv, I—"

"You want to sit down, don't you?" said Marvin, pushing from behind and below. He pushed him to the second step, then the third. "Now get on up—that's right—up, up, *up* you go!"

The Judge did not resist, but neither did he help. Marvin was running out of breath.

"One more," he panted. "Upsy—upsy—NOW!"

One third the distance to the top, and the Judge was safely out of public view. Marvin allowed him to sit down.

"Excuse me, Judge," he said, after settling him at an angle to preclude his tumbling back down onto the sidewalk. "Just sit here a minute and cool yourself off. I gotta see somebody —it'll only take a second."

"But listen, Marv—"

But Marv didn't listen. He leaped to the foot of the stairs and across the few feet of sidewalk to where Mr. Akers was blessing the popcorn with the salt shaker, waving it back and forth, up and down, then in a circle. He looked up at Marvin and smiled.

"Sack of popcorn, Marv?"

"Listen, Mr. Akers, go call Sam Abernathy quick and tell him to get over here as fast as he can!"

Mr. Akers raked up a scoopful of popcorn, filled a paper sack, twisted the top, set it aside and reached for another.

"Why don't you go call him yourself?" he said to the inside of the popcorn machine.

Marvin ignored the question.

"Tell him to come in his car," he added. "We might need it. Tell him it's an emergency and to get here pronto."

"Somebody sick, Marv?"

"Not yet—but they're gonna be if we don't act fast—*real* fast."

Sam Abernathy, the County Tax Collector, was Judge Crawford's closest friend, over Lena Crawford's objections and despite her contention that her husband's personal associates were beneath him. She claimed that Sam brought out the crude and irreverent side of the Judge's nature. The Judge agreed. That was why he liked Sam and enjoyed his company.

With Sam he could cuss in an ungentlemanly fashion, the only way either of them knew how to do it; Sam understood a decent amount of cheating at cards and a reasonable amount of fudging on the golf course. What was more, he was always available, willing and cooperative when a special occasion needed celebrating. They went fishing together on Sundays and blamed one another's unholy influence for keeping them away from church. For seventeen years they had played a single game of gin rummy. With the score standing at 3,236,-428 to 3,236,415, they grew tired of the game and quit. When Sam tried to collect thirteen cents as victor, the Judge accused him of an error in his addition. They got into an awful wrangle about it, but rechecking the figures was so tedious that neither of them would consent to do it. Rather, they resumed the game, and it had been going on ever since, score and all.

So when Marvin Cross sent for Sam Abernathy, he did it with a complete awareness that Sam might have been where the Judge had been and doing what the Judge had been doing. It was a calculated risk. If he lost, his problem would be exactly doubled. In that event, he decided, he might just run out to Smokey Rainwater's Tavern, down a few of his own and triple the problem—for somebody else. Meanwhile, he could do little but keep his fingers crossed and wait.

He returned to the stairwell to find that Judge Crawford had removed his seersucker coat and his necktie and at the moment was fumbling with the buttons on his blue-striped shirt. He had two more to go.

"Whoa there, Judge! Keep your shirt on!" Marvin exclaimed in a fit of simulated laughter.

The Judge caught on. "Haw-haw-haw! Keep your shirt on! That's pretty good, Marv—pretty goddam good! Did I ever tell you about the old maid who sawed the legs off her bed to keep men from hiding under it? Haw-haw-haw!"

Marvin laughed appreciatively and dusted off a few oldies of his own to entertain the Judge until Sam could arrive and decide what to do. He had purged himself of all Little Morons, Little Audreys and had worked his way down to a feeble Pat and Mike story when Sam pulled up and double-parked out front on Main Street. Main Street was narrow. Too narrow, and no one knew why. Probably not even the town designers, though they could have quadrupled the width of the street and the surrounding prairie wouldn't have missed the space. Nevertheless, the street would accommodate only two lanes of traffic, one in each direction, and to make matters worse, it was hemmed in on both sides by foolishly high curbs. So high, in fact, that cars driving along the pavement seemed to be moving through a concrete trough.

Sam Abernathy got out of his automobile and stepped up onto the curb and across the sidewalk.

"What's up, Marv?" he called out, squinting up the stairs into the semidarkness. "Mr. Akers said that—"

The Judge came into focus.

"Oh, no!" Sam slapped his own forehead. "Not today! Please, dear Lord, no, no, *no!*"

Anxiously, Marvin studied Sam's face and manner. He was grateful to see that he was as sober as—a judge?

[*24*]

The Judge was delighted to see his old friend the County Tax Collector. He waved a fat hand at him and let go with a whoop and a holler.

"Well, well, Sam, you ole fart—what in the hell are you doing here?" he yelled. "Come on up and sit down! Marv's got his own private place where his own private breeze blows down from his own private above—'cept it doesn't seem to be blowing right this very minute. We're just sitting here cooling off. Come on up and sit down! Marv, tell Sam that joke you told me about—"

"Look here, Ev," said Sam severely, excitement coming on in one tremendous surge. "How come you went out and got yourself crocked like this? Don't you know you're supposed to meet the Governor in less than two hours?"

"Now, now, don't you worry about the Governor," said the Judge. "He's an ole fart too—just like you are. The Governor's the biggest ole fart in the Lone Star State . . . and when the train pulls in, I'll tell him so—that's what I told him the last time I saw him. It was down in San Antonio. I said, 'Listen here, you ole fart. . . .'"

Sam and Marvin stared at the Judge, then at one another.

"What do you think?" asked Marvin.

"Looks like we got a problem on our hands," replied Sam.

"That's why I called you. He can't get up on a speaking platform like this—not in front of the Governor and everybody in the county." He smiled gratefully at Sam. "I'm sure glad you weren't with him."

"I wish I had been," he said. "Then I wouldn't have to figure out what to do." He shook his head in wonderment. "How in the hell could he get *this* drunk before noon? He must of started right after breakfast. Did you see him around town before this?"

"Not until he came around the corner by the drug store and bumped into it. Do you think maybe we oughta take

[25]

him home and let him sleep it off?"

"We haven't got time."

"He could sleep part of it off."

"That won't do. Once we get him in the sack, we'll never get him out again. Anyway, Lena will blame me for getting him drunk. She always does."

"How about the hotel?"

"That won't do, either. Mrs. Boyd will broadcast it all over town. We don't want anybody knowing about it. It'll cause a big scandal if they do."

"How about the Alamo Rooming House?"

The Judge stirred. "They got bedbugs at the Alamo Room—"

"You keep outa this, Ev," Sam said over his shoulder. "That won't do, Marv. We'd have to rent a whole room for a whole week."

"Maybe not. We ought to be able to get a room for a couple of hours."

"Yeah? You don't know Lovey Jordan like I do, then. She'd charge us for a whole week and make us put up a key deposit to boot."

"Rhoda Fryer's cathouse—"

"Be quiet, Ev!" Sam snapped. "You know, Marv, I think Dice Riley's got a cot in that little loft over the back end of his store, don't he?"

"I don't know. He used to. I haven't been up there in a long time."

"Why don't we see if we can't—"

"Hey, Sam!"

It was lanky, long Artie Whelan, the County Sheriff, wearing his best and cleanest five-gallon hat and his biggest and shiniest star, the one he wore only on holidays and ceremonial occasions. He was standing on the sidewalk at the foot of the stairs.

"You gotta come out and move your car, Sam," he called out. "It's blocking traffic."

Sam was studying the Judge, who was stiff as a poker, stretched out straight and slanted at the exact downward angle of the stairs. What kept him from sliding down onto the sidewalk, Sam couldn't imagine.

"Can't do it right now, Artie," he replied, not taking his eyes off the Judge. "I'm busy."

"That don't matter," said Artie. "Traffic's getting tied up both ways. You'll have to come move it."

"I told you I haven't got time, Artie! Look, Marv, suppose we—"

"And I told you that don't matter," Artie persisted. "I'm gonna give you a ticket if you don't move it, Sam—I'm warning you!"

"Aw, knock it off, Artie!" Sam exploded. "Can't you see I got problems?"

Artie stepped up into the stairwell and craned his neck around Sam Abernathy's rear end. "What's so all-fired important that—"

The Judge by now had succeeded in removing his blue-striped shirt.

"Jeez!" breathed Artie. "He's pie-eyed!"

"You ain't just bird-turdin'."

"Don't he have to meet the Governor at two-thirty?"

"Hell, yes! That's what the problem is."

"Whatcha gonna do with him?"

"Sober him up if we can—and keep him outta sight until we do."

"What if you can't?"

"I dunno. We'll worry about that later. Right now, we're thinking about laying him out in Dice Riley's loft up over the back end of his store."

"Dice Riley's *loft?* You can't do that!" said Artie. "It's

a hundred and forty degrees up there! Dice don't hardly go up there himself in the summertime."

"Tough," said Sam. "Maybe the heat will cook some of the whiskey out of him."

They turned their attention again to the Judge. He was skinning out of his undershirt. He had pulled it up to his fat, pink shoulders. Marvin dived at him and pulled it down.

"Watch it, Judge! Who do you think you are? Sally Rand? Don't you know you can't take off your clothes right here on Main Street?"

"It's hot, Marv!" complained the Judge.

"Well, it's not *that* hot. You want Artie to arrest you for indecent exposure?"

He picked up the soggy blue-striped shirt and unwadded it.

"Now look what you did to your shirt!" He held it by the collar and shook it. "Put this on," he commanded. "Even the County Judge ought to know you can't sit around downtown in your undershirt."

"I'd sit here naked, if y'all'd let me," mumbled the Judge. "This is the hottest goddam spot this side of the Mexican border. And you told me it was cool up here, Marv!" He became wistful. "Do you want to know where it's cool? Well, I'll tell you. In the Rocky Mountains—that's where. The Rock—the big rock—in the Big Rock Candy Moun-tunnnnn-nnnnn! OH-HO-OHHHHHHHH...."

Marvin coaxed the Judge back into his shirt and stuffed the shirttail inside his belt. The Judge squirmed and giggled.

"Watch it there, Marv—hee-hee-hee—*watch out*, Marv! *Marv!* You know how ticklish I am—hee-hee-hee. Get your hands outta my pants, Marv, or I'll have the law on you! Hee-hee-hee! MARV!"

"Pipe down, your Honor," said Marvin, tugging and twisting at the sweating torso. "You want everybody in town to hear you? You've got to go meet the Governor. Remember?"

"The Governor's an ole fart—that's all he is."

Artie Whelan came on up the stairs. "I'll tell you one thing for sure," he said, shoving his hat to the back of his head and hooking his thumbs over the top of his belt. "If you put him in Dice Riley's loft, you're gonna French fry him."

"Yeah—I know," said Sam. "Come on and grab hold."

"I can't stay, Sam—busy day. Town's full of people."

"Aw, come on and grab hold, Artie! We haven't got all day!"

"But I'm supposed to be out there and—"

"Listen, Artie. If you don't help us get the Judge down to Dice's, I'm gonna swear out a complaint against him for disturbing the peace, and you'll have to arrest him and lock him up."

"The heat's making you loony, ain't it, Sam? I can't arrest the County Judge!"

"Okay—come on and give us a hand, then."

Artie looked back down the stairwell. Townie Ledbetter, who had been deaf and dumb since birth, was peering up into the stairwell making signals with his hands. Artie made a few signals back to him and returned to the problem at hand.

"Well, I don't know. . . ." he said, unconvinced. "Maybe just for a few minutes, but as soon as we get him down to Dice's, I gotta get back to my duties."

The Judge didn't want to be moved.

"Where we going?" he asked. "I just got here."

"We're going down the street where you can take a nap."

"I can take one here, if y'all'd just shut up and let me alone!"

"Come on, Ev—let's go," Sam ordered.

The Judge wouldn't go.

They coaxed him to his feet, but they couldn't move him from his tracks. Artie Whelan stood behind and above him; Sam Abernathy and Marvin Cross stood in front and below. They pushed, and they pulled. The Judge wouldn't budge.

"Goose him, Artie," Sam suggested.

Artie was reluctant.

"Jeez—I don't know, Sam."

"Go on and *goose* him—he's goosy as hell."

"Jeez—"

"GOOSE HIM!"

Artie goosed.

"*Yipes!* AR-TEEE!"

The Judge took off.

They overtook him on the sidewalk at the bottom of the stairwell.

He sank onto the bottom step, stretched out his legs and prepared to go to sleep. They pulled him to his feet before he could settle himself comfortably. They propped him against the wall and held him there. They straightened his clothes, then stopped for a little breather.

The Judge tried to free himself.

"If you boys will excuse me a minute," he said, "I believe I'll just get myself a little sack of popcorn. I didn't have much dinner today—"

Artie placed a big hand against the Judge's chest and pushed him back against the wall.

"No, you don't," he said. "You don't need no popcorn. Popcorn's too hot on a hot day like today."

"But all I had for dinner today was some peanut butter and crackers and—"

"—and a snootful of whiskey," Sam interrupted. "So just knock off all this arguing, Ev, and let's get outa here!"

"There's one little detail you boys overlooked," said the Judge.

"Yeah?"

"You didn't ask me if I wanted to go."

"We ain't playing 'May I?', you know."

"Maybe we ought to, then. I'm not sure I want to go down to Dice Riley's store, where—"

"Knock it off, Ev! Marv—grab hold and let's get going."

"But Sam, he said—"

"He said lots of things—come on. Let's go!"

With Marvin Cross tugging at one arm and Sam Abernathy the other, they moved the Judge away from the wall and turned him in the direction of the Fort Worth & Denver railroad tracks, the depot, and perforce, Riley's Grocery & Market. He resisted, but he was no match for the strength and determination of his deliverers. Especially after Sam Abernathy threatened to goose him again if he didn't start walking. Mr. Akers was standing on a chair pouring a new batch of unpopped corn into the top of the machine and couldn't spare the time to wonder what was going on.

Artie followed at the trio's heels, hissing them on faster.

"Don't walk so slow," he told them. "If you don't keep him moving, he'll fall flat on his face."

They quickened their pace. The taller men on either side of the Judge—Sam was six feet tall; Marvin was one inch taller—were taking long strides that the Judge's short legs could not equal. His feet touched the ground only on alternate steps, sometimes not that often.

They marched through the business district along Main Street, past the Marvella Beauty Shop, past Dunlap Insurance Company, past a fly-by-night linen shop that had moved into a vacant store building long enough to stage a GIGANTIC CLOSE-OUT SALE! and past *The Weekly Courier*. They marched with their heads up and eyes straight ahead, ignoring the curious stares and friendly greetings of the people they met, including Sam's young son, Roland. They navigated their way past Delsey Jacobs' Drygoods Store to the corner of Second and Main, where Luther Hoyt was standing on the curb demonstrating his new dentures to Howard Slaton. They crossed Second Street.

On the other side, they lifted the Judge bodily onto the high curb and propelled him past White's Auto Store; past Big Moot Williams, part-time chicken plucker and full-time bootlegger, who stopped scanning the crowd for prospective customers and froze to rigid attention at the sight of Sheriff Whelan; past a group of Girl Scouts who attempted to sell them a pennant and a balloon, to the front door of Riley's Grocery & Market. Without breaking stride, they flung back the screen door and shoved the Judge into the store out of public view.

Mr. Riley, a gaunt, dreary gentleman in his sixties with a mole on his chin, a pair of rimless spectacles on his nose, and a triangular Adam's apple on his neck, was alone in the store swatting flies. With the swatter suspended in mid-swing above his head, he gaped at the foursome who had burst in off the street like an unruly gust of wind. His skinny arm descended slowly. He was unable to find his voice.

Dice Riley had been doing business in the same spot for so many years it had never crossed his mind that he might do it somewhere else, an airy location, say, where he could spread out and let the sunshine in. The store was as cramped, gloomy and depressing as its proprietor. Even when the daylight somehow managed to force its way through the musty front door and windows and the overhead lights were burning, the interior was dark and dingy. Never a great one for newfangled merchandising tricks and techniques, Mr. Riley didn't bother with catchy display racks, colorful posters, gay streamers and enticing advertisements. He hid his groceries in rows of cavernous shelves that could have accommodated John Deere farm implements and let the devil take the hindmost—if the devil could find it amid those dismal surroundings. All in all, Riley's Grocery & Market had the appeal and charm of a harness shed.

So, if Judge Crawford's friends wanted to put him in an out-of-the-way spot where he was unlikely to be disturbed by sightseers and idle curiosity seekers, they selected the ideal place. Nobody ever came into Riley's Grocery & Market for any reason, not even to buy groceries, unless they were habitual customers who settled up only on the first of the month, and sometimes not that often if they needed a new coat or felt a yen to reupholster the living-room sofa.

The Judge's friends steered him past the narrow, cluttered counter and the open-mouthed Mr. Riley, half explaining their intentions and actions as they moved.

"Lord-a-mercy!" Marvin exclaimed. "I don't see what keeps Dice's groceries from cooking in the cans! Haven't you got a fan in this place, Dice?"

"I got some of them cardboard fans from L. T. Ditmore's Funeral Home," said Mr. Riley, whose mind had not yet assimilated all that his eyes had taken in.

At the rear of the store, they pushed the Judge up a flight of plain, unpainted wooden steps to the loft above.

"It's mighty hot up there," Mr. Riley called after them. "Some of them fans are on the desk if you need to fan yourselfs."

"They claim the heat will be good for him," Artie called back.

"Is the Judge in pretty bad shape?"

"You ain't just bird—"

Riley's Grocery & Market was a one-story structure, and to make it two—after a fashion—the proprietor had built a compressed deck above the stock room. It was low and compact, with barely enough space from top to bottom to accommodate a person standing upright. There he did his bookkeeping on an ancient rolltop desk, filed his records in a battered tin cabinet, and stored his cash in a thousand-pound safe. A mammoth ladder-backed rocking chair sat at the top of the steps and a gas heater in a dark corner. Against the back wall was a canvas folding cot puffed high with a feather mattress and covered over with a dark wool patchwork quilt. There were no windows, and what light there was came from the store below and a single unshaded bulb dangling by a cord from the ceiling. What color the loft afforded came from an occasional red or blue patch on the wool quilt and from a Chambers Chevrolet calendar hung on the wall three years previously. The walls and the floor were in their original unpainted state, but the years had rendered them old and dingy, entirely in harmony with everything else in sight. Generally speaking, the loft had the atmosphere of a dirt dugout and the climate of a blast furnace.

"It's warm up here in the winter," Artie said.

"I don't doubt it," said Sam, unbuttoning his shirt.

They stripped the Judge of his coat and necktie and dumped him on the cot, where he all but sank from sight into the billowy feather bed and scratchy wool quilt.

"Jeez! He's gonna suffocate!" said Artie.

"That's his privilege," replied Sam.

They removed his shoes, socks and shirt, then wrestled him out of his wet, limp undershirt.

"How about his pants?" asked Marvin.

"If we don't get outta here, I'm gonna take *mine* off," Artie said.

"He's naked enough already," Sam decided.

Slick with perspiration, Judge Crawford resembled a fat red lobster in boiling water.

"Lord-a-mercy! There's not one breath of air up here!" Marvin said.

"Probably poison us if there was," said Sam.

They stared at the Judge.

"Maybe one of us ought to stay up here with him," Sam said. "Just in case he decides to leave, you see."

"I agree—as long as it's not me," said Artie, heading for the stairs.

"Me, too," Marvin said, mopping his face and unbuttoning his shirt. He followed Artie to the stairs.

Sam remained behind.

Down below, Mr. Riley, flyswatter poised for the next kill, watched Artie and Marvin stagger down the steps and to the front of the store.

"Did you find the fans?" he asked timidly. "Mr. Ditmore gave me a whole handful and said they's plenty more where they came from."

"He don't need no fan," said Artie. "The heat's gonna boil the whiskey outa him or it's gonna stew him to pieces—either one."

Mr. Riley shook his head in dismay. "It just don't look right for the County Judge to go around town drinking like that."

Sam came hurrying down the steps. He had reconsidered the necessity for standing watch over Judge Crawford.

"Phew! How in the hell can you stand it up there, Dice?" he exclaimed.

Mr. Riley swung at the air with the flyswatter. "I haven't been up there myself since it turned off hot like this," he said. "I reckon it must of been May—no, seems like it was April—the last of April, I reckon it was, since—"

He was interrupted by singing from on high.

"She was on-leeeeee a farmer's daugh-terrrrr . . .
And he was a city slick—"

"Oh, God!" Sam wailed. "Now he's gonna sing dirty songs."

Mr. Riley coughed nervously. "If he's singing dirty songs and some lady customer comes in—"

"You don't need to worry," said Artie. "They ain't nobody in the store but us."

"I know, but if they *was* to be a lady come in and—"

"If a lady comes in, I'll go up and hold my hand over the Judge's mouth."

"You know, Sam, we ought to do something about that

shirt and coat," Marvin said thoughtfully. "They look like they came out from under a rock. That won't look so good up there with the Governor and all."

"Yeah—you're right. . . ." Sam bit his lip and rubbed his chin. "Why don't you run down and get Delsey Jacobs to press out the wrinkles?"

"Maybe we ought to go out to his house and get him some clean clothes."

"Naw—we can't do that. Lena will raise holy hell and stick her nose into things and louse us up. Go on and see if Delsey has still got his steam up."

Marvin pulled himself up the stairs, his steps lagging. They didn't lag coming down, though. He made it in two leaps. He was carrying Judge Crawford's blue seersucker coat and his blue-striped shirt. He shook his head.

"He's not going to make it," he said. "I don't care what anybody says—he's plain not going to make it." He fanned himself with the Judge's shirt. "He'll die with heat stroke before he sobers—"

"'. . . and she cast a airty smirch
On the lit-tle village church,
And her pappy turned her pic-ture to the wall. . . . '"

"If a lady customer comes in. . . ."

Marvin hurried out the door.

"Maybe we oughta bathe his face in ice water," Sam said. "You got any ice, Dice?"

"Not what you'd call ice exactly. But the soda-pop cooler's got ice water in it—electrified ice water. It's got coils in the bottom of—"

"'. . . to the wallllllllll,
Tew the wallllllllll,
And her pappy turned her pic-ture to the wallllll.'"

"Lady customers come in here all the time. . . ."

"Get a pan full of ice water, then, and a rag—let's go see what we can do. Maybe we can shut him up."

Artie glanced out onto the street. Automobiles were lined up bumper to bumper. None seemed to be moving.

"Lookit them cars!" he exclaimed. "I oughta be out on the street performing my duties instead of wet-nursing a—"

"Duties hell!" said Sam. "We gotta get the Judge sober."

"I didn't get him drunk."

"Neither did I, but we still got to get him sober. How much time we got?"

Mr. Riley looked up from the soda-pop cooler and at the clock on the wall above the meat counter.

"One hour and forty minutes," he replied.

"Jeez! And we got a six-hour job on our hands!"

"That's how long it takes to drive from here to Seymour," Mr. Riley added.

"Six *hours?*"

"No—one hour and forty min—"

"Hurry up with that water, Dice!"

Mr. Riley was staring down into the ice water, trying to figure out who put all that cream soda in the cooler. Must have been an entire case.

After much clanging and scraping, he came up from the rear of the store carrying a two-gallon galvanized bucket half filled with water.

"Don't look very clean," he apologized.

"Don't worry about that none," said Artie.

They looked into the bucket. The water was murky, but it was ice cold.

"This is the only thing I got to put it in—it's the mop bucket—"

"The Judge won't know what it comes out of," said Artie.

He took the bucket from Mr. Riley and followed Sam up the steps.

Mr. Riley returned to his flies.

> "... and she drank up all the gin
> And went out with traveling men;
> And her pappy turned her pic-ture to the wall."

Mr. Riley peered nervously at the people passing on the sidewalk out front. "I just hope none of them ladies. . . ."

> "At the least romantic glance
> She dropped her silken pants
> And her pappy turned her pic-ture to the walllll."

Mr. Riley turned pale.

"Ow-*oh*—ow-*weeeeeee!* Get that cold rag offa me!"

"Just shut up and lay still, Ev!"

"Wow-WEEEEEEEEEE! Whatcha trying to do—freeze me?"

"Wring this out, Artie. Get back on the cot, Ev—get back before I bust you one right in the teeth!"

"Wow! Ouch! Watch—whoa!"

"Be still, Ev, *dammit!*"

"Aw—WOW—get that goddam ice bag off my titties!"

"Oh, my!" Mr. Riley ran to the front door and looked out.

Marvin came in off the sidewalk empty-handed, wiping his face with his handkerchief.

"I believe it's as hot in here as it is out there," he said. "Delsey says he'll bring the clothes himself when he gets them pressed. He said he saw the Judge at the post office about ten o'clock this morning trying to put a stamp on a letter. Jack Goodnight had to do it for him." He held his handkerchief by two corners and flapped it through the air. "How're they doing up there in the oven?"

"Well—if you want to know the truth, it don't look too good. He's singing dirty little songs and saying some *awful* things! I never heard the likes in my *life!*"

"Hey, Dice!" It was Sam leaning over the railing of the loft. "Call Calvin Turnbough and tell him to get down here with some hot black coffee," he yelled. "And tell him to bring it himself and not to send it by anybody else."

"He might be too busy, Sam. Cafes are always busy when they's a big crowd in town like today."

"Just call him, Dice, and don't argue."

Mr. Riley turned to the telephone by the cash register. Miss Eunice Horton, telephone operator, came on the line.

"Number, please?"

"What's the Little Gem Cafe's number, Eunice?"

"Don't you have a book?"

"I can't find it."

"Well—you're supposed to call Information if you don't know the number."

"That's you, ain't it?"

Miss Eunice was no pushover. She had been around. She had made her living for years selling foundation garments to ladies By Appointment Only in the privacy of their own homes. That is, until one day she called to keep an appointment with Mrs. Otis Bailey, society editor of *The Weekly Courier*, who met her in the front hall, naked as the day she was born, ready and waiting to try on samples. Whereupon, Miss Eunice went pale, marched out of the house, bought up her own samples, turned in her franchise, resigned from the firm and got herself a job at the telephone company the next day. Miss Eunice Horton was nobody's fool. She knew how to deal with the likes of Dice Riley.

"All right, Dice," she said sternly. "Just this one time, but no more. From now on when you want to know somebody's number, you'd sure better ask for Information, or you just might not get it!"

She gave Dice the number he wanted.

Marvin Cross checked his watch and shouted, "Hey, you

[*39*]

guys! We just got an hour and ten minutes!"

"Jeez!" Artie moaned.

Marvin rejoined Artie and Sam in the loft, where they were mopping the Judge's face and chest with dirty water from the mop bucket. Sam stood up straight and mopped his own face with the rag.

"This water's getting too warm," he said. "He's not yelling any more."

As a matter of fact, Judge Crawford was not doing anything. His eyes were closed, and his face wore a benevolent expression, the kind he wore when he acquitted prisoners at the bar.

"Look at that, will you?" said Sam. "Out like a light."

"That's what we put him to bed for, ain't it?" Artie asked.

"I guess so—look, Marv. How about taking the bucket and getting some new ice water?"

"Go get it yourself," Marvin said, dropping into the rocking chair. "I'm pooped. P-o-o-p-e-d. It's at least two hundred degrees out on the sidewalk."

"I think I'll go out and cool off, then," Artie said.

Marvin unbuttoned his sweat-soaked shirt and fanned himself with one of Mr. Ditmore's cardboard fans. Artie staggered across the loft and joined him.

"Jeez! I'm wet as a dishrag," he said, dropping onto the top step. "I oughta get me some short underwear."

"You wear long handles *in the summer?*" Marvin inquired.

"They're summer-weight—made outta cotton. They're two piece, and the bottoms are—"

"Here, Artie—go get some new ice water." Sam was standing over him holding out the mop bucket.

"I gotta get back outside, Sam—honest, I have! All that traffic on the—*holy cow!*" He slapped a hand to his forehead. "I clean forgot about your car out in front of Akers'!" He groaned. "I just *gotta* go out and see about *that!* Give me your keys, Sam, and I'll move it myself."

"You can't run off and leave us with the Judge like this. We've got to get him sober and down to the depot."

"I ought to put him in jail."

"Yeah—you ought. Why don't you do that? We'll turn him over to you, whiskey breath, fat stomach and all, and you can lock him up until time to meet the Governor—hey, Dice! How about bringing us some more ice water?"

But Mr. Riley was talking on the telephone.

"I know, Calvin," he was saying, "but Sam says this is a real emergency. They don't want anybody else in town to know about it . . . well . . . I don't know . . you'll have to ask him . . . *I already tole you three times*! Sam said bring it yourself, and that's all I know. . . ."

Artie descended the steps lugging the galvanized bucket.

"I oughta be outside," he complained. "I haven't—*Jeez!* Lookit all them cars; I'll bet they're backed up across the tracks clean out to the cemetery."

"They're not moving very fast," Mr. Riley observed. "I been looking out the window at Velma Agnew sittin' in her car for a long time now. Don't look like she's moved more than a foot in the last—hold still, Artie—"

He moved toward the sheriff and swatted at his head. The sheriff dodged.

"Oh," said Mr. Riley, disappointed. "It got away."

"Where's the soda-pop cooler, Dice?"

Mr. Riley waved his flyswatter toward the rear of the store. "Back there by the door," he said.

Artie went to refill the mop bucket.

Calvin Turnbough arrived with the hot coffee. Calvin was a large man, on the beefy side, pleasant enough in manner and appearance but, for some people's taste, a bit too ready with the advice and counsel. Back in his youth he had worked his passage to Panama on a banana boat and claimed the experience had taught him how to keep cool in the hottest of weather.

"Whew! You can fry an egg on that sidewalk outside," he said. He placed the carton of coffee on the counter and wiped his face with his handkerchief. "When are you going to put a fan in this place, Dice?"

"Bothers my sinus."

"You can put a thirty-inch blower in the rear, and it'll circulate the air."

Artie emerged from the gloom, mop bucket and new water in hand.

"The air in this store is the same air that was in it last week," he grumbled. "Dice ain't had any new air in this store since spring."

"Oh—hello, Artie," Calvin said. "Looks like you got a traffic problem outside. Some car is probably stalled up the street. You might oughta go take a look and see what you can do. Cars are backed up across the tracks."

"Why, thank you kindly, Calvin," said Artie. "That's mighty nice advice. There ain't anything wrong with that traffic that a coupla sticks of dynamite won't take care of."

"I been lookin' at Velma Agnew since—"

"Dice, why don't you put that soda-pop cooler up front where people can find it?" Artie interrupted. "They ain't nobody gonna go scratching around the mops and brooms looking for a soda pop."

"They know where it is—them that wants any soda pop."

"But what if they don't?"

"They *do*, though, Artie! That's what I'm trying to tell you!"

Calvin walked back to the front door and opened his shirt to the outside air.

"Business good at your place, Calvin?" asked Dice.

"You'd think it was," said Calvin over his shoulder. "That is, if you'd count all the people and not look too close at what they're doing. A while ago, I looked down the counter and there wasn't an empty stool. Not one. There were two cups of coffee in sight, and that's all. Everybody was just sitting around talking. Ruby Fletcher didn't have anything to do. Not a thing. Can you imagine that? Most of the booths were full, and *all* the counter space was taken, and the waitress didn't have anything to do but lean against the dessert cabinet and make goo-goo eyes through the kitchen door at Shorty Mayfield."

"Shorty Mayfield? I heard you fired him last week."

"That was last week."

"It seems like you fire him an awful lot, Calvin."

"Well, you know how it is when—"

"Come on with that coffee, Calvin," Artie called back as he struggled up the steps with the bucket of water.

Mr. Riley looked doubtfully at the cardboard carton on the counter. "It's mighty hot weather for hot coffee, ain't it?"

"That's what you told me to bring, isn't it?"

"I reckon so. I don't drink much coffee myself. Not any more. Gives me heartburn. I drink one cup at breakfast with cream and no sugar. I used to put sugar in—"

"Wow—ow—wow-*weeeeeee!* Ouch! Hey! Watch it, Sam! *Don't!* Get that goddam ice water offa me—wow-WEEEEEEE!"

"Now look what you did! You woke him up!"

"Yeah—ice water does that."

"They're making a lot of noise," Calvin observed.

"And all them cusswords!" said Mr. Riley. "I never heard anything like it in my life! The Judge has been saying some *terrible* things. Why, if Missus Riley, my wife, was to come in the store right now and hear all the things he's been saying—"

"Hey, Calvin! How about that coffee?" Sam Abernathy's voice was loaded with impatience.

"I gotta catch my breath, don't I?" Calvin replied. He picked up the carton. "Just keep your shirttail in!"

He started for the unpainted wooden steps.

"There ain't no fan up there, either, Calvin," Mr. Riley called after him. "There's some L. T. Ditmore Funeral Home fans on the desk if. . . ."

Calvin stopped at the top of the steps and grasped the railing.

"Phew-weeeeee!" he shouted. "This place smells like the inside of an old shoe—nine shades hotter than Hades!"

He put the coffee on the desk and stepped over to view the body.

"Holy mackerel!" he said, staring down at the perspiring County Judge deep inside the thick nest of feather mattress and wool quilt. "You planning on *him* greeting the Governor before this time next week?"

"Unless you'd like to do it for him," Sam said, taking the coffee from the desk. "I think he's getting worse. Here—Ev—sit up and drink this coffee Calvin brought. He brought it just for you . . come on . . ."

The Judge wouldn't sit up.

"Lemme alone," he grumbled. "I'm sleepy—lemme alone."

"Come on, Ev—stop being mule-headed. *Ev*—SIT UP!"

"A while ago you boys wouldn't *let* me sit up—and now you won't let me stay down—lemme alone."

"Just one little taste, Ev—come on. Just one little taste. . . . Come on now, *please, GODDAMMIT!*"

"I don't want any of Calvin Turnbough's coffee . . . probably made it himself . . . get away and lemme alone . . ."

"You got to taste this coffee, Judge," Calvin said.

"Shut your big mouth and get outta here!" the Judge screamed.

"Jeez! He's getting mean now," Artie said. "They ain't nothing harder to handle than a mean drunk."

"You can't blame him," said Marvin. "Hot coffee on a day like this is like pouring oil on a fire. When I used to get the

[*44*]

chills, they'd cover me up and give me hot coffee to make me sweat."

"Hot tea'll warm you up quicker," Artie said.

"You guys are spinning your wheels," Calvin said wisely. "Anybody *that* drunk won't be sober enough one measly little hour from now to even *walk*, much less meet the Governor. You might as well forget him and get somebody to memorize his speech and take his place at the depot."

"How about you?" Sam asked, looking around irritably.

"Me?"

"Yeah—you. You want to take his place?"

"You think I'm crazy or something?"

"Okay—if you're gonna stand around and have ideas, how about having a good one for a change?"

"Forty-five minutes in a cold shower is what I'd recommend."

"Oh, for God's sake, Calvin! Do you see any cold showers around here to put him in? We've got to be practical about this thing."

"They've got cold showers at the hotel."

"Is that right? I'll bet they got 'em at the Adolphus Hotel in Dallas, too."

They took turns trying to force Calvin's coffee down the Judge's unwilling throat, but they got nothing for their troubles but a hot slosh on the backs of their hands or a splash across their stomachs. They were tired. They were hot. They were disgusted. They were desperate.

Sam stepped away from the cot and dropped into the chair at the rolltop desk. He stared at the Judge, his exasperation complete.

"We ought to drown the old bastard in that hot coffee," he said. "Can you beat it? He's the one who invited the Governor. The one and only time in the history of this town that the Governor decided to visit us, and Little Short

[*45*]

Drawers here has to go out and get skunk drunk."

"If the Governor was drunk too, maybe it wouldn't matter," Artie Whelan suggested.

Sam turned his eyes onto Artie.

"You're getting almost as intelligent as Calvin," he said.

"He must of been out celebrating," Artie went on. "You know how he celebrates special occasions."

Sam shook his head and snorted. "I just don't see how you figured that out, Artie," he said. He turned back to the Judge and stared at him again. Then suddenly, he said, "Pour the rest of that ice water on his head, Artie. Just turn the bucket upside down and let him have it."

Artie looked around as though he were hearing spooks.

"Not on Dice's feather bed and wool quilt, Sam! It'd smell for a month."

"If you could just switch him from hot to cold real quick," offered Calvin, "it would be like a shock treatment. That might do it."

"Sounds reasonable," Sam agreed. "The only trouble is that he don't have any hot and cold switches on him."

"You oughta get him out of here, though. Look at him—he's drowning in his own sweat."

"And where do you suggest we might take him?"

The question drew a blank. It did put an idea in Sam Abernathy's head, though. He got up from the desk and stepped to the edge of the loft.

"Hey, Dice!" he called down into the store. "What's in your big refrigerator vault?"

"A coupla sides of beef and some chickens," Mr. Riley replied. "And a few watermelons and a coupla cases of milk—"

"Whatcha got in mind, Sam?" Artie asked. "Whatever it is, I wish you'd hurry it up. Every time I look out front I still see Velma Agnew, so them cars ain't moving! I gotta get back out on the street and do my duty. Folks will think it's kinda funny for all this crowd to be in town and the Sheriff's not nowhere in sight."

Sam paid no attention to Artie. He was listening to Mr. Riley without digesting his meaning.

"—and some fresh butter, a case of tomatoes and lettuce. I got in some real fine lettuce this morning—big, leafy green—"

"You got room in the icebox for Judge Five-by-Five?" Sam broke in.

"You ain't thinking about putting him on ice, are you, Sam?"

"Why not? We tried everything else. How much time have we got, Marv?"

"Fifty-five minutes."

"Jeez!" Artie said.

"Sam, I'm telling you, it won't do any good," Marvin Cross argued. "We started too late. You'd better get hold of Fred Sellers or somebody else who can make speeches and tell him the Judge is sick—"

"Is there anything in the refrigerator for the Judge to sit on, Dice?" Sam asked.

"They's not any chairs or davenports, if that's what you mean," said Mr. Riley. "Nobody ever wanted to sit down in there that I know of, so I never put no—"

"Find something, then—a crate or keg. Turn it upside down."

Sam turned back to the others. They were watching him in disbelief.

"Sam, you can't put him in the icebox without any clothes on!" Calvin protested. "He'll come down with double pneumonia."

Sam turned to Marvin. "When did Delsey say he'd have his clothes ready, Marv?" he asked.

"He didn't say. He just said he'd bring them down here when he gets them pressed."

"We can't wait, then," Sam decided. "He can wrap up in that wool quilt."

They gathered around the Judge, who by now was awake again. At least, his eyes were open. He was not moving a muscle.

"Looks like you boys could fan me," he said plaintively. "If you won't let me get up, looks like at least you could fan me."

"We're gonna take you where it's real cool, Ev," Sam said with new patience. "Come on and get up."

The Judge stared at the ceiling.

"How come he don't bat his eyes?"

"He's too stiff."

"Maybe he took the paralysis."

"That ain't what's making him stiff."

They pulled him off the cot and managed to stand him on his feet. He demanded his shoes and socks. They promised to bring them later.

"*Now!*" he ordered. "This floor's got splinters in it, and I don't want any splinters in my feet."

"Quit worrying about splinters and *move!*"

"Not until you get my shoes," he said. "And my shirt and my undershirt. I'll not run around in a public place of business without my clothes on."

"That didn't seem to bother you outside on the street."

He tried to focus on the occupants of the loft. They seemed to have multiplied.

"Jeez! Lookit his pants! Looks like he wet 'em!"

"That's just sweat."

"The people at the depot won't know that, though."

"Maybe we ought to take them to Delsey, too."

"Not if I've gotta do it, we don't," said Marvin. "I'm not going back out on that street until the first frost. Must be two hundred degrees outside."

"Aw, go on and take 'em, Marv. We'll get him into the refrigerator while you're gone."

[*48*]

Marvin weighed his choices, juggling another hot walk down Main Street against another tussle with the Judge. Main Street won. He sighed.

"Okay," he said. "Take 'em off and give 'em to me—but I'm serving notice on all of you, this is the last time."

The Judge's trousers fell to the floor.

"Hey! What the—"

"Just lift your foot, your Honor."

"Are you trying to show my—"

"*Lift your foot, dammit!*"

A small struggle ensued.

"Now lift the other one—NOW!"

Somebody tossed the soggy trousers to Marvin Cross. He emptied the pockets and departed.

The others walked the Judge to the head of the steps. He pulled back.

"Now if you boys think I'm going to walk around the grocery store in my drawers, you'd better back up and think again."

Mr. Riley looked up from the counter and turned faint at what he saw.

"JUDGE CRAWFORD!" he shrieked. "Go put your *clothes* on!"

"Go open the door to the refrigerator, Dice," Calvin called.

"It just don't look right for him to be standing up there like that!" Dice said, his Adam's apple working frantically.

"Goodgodamighty, Dice!" Sam yelled. "Quit arguing and open the refrigerator, and we'll get him out of sight for you!"

Dice hurried to the refrigerator at the rear of the store and swung the big door back.

"Hurry it up, *please*," he moaned. "That just don't look decent for the County Judge to run around without no clothes on in a grocery store that's downtown on Main Street."

They walked the Judge down the steps and to the open refrigerator.

The icy air hit his body. "Wow! Does that ever feel good!" he exclaimed. "That cold air feels mighty good." He patted his round stomach and inhaled deeply. "I think I might just step inside and cool off for a few minutes," he went on.

Then he remembered his friends.

"—that is, if you boys will excuse me for a few minutes," he added.

"Go right ahead, Judge," they urged. "Go right on in. See there? Dice has even put an egg crate in there for you to sit on."

"Oh—well, now—that was right nice of Dice, wasn't it? Right nice, indeed it was. Yes it was, indeed."

He stuck one bare foot inside and withdrew it.

"Ouch! That floor is as cold as a witch's tit!"

"Oh, my!"

Mr. Riley raced to the front door.

"I told you to *get my shoes!*" the Judge shouted.

"Run get his shoes, Artie," said Sam.

Artie took off for the loft.

"Some of you boys like to come in and sit a spell?" asked the Judge.

"Not right now, Ev," Sam replied for all of them. "Thanks, just the same. Just go ahead and enjoy yourself. We might come in later."

"Oh—well, I won't stay long. Just long enough to cool off a bit."

Artie returned with the shoes. By pooling their remaining strength, they managed to shoe the Judge and push him into the refrigerator. They clanged the door shut.

For the second time, Marvin returned empty-handed from Delsey Jacobs' Drygoods Store.

"Man-oh-man! Everybody down at the depot is going to get the heat prostration!" he announced. "And Callie Davis is getting suspicious about those clothes I keep bringing in."

Calvin Turnbough looked worried. "He's going to freeze in there without his clothes," he said. "I'm going to give him the quilt."

The others moved away from the door toward the meat counter. Calvin fetched the quilt from the loft and threw it inside the refrigerator.

While they waited for the Judge to sober up or freeze up —whichever happened first—they nibbled on a wheel of cheese that lay atop the meat counter and chomped on dill pickles that floated in a nearby barrel. Mr. Riley looked on apprehensively, trying to keep track of quantities.

"I can cut some of that cheese off and weigh it real easy," he said.

They weren't interested.

They waited. They talked. They ate. They were five: Sam Abernathy, Artie Whelan, Marvin Cross, Calvin Turnbough, and their reluctant host, Dice Riley.

"This is pretty good cheese, Dice."

"It's forty-nine cents a pound," he replied hopefully.

"It would taste better if we had some crackers."

"—I'm running a Special on cheese this week—"

"It sure would go good with a cold bottle of beer, wouldn't it?"

"—regular price is fifty-one cents a pound."

From inside the refrigerator came the distant sound of a knocking on the door. They all stopped chewing and looked at one another.

"Don't answer him," said Sam. "A little cold weather won't hurt him."

"I got it set on thirty-five degrees," said Dice.

"How long do you think we ought to leave him in there, Sam?"

"Until time to go."

"I wonder if he's got his speech memorized."

"The Judge? He don't need to memorize a speech. He'd talk with somebody choking him."

"The pickles are by the pound, too," ventured Dice. "They're twenty-nine cents in bulk like that. Del Monte and Heinz's are higher."

"I'll bet Lena is out looking for him and having a purple-tailed hissy."

"Was he supposed to go home to get her and take her to the train?"

"Damn if I know. She'll have to meet him at the depot, I guess."

Two pounds of cheese and a dozen dill pickles later, Delsey Jacobs burst through the front door with the Judge's freshly pressed clothes on hangers. He stopped at the front counter and squinted into the gloom.

"Come out—come out—wherever you are!" he sang out playfully. "I know there's somebody here somewhere—come out!"

He looked down at an open box of two-for-a-penny Mary Janes on the counter. He picked one up and turned it over in his hand.

"How long have you had these, Dice?" he asked. "Did they come with the building? They're covered with dust."

Delsey Jacobs, father of six children and another en route, was the only Jewish merchant in town, Superintendent of the First Methodist Sunday School, and owner of a forty-acre farm north of town that he hadn't the foggiest idea what to do with. He bounced when he walked and bubbled when he talked, which meant that he was always bouncing and bubbling, for he was in constant motion and talked incessantly.

He made his way through the store to the meat counter.

"You know, Dice," he said as he bounced, "a couple of buckets of white paint on these walls might make it possible for your customers to read the labels on the cans. I said *might*.

What a day! If the Governor ever comes to town again, I'll go broke. There must have been two hundred people in the store today. Callie sold one of them a package of bias tape, and made an exchange on a four ninety-five sweater for another. Now don't ask me what kind of mentality thinks about *sweaters*, of all things, on a day like this. Anyway, that's my volume of business for the day."

He surveyed the Judge's friends lounging before the meat counter.

"This scene needs a pot-bellied stove," he said. "Didn't any of you eat dinner today? Slice me off a piece of that cheese, will you, Calvin?"

Calvin cut off a sliver and handed it to him.

"It's forty-nine cents a pound this week," said Mr. Riley.

"You're overcharging again, Dice," said Delsey. "So I said, 'Callie, why don't you try *something* on *somebody*—anything at all—maybe those black bloomers with elastic in the legs. Who knows? They might buy them.' What did you do with the Judge? Send him down to the depot in the raw?"

"We've got him on ice for the time being," said Sam. He explained their strategy.

"Well, when you get him out, send him down to the store. I want to advise him about his wardrobe." He lifted the Judge's coat and turned it around, then back again. "Just look at this! *Where* did Everett Crawford get it? Did Lena make it? I understand she sews. If she made *this*, you might send her along with Everett. I want to advise her, too. Look at these *stitches!* I've seen better tailoring on cotton sacks."

"The Judge never was much of a clotheshorse," said Marvin. "You remember that old gray coat he used to wear with the leather patches on the elbow? He wore it to—"

Marvin Cross' words and face froze. His eyes widened. His hand pointed to the front door. They all turned to follow his gaze.

Mrs. Purdy Robinson was coming through the front door.

With the shoulders of a stevedore, Mrs. Robinson was built like a triangle with the apex at the bottom. Formidable in manner as well as appearance, she stalked with a heavy tread and seemed always to be smelling an unpleasant odor. She was the wife of the local hardware merchant and the town's leading authority on other people and their affairs.

"Get rid of her, Dice!" Sam hissed.

"How can I do that?"

"That's your problem."

"Well, now—I don't know as how I can do that, exactly. I never did run anybody out of this store yet."

"Then let Mrs. Purdy Robinson be your first."

"Go on, Dice!" whispered Marvin Cross. "She's got the longest tongue in town."

"And it's always flapping," said Delsey. "I understand her tongue gets sunburned in summer and frostbitten in winter."

With an anxious glance at the dwindling wheel of cheese, Mr. Riley detached himself from the group and moved up front to meet Mrs. Robinson. She was standing inside the door looking over the premises as though searching for the best spot to plant the dynamite. She ignored Mr. Riley's greeting.

"What's going on back there, Dice—a convention?" she asked imperially.

"They're just waiting till time to meet the Governor, Mrs. Robinson. What can I do for you today?"

"I want you to fix me a rolled roast," she said, moving past Dice, her eyes fixed on the group at the meat counter. "I was on the way down to the depot myself," she went on, "and I thought if you're not going, maybe you could fix me the roast, and I'll come back by afterwards and pick it up. What's that they're all eating?"

"I'm having a Special on cheese this week—forty-nine cents until Saturday."

"Your Specials don't usually attract much attention, do they, Dice?"

She stopped and lifted a box of pancake flour from a shelf.

"The last box of this you sold me had bugs in it," she said. She returned the box to the shelf. "What's Artie Whelan doing back there? Is somebody in trouble?"

"No, ma'am. They ain't nobody in trouble. He just stopped in to cool off."

"*Cool off?* In *here?*"

"Well—the sun don't come in here much."

"Neither does the air."

She moved on down the shelf with the unhappy Mr. Riley in tow.

"Seems to me like they ought to be getting down to the depot," she said. "Why are they waiting *here?*" From her mouth it was an accusation rather than a question. "I've never heard of people congregating in this store like they do at the Little Gem or the City Drug Store."

"Sometimes they do. How big a roast did you have in mind, Mrs. Robinson?"

"Oh, maybe three, three and a half pounds—no more than four. Purdy's sister from Merkel is coming Saturday with that good-for-nothing husband of hers, and I thought it would be good to have for Sunday dinner. I guess the poor thing needs to get a square meal inside her stomach without worrying about how to pay for it. She's got her hands full with that shiftless husband, let me tell you right now. You know, he's gone off and left her three times, but she always takes him back. He never was worth a pewter nickel. I've told her again and again that she would be better off without him, but she won't listen. And of course, as you might know, Purdy sides in with her."

She stopped to examine a box of rice, but not really.

"They all look hot and sweaty," she said. "What have they

[55]

been doing—digging ditches?"

"Well, it's like I said—it turned off hot today, Mrs. Robinson."

No one at the meat counter said a word. Not a blessed word. They only listened. Mrs. Robinson, followed by Mr. Riley, continued her stroll through the shelves past the macaroni, past the dried beans, alongside the hominy grits and the Quaker Oats. They emerged at the other end of the shelf, squarely in front of the meat counter.

"Oh, hello, Sam," she said. "Calvin . . . Marvin. . . ."

"Why, hello, there, Eula!" said Sam. His eyes darted to the refrigerator.

The others began to babble.

"Hello, Mrs. Robinson."

"Sure a scorcher today, ain't it, Eula?"

"How's Purdy, Mrs. Robinson?"

"Too bad the Governor can't come on one of our cooler days," she said.

"That won't be until next winter," said one of the Judge's friends.

"It gets cooler in—"

"Delsey—that's not your coat, is it?" Her eyes had fixed themselves on the blue seersucker suit.

"Dear me, no!" said Delsey with a light chuckle. "I'm out gathering up old rags for the rummage sale at the church." He examined her clothes appraisingly. "We'll take dresses, too," he added.

"Mmmmmm—I didn't think that coat would fit you," she said. "The sleeves look too short . . . oh, Dice? Be real careful now about how much fat's in the roast. You know how I like them."

"Yes, ma'am. I'll fix it real good for you."

"Jessie Atwater was telling me down the street that she saw Lena Crawford looking for the Judge," she said. "You seen him, Sam?"

"The Judge? He's supposed to be down at the depot, isn't he?"

"Yes—that's why Lena was looking for him." Her eyes had returned to the blue seersucker suit. She studied it with perplexity. "I understand Lena was in a real snit," she went on. "You know how she can get when things don't go to suit her. Anyway—she's supposed to be on the platform with him—along with the Cliftons and Shumakers and Duckworths. Jessie said Lena hadn't seen the Judge since breakfast. They tell me that Gertrude Clifton's gall bladder is giving her trouble again—what's that banging noise?"

From inside the refrigerator came a distant sound like the beat-beat-beat of the tom-toms.

They all looked at Sam Abernathy. Sam Abernathy looked at Mrs. Robinson. Mrs. Robinson looked at Mr. Riley. Mr. Riley chose that exact moment to take in after a fly. They all started talking at once.

"Might be your water pipes, Dice."

"You oughta have 'em looked at, Dice."

"If it was me, I'd call Willis Shumaker to come see about them. He fixed mine real good."

"It's not the water pipes," said Delsey. "The place is falling apart. I've been trying to tell Dice for a long time that the roof was going to cave in on him. You should listen to me sometimes, Dice."

"I had a knocking like that under my house once, and it was the water pipes all the time."

"Whatever it is," said Mrs. Robinson, "I'd be real careful about turning it over to Willis Shumaker. The prices he charges for only—" Her eyes strayed to the clock above the meat counter. "Oh, my heavens!" she exclaimed. "Twenty minutes! I'd better get on down to the depot. I probably won't be able to get close enough to see anything. You boys better hurry."

She overtook Mr. Riley, who had chased a fly as far as the

vegetable counter. "Dice, if that roast is not ready when I'm ready to go home, Purdy can stop in and pick it up," she said.

She sailed through the front door.

The men at the meat counter swung into action.

"Let's get him out and dressed!" Sam commanded. "You gotta help us, Delsey."

"I've got to get back to the store, Sam," he replied. "I left Callie there by herself, and she might sell something. I'd kinda like to look on—you know, for old time's sake."

"Now don't *you* start that, Delsey!" Sam said threateningly. "It's gonna take all of us to get the Judge dressed and down to the depot."

"I just don't want to be a party to putting this seersucker contraption on a good friend and public servant. I think far too much of him and the community for—"

"Aw, cut out the jabbering, Delsey! We've got things to do, so just knock it off and lend a hand."

Judge Crawford was sitting hunched in a fetuslike position on the egg crate, wrapped to the ears in the wool patchwork quilt. Nothing was visible but his round fat face—but not the same face they had stored in the refrigerator to begin with. This one was a pale, frosty pink, the exact hue of the marble that surrounded the front door of the First National Bank. His eyes were glassy. His lips were blue.

"*Brrrrrrr,*" he murmured without moving. "The coldest goddam place this side of the North Pole. Didn't you boys hear me knocking on the door?"

"We heard you. We've been chewing the fat with Mrs. Purdy Robinson."

"Come on, Judge—time to get your clothes on and down to the depot. The train's due in twenty minutes."

"Eighteen!" somebody corrected.

"You don't need to be so exact!"

"I think I'd better go on ahead and see about the traffic," said the Sheriff.

"No, you don't!" said the Tax Collector. "You gotta help us with the Judge. Anyway, the traffic is already too snarled up for you to do anything about it."

"Velma Agnew ain't out in front any more," said Artie. "But it seems like I've been seeing Liles Greenwood's blue pickup for a mighty long time. I think traffic's stopped cold again."

The Judge flung off his wrappings and bolted for the open door. "The coldest goddam place in—"

He ran smack head-on into the door jamb.

"He's still drunk!"

"What else did you expect? Come on!"

"Did it hurt you, Judge?"

"Don't worry about the Judge," said Sam. "The Lord looks after crazy people and drunks. Come on—let's get him dressed and outside in the sun."

"Hey, lookit! His upper plate fell out!"

"Well, quit your gawking and put it back in!"

They stuffed the Judge into his clothes and his teeth into his mouth. His necktie was crumpled and curled up on the end. Delsey traded with him.

The clock showed fifteen minutes past two.

"Maybe we can walk it off of him," Calvin suggested. "I heard once that you can walk whiskey out of your system— one mile for each ounce."

"Well, now, that's right nice to know, ain't it? In this case, that means we'd have to walk him all the way to Fort Worth and back."

"We ought to try, though."

"The depot's not far enough way."

"We'll *make* it far enough," said Sam with sudden decision. "Somebody tie that other shoe—we'll take a detour."

"We haven't got time! It'll be all we can do to get him to the depot and on the platform before the train's due in."

"Trains are never on time."

"Unless you want them to be late."

They pushed the Judge to the front door.

"We'll make it if all of you'll stop blabbering and do like I tell you," said Sam. He stood in the door and looked them over. He shook his head in obvious doubt. Then he took a deep breath. "Well—here's what we'll do. I'll lead the way. The rest of you make a screen of yourselves around him so nobody can see him."

"He looks better than we do—him with his pressed clothes and all."

"Shut up and listen!" Sam snapped. "Just follow me and don't try to explain anything to anybody on the street—not even if they ask you. Just keep your traps shut and let 'em wonder."

He pointed a weary finger at Judge Crawford, who was standing by submissively, waiting with a patience that none of them trusted.

"And that goes for you, too, Ev—we don't want any more trouble outa you! Just stay along with us and *no dirty singing!* You got that?"

The Judge nodded benignly. His eyelids were beginning to droop.

"Stay awake and listen!" Sam stormed. "Somebody zip up his pants."

Marvin reached for the Judge's fly.

"Watch it—*Marv!*"

"Now, Ev, listen to what I'm telling you," Sam continued. "And listen real hard. Just walk along with us and keep your mouth shut. You can be thinking about what you're gonna say to the Governor."

"That ole fart!"

"Ev—I'm warning you!" Sam shouted. He sighed. "You know . . . we might just be asking for it, taking him down there like this in front of all those people. . . ."

"This is sure as hell a fine time to start worrying about *that!*"

"I been telling you, Sam—he's not gonna make it," said Marvin Cross. "And even if he does, I won't. I'll bet I lost ten pounds already, and we're not even at the depot yet."

Sam was studying the Judge. "I wonder if he even remembers that the Governor's coming today and he's supposed to greet him and—"

He broke off and got hold of himself with new resolution.

"It's do or die," he said. "Come on—let's go."

Silently, they filed outside.

The heat from the sidewalk hit them full blast. As hot as it had been inside Riley's Grocery & Market, they were not prepared for the shock of the withering heat outside. The blistering glare of the sun blinded them. The wind lashed at them and parched their faces. The temperature had gone up another few degrees. Or so it felt.

"Godamighty!"

"We're all gonna faint and fall on our faces."

"Be sure and walk slow, Sam."

"Just shut up and follow me," said Sam.

Judge Crawford's friends formed a ring around him, shutting off the hot wind, a blessing he was in no condition to appreciate.

"I'm hot," he complained.

"Shut up, Ev," Sam ordered.

With a final glance at his group, he took a deep breath.

"Okay," he said. "This is it. Start walking."

They started walking: five men in a tight little cluster, at the core of which was a sixth, too short and too surrounded to be visible to the public eye. They marched off down the

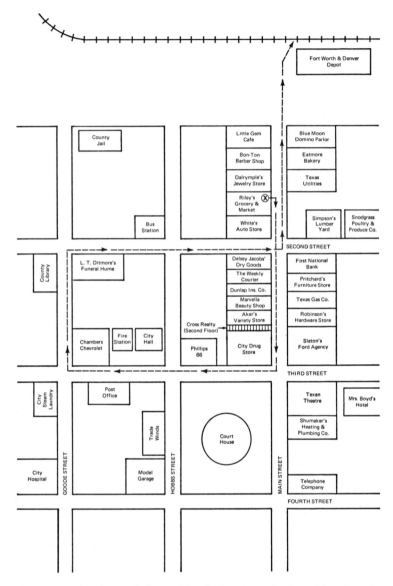

Route to the depot followed by Judge Crawford and his friends

street, leaving Mr. Riley in the store alone with his flies and a heart brimming with relief.

"*Psst!* You're going the wrong way," hissed Calvin Turnbough.

"Don't you think I know that?" said Sam from the corner of his mouth. "We're going in a roundabout way to give him a chance to walk off some of that jag."

"We haven't got time—"

"Cut out the bad-mouthing and follow me like I told you!"

If they were an odd-looking assortment, their actions looked even odder. They seemed to be out of touch with the times and out of step with the town. While the crowds streamed north on Main Street to the depot, Judge Crawford and his friends paddled upstream in the opposite direction. They marched south across Second Street, a flying wedge that parted the oncoming citizens and left them wide-eyed and open-mouthed. Dripping with sweat and puffing from exhaustion, even before they had navigated the first half of the city block, they marched briskly in what they assumed to be a military cadence but in truth was a rabble. Their heads were up and their eyes were fixed straight ahead. They ignored the curious stares and half-asked questions of their fellow natives.

As they passed Delsey Jacobs' Drygoods Store, Callie Davis was leaning on the glove counter staring idly into the street. Delsey attempted to peel off in response to her excited reminder that they were headed in the wrong direction.

"Don't listen to her, Delsey," Marvin Cross muttered.

"You're too late—I heard her already."

But Delsey Jacobs, with the rest of them, marched on.

"Holy cow! Lookit his eyes!"

"What's the matter now?" asked Sam over his shoulder. "Has he got 'em shut again?"

He did not slow his pace nor miss a step. He was afraid to look around at the Judge.

"His eyes are on fire!" Artie exclaimed. "They're the drunkest looking part of him!"

They marched on past *The Weekly Courier*, past the Marvella Beauty Shop, past the linen shop's GIGANTIC CLOSE-OUT SALE! to Akers' Variety Store, where Mr. Akers was still sacking popcorn for the stragglers. He looked up at what appeared to be a posse moving in. He dropped a half-filled sack of popcorn.

"Marv, peel off and go into Akers' and get him a pair of colored sunglasses to hide his eyes with," Sam ordered, head up and eyes still to the front.

"What kind of glasses?"

"*Colored*, dammit! You can come out the back door and catch up with us around the corner on Third Street."

Marvin dropped out of the formation, raced through Akers' Variety Store and out the back door with sunglasses in hand. He caught up with Sam Abernathy's platoon on Court House Square. They were crossing the alley behind the City Drug Store. He fell back into formation.

"That Higgins girl was screaming at me to come back and pay her," he mumbled as he fitted the sunglasses onto the Judge's perspiring face.

"They hurt my nose!" complained the Judge.

"Tough luck."

"I can't see—"

"You don't need to see nothing—"

Third Street was deserted, except for Old Man Bartlett, who was crossing the intersection at Goode Street in his vegetable wagon cussing at Raymond, his horse. They marched west on Court House Square, past Phillips 66, past the City Hall, past the Fire Station, where Wes Caldwell was propped back in a cane-bottomed chair on the sidewalk, chewing a matchstick. He watched the extraordinary group approach, march past and out of sight around the corner by Chambers Chevrolet, too stunned to say a word. And no one said a word to Wes, not even Sam Abernathy, who was his brother-in-law.

Alongside Chambers Chevrolet, they marched one block north past L. T. Ditmore's Funeral Home.

"I should have worn a track suit," said Delsey Jacobs. "I sell them, you know—five ninety-five, including jockey strap."

"Slow down, Sam!" said Artie.

"Can't do it—might miss the train."

"The Judge can't walk this fast—his legs are too short."

"Then tell him to run."

"I'm plum wore out myself, Sam."

"Me, too. I promise you, Sam, I'm gonna get the heat prostration."

"You'll live," said Sam. "We gotta get the Judge sober."

"Well, that don't include me. I ain't drunk."

"We got ten whole minutes, Sam. *Slow down!* Sweat's running down inside my pants. It'll look like I wet 'em."

"If they're already wet," said Sam, "it'll already look like you wet 'em, so that's no excuse for slowing down. Anyway, I haven't exactly got the chill bumps myself."

"I think I'm gonna collapse—I'm promising you—"

"Save it until we get to the depot."

"I'm outta breath!"

"Me, too," said Delsey. "I ran out when we passed the Marvella Beauty Shop and Clara Baker yelled at Artie. I think she's got the hots for you, Artie."

"Clara Baker ain't had the hots for nobody since before me and you was born," Artie replied between gasps.

"I understand she didn't have them then," said Delsey. "I hear she's a lady eunuch."

"Lord-a-mercy, Delsey!" Marvin Cross exclaimed. "Don't you *ever* run down? Why don't you save your breath?"

"You're just jealous because you don't have any."

"I did have—before today."

They rounded the corner at L. T. Ditmore's Funeral Home, turned east on Second Street and headed back toward Main Street. Two blocks later, they made one last turn—left on Main Street—and came abreast of their starting point, Riley's Grocery & Market.

Mr. Riley was standing in the door, flyswatter in hand. His eyes bulged, and his jaw dropped.

"Where y'all been?" he called out.

No one replied. They stumbled past.

On they marched, five sweaty, bedraggled citizens surrounding a sixth, who by now was sweatier and more bedraggled than the lot of them combined. Shut away from the outside air and inside the tight circle of his friends where he absorbed their body heat, the Judge was hissing like a hot poker in a bucket of water. He tried to complain, but nothing came from his mouth except a weak gurgle.

They made it past August Dalrymple's jewelry store, Mr. Dalrymple was standing in the door.

"Good afternoon, gentlemen," he said politely.

They made it past the Bon-Ton Barber Shop, too tired to know that they were too tired to make it. They reached the Little Gem Cafe. Calvin Turnbough decided that he had had it, Governor or no Governor.

"I'm getting off here, I don't care what anybody says," he gasped. "You don't need me any more, anyway."

"Stay where you are, Calvin!" Sam commanded sharply. "The first man that steps outta this formation is gonna get shot!"

"That wouldn't be so bad," said Delsey.

Artie Whelan locked his arm through Calvin's to prevent his defection.

"Get your clappy hands offa me, Artie!" Calvin growled.

[*66*]

"Knock it off, Calvin!" Sam ordered. "You're getting worse than the Judge. We've nearly got it made now."

They angled across the wide U-turn space toward the Fort Worth & Denver depot, where the crowd sweltered and waited for the Governor's train to come in.

"Coming through!" Sam bellowed as they reached the edge of the crowd.

The people turned and looked without comprehension.

"*Coming through!* ONE SIDE, PLEASE! HOT STUFF! *HOT STUFF!*"

The crowd parted obediently, if not understandingly, to make an aisle for the steamy group's passage to the platform. A few more yards and there it was, high above the people's heads and draped in Lone Star bunting. The sight was more welcome than a tax refund. Without bothering to sort them out, they knew that the three and a half couples staring down over the bunting at their approach, rigid with disbelief, were the Cliftons, the Duckworths, the Shumakers, and Lena Crawford, who had been a widow since breakfast.

At the edge of the platform, they released the Judge from custody and shoved him up the steps into a tangle of down-stretched hands. The hands pulled him on to the top.

The Welcoming Committee was complete now, down to and including the Official Greeter.

Half-crazed with anxiety and half-wild with rage, Mrs. Everett Philander Crawford contorted her face into a dreadful public smile.

"*Where* in heaven's *name* have you *been?*" she breathed furiously through clenched teeth.

The least of her husband's concerns at that moment was a trip report. He said nothing.

Panting and gasping for breath, the Judge stood on the platform looking for all the world as though he had at that very moment been fished out of the creek. His blue seersucker suit was dark with great swatches and circles of perspiration; his shirt collar was crushed and wilted, a messy roll of wet cloth around his neck; his trousers were soaked and wrinkled; his borrowed necktie was askew while curling up at the bottom. Streams of perspiration gushed from under his wide-brimmed straw hat and splattered down over his face, drenching his colored sunglasses and shutting out his vision, but it didn't matter. He couldn't see, anyway.

Lena Crawford worked hard to maintain her dreadful smile for the public.

"*What* have you been *doing?*" she muttered from the side of her mouth and through her clenched teeth. "You're a disgrace—*look at yourself!*"

Her husband didn't bother.

He collapsed against the railing and panted. Like his old one-eyed airedale after chasing the meter reader, he panted with his tongue hanging out and his fat round body shaking like his old Whippet with a cylinder missing. With foggy vision, he peered down over the railing for a glimpse of his recent captors—or deliverers, as the case may be. They had tumbled onto the ground below, steamy and soggy. He could not distinguish one from the other. The County Judge was on his own.

And none too soon.

The train whistled in the distance. The crowd turned eagerly to watch it snake into view around the grain elevator and clang into the station. The engineer leaned from his cab and waved. The crowd cheered him past and bunched in close for their first view of the Governor.

The Judge rose magnificently to the occasion. He could never explain afterwards how he did it, and for the best of reasons: he remembered nothing about it. He shook the Governor's hand, gave the Governor's lady a 90-proof peck on the cheek and introduced them to the other members of the Welcoming Committee.

"I hope he doesn't breathe on the Governor," a tired voice gasped from somewhere under the platform. "His breath would shrivel a mesquite tree."

Otherwise, all was silent from that particular quarter. All, that is, except the sounds of heavy breathing.

The Judge signaled the high-school band to begin the program. The band played two choruses of "The Eyes of Texas"; the high-school glee club sang an arrangement of "Beautiful, Beautiful Texas"; the sixteen-year-old Ida Bell Clifton presented a bouquet of American Beauty roses to the Governor's lady; Judge Crawford followed with an Official Greeting and Welcoming Speech carefully timed to end after four minutes; the delegates from the local civic clubs joined him on the platform and presented the Governor with a ceremonial scroll; then the Governor stepped to the front of the platform to respond with whatever was in his heart and on his mind.

"My fel-low Tex-unnnnns," he bellowed. "I am deeply honored by the privilege and pleasure of standing on this platform today alongside my old friend, Judge Everett Crawford—YOUR friend and MY friend—and to gaze with proud eyes on your fair city—truly one of the real jewels of the Texas Panhandle. It touches my heart to see the GREAAAAAAT and VAAAAAST assembly of dedicated and loyal Tex-unnnns who have taken time away from their manifold businesses and varied personal pursuits to demonstrate their devotion to the Chief Executive of this GREAAAAT and GLORRRRRRR-IOUS Lone Star State and to let him know that—"

The engineer tooted his departing whistle three times and broke up the meeting.

The Governor's party scampered aboard the train. If the Governor himself was angry that he had not been permitted to finish his speech, he was too good a diplomat and too much the politician to let it show. He stood on the rear platform of the train and waved exuberantly at all the voters. The voters waved back and cheered him and the train out of sight. As the last car disappeared over the first rise in the distance, the County Judge fell over in a dead faint.

The other members of the Welcoming Committee, led by Mrs. Lena Crawford, gathered around the fallen Judge to administer first aid. Onlookers assumed that he had been out in the sun too long and was suffering a heat stroke. Everybody, that is, except the Judge's friends, Sam Abernathy, Marvin Cross, Artie Whelan, Calvin Turnbough, and Delsey Jacobs. They knew better. Anyway, they couldn't have cared less.

They were suffering heat strokes of their own.

2.

≈

Willis Shumaker's Resignation

Nobody knew why Willis Shumaker resigned from Rotary Club, not even his wife, Mattie. He explained it to her in great detail, but she didn't understand. So she followed the lead of their friends and invented excuses for him that sounded reasonable. His business was taking up an awful lot of his time these days, they said, or he hadn't been feeling well lately, or he thought it best to pare down his activities and make room for others to do their fair share. They all missed it a country mile.

Shumaker's Heating & Plumbing Company took no more of its owner's time than it ever had; physically, Willis was in the pink, and he retained his membership in all other organizations, holding offices in most and doing enough committee work to kill a lesser man. Even after he resigned from Rotary, he was more active in the community than the next five men combined. What was more, he struck people as the happiest and most contented man in town.

At a regular Thursday luncheon meeting when Mr. Hightower, the high-school principal, was scheduled to speak on

"Youth, Tomorrow's Leaders," Willis Shumaker submitted his resignation and sidetracked the meeting so completely that Mr. Hightower never got the opportunity to make his speech. It was by far the most sensational resignation the Rotarians knew anything about, even more sensational than when Wilmer Thatcher ran off with his own mother-in-law and they threw him out. When Willis resigned, it was the only time a past president, past secretary, past treasurer, past membership vice president, and past chairman of the Ways and Means Committee—all rolled into one—quit the club without dying or moving away from town. Willis had filled all these offices and to while away the time in between had served on every committee imaginable. If the constitution and bylaws had permitted and Willis had consented, the Rotarians would have elected him to all offices and put him in charge of everything. He was a real go-getter.

He was a fine, Christian, civic-minded citizen, sole proprietor of Shumaker's Heating & Plumbing Company on the Main Street side of Court House Square, next door to the Texan Theatre. He was the father of three teen-aged children, a 32nd-degree Mason, deacon in the First Baptist Church, secretary of the School Board, member of the Boy Scout Commission, a director of the Chamber of Commerce, and president of Plumbers and Steamfitters Union, Local #810, with a membership of four, all of whom, it so happened, were employed by Shumaker's Heating & Plumbing Company. Although he frequently urged his union colleagues to elect each other president occasionally, they wouldn't hear of it. It just proves how Willis was held in esteem by everyone, including his employees.

He was on the board of governors of the Country Club, a member of the City Council, and a director of the American Red Cross, local chapter. He was an Elk, a Volunteer Fireman, commander of American Legion Post No. 34, and Lord only knows what else. If there was a convention anywhere that needed a local delegate, people automatically thought of Willis Shumaker first. Had he accepted all such assignments that were offered him, he would have been on the road all the time. Three times in his life he had been elected local Man of the Year. If you wanted a job done well, all you had to do was give it to this busy man and worry no more about it. He typified the Rotarian at his finest.

The Rotary Club met at the hotel every Thursday at twelve o'clock. Members who arrived after the dining-room doors were closed paid a tardy fine of five cents a minute, excuses and alibis notwithstanding. The largest tardy fine on record ($1.35) was levied against Dr. George Odom, veterinarian, who had stayed too long with a sick horse east of town. At a few minutes before twelve o'clock on Thursdays, if you chanced to be walking by the corner of Third and Main Streets, you might get run over and knocked down by Rotarians trying to get a foot inside the lobby before the doors closed. They hurried, scurried, scampered and raced one another around the corner from Main to Third and along the side of the Texan Theatre to the hotel, which occupied the corner across the alley. It was said that nobody was more resolute than a Rotarian determined not to bring up the rear on Thursday.

The hotel, where the Rotary Club held its weekly meetings, was a hybrid. It had come into this world as a frame residence; then after the addition of three rooms upstairs and four on the rear, the living room–lobby was expanded to take in the porch, a new concrete facing was substituted for the brown clapboard siding, and an electric sign was hung out front on the Third Street side. Through the years, rooms had been added helter-skelter to the structure, giving a kind of crazy-house feel to guests who wandered around unescorted through the zigzag corridors in search of their rooms. So, despite the attempts at commercializing the hotel's appearance, it was still a family residence that had simply got too big for its britches.

Mrs. Boyd, owner of the hotel, usually set places for twenty-five, but seldom more than twenty showed up, including guests. She set a decent table, even though she tended to cook the roast beef too dry and serve the tables too early (during the sing-song). No one complained about the cold food and iced tea with melted ice, though, because fellowship, not food, was the primary object of the meetings; and you couldn't find a jollier, more congenial bunch of fellows in the entire State of Texas than those gathered in Mrs. Boyd's dining room each Thursday at noon. There was a small undercurrent of feeling that the meetings should be moved to the Little Gem Cafe's new banquet room, since Calvin Turnbough, the proprietor, was a Rotarian. Mrs. Boyd, however, had been serving the Rotary Club for twenty-seven years with staunch loyalty, and no one seriously proposed such a switch. To lose the Rotary luncheons would be a blow to her business, and the Rotary Club was committed to helping businesses, not destroying them.

The Rotarians began drifting into the hotel about ten minutes to twelve, milling about the lobby, sometimes visiting, sometimes listening to the news on the radio, sometimes reading the newspapers, sometimes politicking, and sometimes transacting a little business in passing. Promptly at twelve o'clock—if the whistle at the Cotton Compress blew promptly, that is—Mrs. Boyd opened the double doors to the dining room, and the Rotarians filed inside to stand behind their chairs. Nobody was assigned regular seats, except the President, the Program Chairman for the day, and whoever was on the program. They always sat at the head table.

Miss Addie Barker, who had been playing the piano for Rotary luncheons for thirty years, sat at the upright piano by the kitchen door, waiting for Purdy Robinson, the song director, to select a song from the *Rotary Song Book* and announce the page number. His selections were always familiar, tried and true: "There's a Long Long Trail A-winding," "Grandfather's Clock," "America," "Rotary Forever" and, at Christmastime, "Jingle Bells" and "Silent Night." Purdy was not a first-class song director, not even by the most charitable of judgments, but he was willing, he was available, he sang loud, and he kept everybody at it. That's what he was for. Singing got everybody into a good frame of mind and a sociable mood. That was important.

With the singing over, Miss Addie usually slipped out through the kitchen door, one of the preacher members said grace, and everybody sat down to eat, to socialize, and to enjoy good fellowship. They visited, discussed the news and weather, swapped jokes, told business experiences, and compared waistlines. Sometimes they rawhided the pants off a fellow Rotarian, like the time they ganged up on Artie Whelan, the Sheriff, and gave him fits about his trip to Amarillo, where he got a traffic ticket for overparking. The fact that he was in the law-enforcement business himself wasn't enough to get him off the hook with the Amarillo police. He like to never have lived it down.

After dessert—cottage pudding, fruit Jello, or one scoop of vanilla ice cream—everyone pushed back from the table, passed around the toothpicks, unwrapped the chewing gum and lighted up cigarettes and cigars; and the business meeting got under way.

The first order of business was the introduction of guests. There were always a few: business associates from another town, a visiting relative, an ex-resident of the town back on a visit, or a local citizen who for one reason or another was not a Rotarian. After each introduction, usually performed in a light vein with humorous touches, and after the applause, the President welcomed them in behalf of all Rotarians and said he hoped, when they got back home, they wouldn't forget to tell everyone what a real, live-wire, go-getting Rotary Club looked like and how it operated.

The Secretary read the minutes of the previous meeting and someone made a motion they be approved. The motion was seconded, and everyone who agreed signified by saying "Aye." The Treasurer read the financial report that often didn't vary by a thin dime from week to week, and it was likewise approved. Old Business didn't take up much time, for they seldom left any dangling. New Business might consist of a plan for contributing to the County Library, or a resolution supporting the local churches in their summer revival meetings, or a discussion of the impropriety of the Rotary Club taking an official position in the coming elections. Once a year, somebody proposed a rising vote of thanks to Miss Addie for her fine piano-playing. Someone always tipped her off when it was on the agenda so she could hang around for it. Although she knew what was in store and had ample time to prepare her emotions accordingly, she always wept and said a team of wild horses couldn't keep her away from Rotary on Thursdays. With the business meeting out of the way, the President turned the meeting over to the Program Chairman for the day.

Each Rotarian took his turn. If he was lucky, his day fell in a week when a revival meeting was in progress, enabling him to snag the visiting evangelist for an inspirational talk, or during a political campaign when a member of legislature was in town and available for a little nonpolitical speechmaking. In May, the winners of the high-school Interscholastic League competition came in and delivered their winning declamations, extemporaneous speeches or orations. Around Thanksgiving, if the high-school football team had had a good season, the coach was invited to speak on what makes a winning combination. If the season had been a flop, the coach was invited to speak anyway, on teamwork, sportsmanship or physical fitness.

Sometimes the programs were unadulterated entertainment. The most popular program in years took place when Mrs. Jack Goodnight's nephew, who played the guitar and sang with a string band on the radio in Ardmore, Oklahoma, staged a twenty-minute program, just as he would have done in the broadcasting studio. Some thought the program was not high-minded enough, but even those few had to admit they got a big kick out of it. Once a year on Ladies Day, the wives took complete charge of the meeting and would not allow their husbands to do a solitary thing but look on. One of the highlights of the year, Ladies Day was never serious. Everyone simply relaxed and had loads of fun, especially if one of the wives did a takeoff on her husband making a speech or singing a Rotary song, and one of them always did.

The meeting usually adjourned by one-thirty, and the Rotarians returned to their businesses more sluggish than energetic. The Treasurer remained behind to settle the bill with Mrs. Boyd. If there was a shortage of money, he made up the difference from the club treasury or from his own pocket and at the next meeting tracked down the culprit who had neglected to pay. For two Thursdays in a row, Sam Abernathy forgot to pay, and he got razzed something awful about it. The County Tax Collector, of all people, forgetting to pay!

When Willis Shumaker was elected President, Mattie Shumaker was beside herself with joy. Despite the many honors and offices that had been bestowed upon him during the years, this one was somehow different. It seemed to have prestige unequaled by all the others combined. It was a dream come true, to think that Willis Shumaker was President of the Rotary Club and she, his wife, was automatically the Honorary President of the Rotary Ladies Auxiliary. Unfortunately, the Ladies Auxiliary didn't meet but twice during Willis' term of office, and Mattie didn't have much to do. Once, they met to plan the annual Ladies Day, and the second time was to organize the refreshment booth at the Rotary's Donkey Baseball Game. At the end of Willis' term, the ladies gave Mattie a silver card tray engraved with her initials. She got choked up while protesting that she didn't deserve such a remembrance. They said if she didn't, they didn't know who did.

The Rotarians presented Willis with a plaque and engraved his name on the scroll of Past Presidents that hung in the hotel lobby. He admitted quite openly that it was a load off his mind not to have to preside over all those meetings, but no one took him seriously. Anybody who could preside as well as Willis Shumaker certainly didn't need to fear doing it. As past president, he continued to attend meetings regularly like the good Rotarian he was. He missed only once in eight months, and that was when he was in Houston on business.

It might have been nine months afterwards, maybe ten, but less than a year anyway, before he missed a meeting for no apparent reason. He walked into the house on Thursday at noon and almost startled his wife out of her wits.

"Willis Shumaker! How come you're not at Rotary Club?" she demanded.

"I just didn't feel like going," he said.

"Are you sick?"

"No. I feel fine."

"Then how come you didn't go to Rotary?"

"I told you—I just didn't feel like going."

"If you didn't feel like going, you must be sick."

"You can feel like not doing something without being sick, Mattie. I just didn't want to go. Nothing's wrong with me physically, if that's what you think."

"Didn't *want* to go?" She narrowed her eyes and looked

him over carefully. "That's no excuse!"

"It's the only excuse I've got."

She picked at him while she prepared his dinner, but she could get nothing out of him.

That afternoon she told a neighbor that she was afraid that Willis was coming down with something, but she didn't know what.

"But whatever it is certainly didn't affect his appetite," she said. "He ate enough dinner for a harvest hand. I couldn't fill him up."

Calvin Turnbough asked Willis the next day why he hadn't come to Rotary Club.

"I just didn't feel up to it, Calvin," he said.

"I see," said Calvin, but he really didn't.

Willis didn't miss another meeting for three months. And then—

"Willis, did somebody make you mad at Rotary?" Mattie asked when he appeared without warning for dinner on a second Thursday.

He assured her that in the human relations department he was hitting on all six. He seemed strangely happy.

"You've never missed Rotary like this," she said, her worry now out in the open. "And you act so *peculiar* about it. Maybe you ought to go see Dr. Beasley."

"You mean to get a shot or a pill for missing Rotary?" He laughed. "I've only missed twice," he added.

"But it's not like you to miss even once," she said, still suspicious. "If you ask me, I think something's bothering you that you won't tell me about."

"If you want to know the truth," he said, "I got to thinking about Mrs. Boyd's dried roast, and I almost threw up. She's got a one-track mind when she gets in that kitchen. She buys the cheapest cut of meat she can find, then she cooks the daylights out of it. Dry roast, watery mashed potatoes, lukewarm creamed peas, wilted salad, one little square of hard corn bread, iced tea without ice, and soggy pudding—it's about time again for bread pudding made out of her leftover biscuits. I think she starts saving the biscuits two weeks in advance."

"Now everybody knows that Mrs. Boyd sets a good table," Mattie said. "You've never complained about it before."

"It took me almost twenty years to get sick of all her leftovers. You know, I'll bet she doesn't even have any garbage cans. Why would she? She doesn't need them. But if she does, I'll bet they're clean, new and shiny inside."

Later, several Rotarians asked why he hadn't come to Rotary that day.

"I didn't feel like it," he told each of them.

Each of them recommended that he see Dr. Beasley.

When he missed the third meeting, Mattie was too upset to prepare his dinner. She sat down at the kitchen table across from him and, as the saying goes, put him through the wringer.

"There's more to this than Mrs. Boyd's food," she concluded wisely, "and I want to know what it is."

"All right, you've got me cornered," he said agreeably. "It's all those silly songs. I almost stayed in bed this morning when I woke up and remembered it was Thursday and that I had to face Purdy Robinson with his head in that songbook and waving his hand like he's treading water. Last week we sang 'My Darling Nellie Gray' and 'Carry Me Back to Ole Virginny.' Today it'll probably be 'Flow Gently, Sweet Afton' and 'Home on the Range.' "

Mattie tried to understand his criticism.

"What would you like to sing, then?" she asked.

"Nothing. Nothing at all. To hell with the singing!"

"*Willis Shumaker!* Watch your tongue!"

Marvin Cross sat down on the stool next to him the following morning in the Little Gem Cafe and said some of the fellows were beginning to wonder what was wrong with Ole Willis Shumaker these days. He wasn't coming to Rotary as regularly as he used to.

"Nothing's wrong, Marv," Willis said. "Believe me."

"But it's not like you to miss Rotary so much," Marvin persisted.

"Three meetings in a year and a half—that's all. Lots of people miss more than that."

"Everybody's not as active and interested as you are, Willis. And not everybody's one of our past presidents."

Willis waited four months before he allowed himself to miss another meeting. Mattie decided that the time had come for a showdown.

"I've had about as much of this as I can take, Willis Shumaker," she said over the dinner table. "You've *got* to tell me what's eating you about that Rotary Club. It's nearly driven me out of my mind."

"Lots of things," he said. "Today it's Fred Sellers."

"What did he do?"

"Nothing—but he's going to. Today he's going to make a speech."

"Well, what's wrong with that? Fred Sellers is the best public speaker in town."

"Probably. But it wouldn't hurt him to get a new speech."

"You mean he makes the same speech every time?"

"Just about. Today it's 'Civic Clubs and the Community.' Last time he had three main points about 'Rotary's Moral Responsibility to the Community.' Same thing. If it wasn't Fred, it would be somebody else with three main points. Everybody's got three main points. They talk about 'Leadership in Business,' or 'Community Morale and Welfare,' or some such drivel."

"*Drivel?* Willis, I think that's an awful thing for you to say!"

"Well—after thirty or forty times around, that's the way it sounds to me."

Mattie threw up her hands. "First you come in and say you don't feel like going. Then you say you're tired of Mrs. Boyd's food. After that you won't go because you don't want to sing 'My Old Kentucky Home.' Now you tell me you don't want to listen to Fred Sellers make a speech. How can I tell what's wrong with you when you tell me so many things and a different one each time?"

"Put them all together, and they spell MOTHER," he said playfully. "It's the combination, Mattie—the combination is what does it."

Before the afternoon was over, Mr. Hudgins stopped in at Shumaker's Heating & Plumbing Company to tell Willis what a good speech he had missed at noon and what a spellbinder Fred Sellers was.

"We missed you, Willis," said Mr. Hudgins kindly. "Hope nothing's wrong at home or with the business here."

"Everything's fine, Frank. Things are just fine."

"Naturally, I'll take your word for it," said Mr. Hudgins. "But just remember one thing, Willis. You've got lots of friends in that Rotary Club, and any of us are standing by to help out in any way we can. All you've got to do is call on us."

One day while driving home from work, Willis rolled up the windows of his automobile, glanced in the back seat to reassure himself that he was alone, and said aloud, "The Rotary Club is driving me crazy."

The admission lifted his spirits. So high, in fact, that he lost his head and said it again.

Three blocks later, his exhilaration took him one step further.

"I think I'll quit," he said aloud.

It was a catharsis. It was a release. By the time he arrived home, he was in such high spirits that Mattie would have accused him of drinking had he not been a dedicated teetotaler. That night he slept more soundly than he had slept in months.

After supper a few months later, while Mattie was clearing the table and after the children had scattered throughout the house to do their homework, Willis let it all out.

"I've decided to resign from Rotary Club," he said suddenly.

Mattie was halfway through the kitchen door. She turned back.

"You've decided to *what?*" she asked.

"You heard me."

"What in heaven's name are you talking about?"

"Just what I said—I intend to resign from Rotary Club."

Mattie returned to the dining table, a sticky, messy dinner plate in each hand. The silverware slid off onto the carpet. She seemed not to notice.

"Are you out of your mind?" she asked, dropping into a chair.

"No."

"Then why on earth would you think about resigning from the Rotary Club?"

"Because I'm tired of it," he said. "I'm tired of the meetings. I'm tired of the singing. I'm tired of the programs. I'm tired of the food. I'm tired of everything about it."

"Willis Shumaker, you've gone mad. Stark raving mad! You know as well as I do that you can't get along without the Rotary Club."

"Why not?"

"You just can't, that's all. You've been a Rotarian for years."

"Maybe that's the reason I'm tired of it. I hate it."

"*Hate* it? Willis, have you got a fever?"

"No."

"Then how can you say you hate Rotary? You've never hated it before."

"I never hated mutton, either, until one time I ate too much of it and got sick."

"That's no reason to resign."

"It'll have to do until a better one comes along."

"The Rotary Club does a lot of good for the town."

"For instance?"

"It promotes community progress."

"How?"

"Well—it just does. Businessmen's clubs always do."

"So does the Chamber of Commerce, and I'm a director of that."

"But you've got to do your part everywhere."

"You're kidding! You're telling *me* about doing my part? I do it all the time. I always have. Just the other day I was counting all the elective offices I hold or have held in this town—civic and religious. I'm not sure I counted all of them, but I counted *twenty-seven*."

"Well, good grief! That doesn't mean—"

"Besides those twenty-seven offices, I played first base in the Donkey Baseball Game last year. I was bridesmaid at the Womanless Wedding two years ago. I had a leading part in this year's Black Face Minstrels for the March of Dimes. I worked the ticket booth at every home football game for three years in a row. The only reason I didn't run for mayor when they asked me was because I didn't have time to campaign. I even preached once when Brother Wallace couldn't get home from Wichita Falls because of that washout on Pease River. So don't tell me about doing my part."

"But the Rotary's good for your business."

"How can that be? I've got a monopoly. I'm the only plumber in town."

"I wish you wouldn't call yourself a plumber, Willis, I've asked you again and again not to do that."

"What am I if not a plumber?"

"You *own* the company. You're a *businessman*. And that's another thing. Being a Rotarian improves your business relations by bringing all businessmen together each week," she said.

"I'm surrounded by Rotarians seven days a week. Anywhere I go—to church, to the Little Gem, to play golf, to the barbershop, just name it—and I've got Rotarians all around me. Eating together at Mrs. Boyd's every Thursday doesn't add anything to that."

"The Rotary Club is always taking on worthwhile projects."

"Refresh my memory."

"They gave a hundred dollars to the County Library Fund this spring."

"And so? I could have raised a hundred dollars in one afternoon by walking up and down the street and asking for it. Fannie Hoffmyer and the B. and P.W. Club raised three hundred and fifty dollars in one night."

"The Rotary Club bought that little Waldrip boy on Northside a pair of glasses."

"They cost fifteen ninety-five because we got them at cost, and Dr. Beasley gave his services free."

"Well, there you are!" she said in triumph. "Dr. Beasley is a Rotarian."

"Dr. Beasley is a human being. He gives his services free many times when people can't afford to pay. Being a Rotarian is not what makes him kindhearted."

Mattie got up and finished clearing the table, but before she surrendered she fired one last shot.

"You know yourself that you've always been thrilled to death to be a Rotarian."

"The thrill has gone."

"You strutted like a peacock when you were elected president of the Rotary."

"It was an honor."

"Then how can you say you hate it or that you're tired of it?"

He changed his tone abruptly. "Mattie? Why don't you wear that gray coat with the fur collar any more?"

"Well, for heaven's sakes! I wore it six years!"

"But you loved that coat," he reminded her. "And it's not worn out. It's the same coat. The cloth is good, and it still keeps you warm. Why did you stop wearing it?"

"I got sick and tired of it, if you must know."

"That's why I intend to resign from the Rotary Club—I'm sick and tired of it."

"But that's not the same thing as getting tired of an old gray coat."

"Seems the same to me—anyway, that's why I'm resigning."

"What will you tell everybody? That you're sick and tired of it?"

"Certainly not. I've got more sense than that. Don't worry. I'll walk out the door with all my friendships intact."

"I wish I could be sure of that," she said, shaking her head in bewilderment. "You'd better get into bed and get a good night's sleep. Maybe you'll feel better in the morning."

He did. He had never felt better in his life. He began working on his letter of resignation that very morning. In the days following he returned to it again and again until he saw that he could improve it no more. Then he laid it aside, pleased that he had done his best.

Meanwhile, he attended Rotary luncheons on Thursdays,

fiendishly enjoying them while marking time until the appropriate moment to submit his letter of resignation. Respectfully, he laughed at all jokes. Dutifully he chuckled at the ridiculous antics of silly wives, including his own, on the day they took charge of the luncheon. He could endure the spectacle only because he knew that never again for the rest of his life would he be compelled to witness another Ladies Day. He didn't even lose patience with the endless wrangling over a resolution for or against—he wasn't sure which—the proposed bypass around the south end of town. He applauded appreciatively for the tired clichés and worn-out speeches of the program guests. He drowned the roast beef in ketchup to moisten it and give it flavor. He licked the platter clean, looking forward to the day when he would no longer be concerned with the taste, texture and dryness of the one and only entrée that Mrs. Boyd's imagination permitted her to prepare. Under Purdy Robinson's seesaw song directing, he all but shouted the words to "I've Got Sixpence" and "Down by the Old Mill Stream." To outward appearances, Willis Shumaker was the most enthusiastic of Rotarians. No one would have suspected that his happiness and jubilation was analagous to that of a student on the last day of school.

Came the day. He carried his letter to the Rotary Club. A moment before the double doors opened, he handed it to Lefty Aiken, Membership Vice President, and requested that he read it when Booby Duckworth, President, called for New Business.

Lefty stuck it in his pocket without reading it. After the singing was over, grace had been said, and the Rotarians had started whacking away at the dry roast beef, Willis glanced across the room to find Lefty Aiken regarding him with mystification. Just before dessert was served—fruit Jello it was that day—Lefty got up from his chair and came around to lean over Willis' shoulder.

"Willis, are you sure you want me to read this?" he whispered.

"I'm sure," said Willis. "Dead sure."

"But it doesn't give any reasons."

"That's okay," Willis said smugly. "Just read it as it is, and I'll take care of the rest of it."

"We've been friends a long time, Willis, and I don't like to be a party to something you might be sorry for later on."

"I won't be sorry, Lefty. But thanks just the same."

Lefty sighed and returned to his seat, too bewildered to enjoy his dinner and the good fellowship that went with it.

When Booby had finished welcoming the guests and called for New Business, Lefty Aiken got to his feet and announced that he had been handed a letter by a fellow Rotarian who desired that it be read to the membership. Here is what he read:

"To my fellow Rotarians:

"Please accept my resignation from the Rotary Club effective this date. I will aways treasure my associations in this club, and I will aways be grateful for the highest honor you could bestow on any member, namely the privilege of serving as your President. My personal relations with any of you, individually or collectively, have nothing to do with my decision to terminate my membership. I will always consider each of you a true friend.

"Your approval of my resignation without discussion will be appreciated.

"Yours very truly,
"Willis Shumaker"

Lefty sat down. Had anyone dropped a pin at that moment, it would have created a crashing, banging noise.

Booby got to his feet and coughed nervously.

"I won't pretend that I'm not surprised," he said slowly.

"But in deference to our fellow Rotarian's wishes, I feel duty bound to ask for a motion without discussion." He looked across the room at Willis, obviously wishing for a way out. "Although I will have to say, both as your friend and as your President, Willis, that I would like nothing better than to persuade you to reconsider this step you have decided to take."

He paused for a moment and watched Willis carefully for agreement. Willis shook his head and smiled. Every eye in the room was fastened on the President. No one dared look at Willis.

Booby gulped noisily.

"In that event," he said, "do I hear a motion that this resignation be accepted?"

No one said a word.

Booby repeated the question.

Again silence.

Willis himself got to his feet. "Mr. President," he said, "I move that this letter of resignation be accepted."

Eyebrows went up. Feet shuffled. Chairs scraped the floor. A hubbub of activity set in without anyone actually doing anything. That is, no one except Willis. He sat down.

"This is somewhat irregular—er—isn't it?" Booby stammered. "I'm not sure it's proper."

Willis stood up again. "I don't think you'll find it prohibited by our constitution and bylaws," he said.

Booby was by no means assured. He didn't know that much about procedures.

"Maybe it's not proper parliamentary procedure," he said.

"It isn't exactly *good* parliamentary procedure," Willis said, "but I don't think you'll find it prohibited by Roberts' *Rules of Order*."

Booby looked over the room and caught the eye of Ennis Grissom, the Parliamentarian for that year. Ennis was trying to look the other way, but he got caught.

"Is that right, Ennis?" Booby asked.

Ennis nodded.

Booby stared at Ennis for a moment, then turned back to the room at large.

"Well—okay," he said helplessly. "Do I hear a second?"

He didn't. He waited for an awkward moment or so.

Marvin Cross stirred. "Second," he mumbled.

"All in favor let it be known by saying 'Aye,'" Booby directed.

A chorus of "Ayes" went up from around the room.

"All opposed let it be known by saying 'Nay.'"

A chorus of "Nays" went up from around the room.

"I couldn't tell much difference," Booby said wonderingly. "Sounded all the same to me."

A general nodding of heads confirmed his judgment.

"This is rather unusual," he said. "Maybe we'd better have a show of hands so we'll know for sure. Allinfavorletitbeknownbyraisingtheirrighthands."

Lefty Aiken counted the hands.

"Eleven," he announced.

"Allopposedletitbeknownbyalikesign."

Lefty counted the hands again.

"Eleven," he said again. "It's a tie, Boob—Mr. President."

"Well, this is *really* unusual," said Booby. He ran a hand over his bald head. He looked at his hand. It was wet. "The first time in my experience, as a matter of fact," he went on. "I guess the only thing to do is vote again. Allinfavorletitbe—"

"Mr. President!" Willis was on his feet again. "I believe that Section XII of our constitution and bylaws requires that in case of a tie, the President must cast the deciding vote. In that case, therefore, another vote would not only be unnecessary, it would be unconstitutional as well."

Most Rotarians were less than experts on the constitution and bylaws of their organization, and they were pleased that their past president was. They took his word without question and admired him openly for being so knowledgeable.

Calvin Turnbough stood up. "Mr. President, I move that we waive that particular provision of the constitution for this one specific matter of business only, so that we can cast another vote on this unusual matter. Somebody might want to change their vote, and we ought to give them a chance."

By now, Booby Duckworth was ready to faint, and he was grateful for Calvin's coming to save him. "Now that sounds like a fine idea," he said. "Maybe we ought to do what Calvin says. Allinfavorofwaivingthe—"

Willis stood up and interrupted once again. "Mr. President! According to Section VI of our constitution and bylaws, no provision of said constitution and bylaws can be waived unless it is so recommended to the full membership by the board of directors after meeting and study in executive session. Therefore, any vote to waive the provisions of Section XII of the constitution at this particular time is out of order."

"What'll we do, then?" Booby asked.

"Either get Brother Rotarian Turnbough to withdraw his motion, else this membership will have to vote on his motion, but we won't be voting on what he *said*. Understand? We will actually be voting on whether or not the board of directors shall consider it in executive session. So if we have a vote, I think it should be clear to all members exactly what it is we're voting on."

"Now let me get this straight," said Booby. "Does this mean that before we can get rid of this rule about breaking the tie, we've got to have a meeting of the directors and talk about it then come back and vote on it?"

"It does."

"When?"

"As soon as possible—preferably before the next meeting next Thursday."

"What'll we do with this tie vote in the mean time?"

"Table it—unless you can get Calvin to withdraw it."

"How about it, Calvin?" Booby said. "You wanna withdraw it?"

Calvin stood up. "I don't hardly see how I can do that, Mr. President. My conscience just won't allow me to do it. I'm sorry, but that's the way I feel about—"

"Okayokayokay, Calvin," said Booby. He wiped his head again. He turned back to Willis. "Now, Willis, do you mean to tell me that we'll just have to break up this meeting and leave the motion hanging?"

"We have no choice," said Willis.

Booby sought out Ennis Grissom again. "That right, Ennis?"

Ennis shrugged. He didn't know.

"Well, you really handed me one this time, Willis," Booby said. "I don't know when I could meet with the directors. I've got to go down to Quanah this afternoon, and I'm supposed to be in Childress all day tomorrow. That takes us up to Saturday, and you know as well as I do that we can't get anybody to meet on Saturday, and we sure as hell can't meet on Sunday. And next week I've gotta be in Austin until Wednesday—I might not even be here for next Thursday's meeting. So when you add all—are you *sure* we've got to do it this way, Willis?"

Willis nodded.

Booby looked at Ennis.

Ennis nodded.

Booby turned to Calvin. "Maybe you ought to withdraw your motion after all, Calvin, seeing as how it's so hard to have a meeting of the directors and all."

Calvin stood firm. "I don't see how I can very well do that,

Mr. President. I just don't think it's very democratic for this club to want to do something and not be able to do it. It just don't strike me as very *American!*"

The membership broke out into loud applause.

A windy free-for-all ensued, during which Booby Duckworth banged the table with his gavel so often and with such force that Mrs. Boyd opened the door and looked in to see if he was tearing up her furniture. Deaf-and-dumb Townie Ledbetter, who was washing dishes for Mrs. Boyd that week, had come in from the kitchen and was sitting on the piano stool outside the door. Mrs. Boyd waved him to get back into the kitchen. He grinned happily at her, waved back, and stayed where he was.

Everyone talked at once. A few Rotarians suggested that they remove the constitution altogether. Others said this was an occasion that called for cool heads and thoughtful minds, else somebody might fly off the handle and do something they would regret later on. No constitution at all would mean anarchy. Yes, but why have a constitution if in reality it was a dictatorship? Yes, but there were proper ways and improper ways to get things done, and the Rotarians would be eternally sorry if they chose the *improper* way. Motions were made and seconded; motions were made and not seconded; some motions were discussed; some were not. Some were not even heard. Some members called for a vote. Some member made a motion that the meeting be adjourned.

Eventually, Booby had had enough. He threw up his hands and called a halt.

"All right—*all right*—ALL RIGHT!" he shouted.

No one took him seriously.

"Everybody quiet!" he continued to shout. "Qui-et! *Qui-ett!* Everybody LISTEN to me! Listen, listen, *lis-sunnnn,* LISS-SUNNNNNN to *ME!*"

A wave of quietness swept the room.

"I can't do any presiding with everybody talking at once," he said. "Now let's get this business straightened out. Most of us have got to get back to work. I know I sure as hell do. We're gonna be here all day if we don't get some order into these proceedings and *finish!*"

The last of the talking subsided. The Rotarians listened expectantly.

"Okay—that's more like it," Booby said. "*Now.* Does anybody know how many motions there are before the house? Because I'll be real honest with you—I lost count. Does *anybody* know?"

A rumbling started up from the tables.

"OR-DERRRR!" Booby shouted quickly. "All I asked was a question. I didn't ask everybody to start yapping again!" He turned to Ennis Grissom, Parliamentarian. "How many motions are there, Ennis?"

Ennis looked panic stricken.

"Five—I think."

"Okay—five it is," Booby decided.

"I counted six," said Calvin Turnbough.

"I know of eight," said Frank Hudgins.

Booby banged his gavel twice.

"*Five*, me and Ennis said!" He banged his gavel again. "We got *five* motions before the house—not six, and not eight, and not any other number. We got FIVE! And we're gonna get rid of the whole shebang—right now. Now the way we're gonna do it is start with the last one and work our way back to the first. I hope none of you got any objections, because that's the way we're gonna do it anyway!"

Ennis Grissom half rose from his chair. "Mr. President, I believe that the proper procedure is to take the first one first," he said. "Technically speaking, all others are out of order. Besides, some of the later motions might hinge on an earlier motion, and it doesn't make much sense if we vote on—"

[*94*]

"OVERRULED!" Booby announced without hesitation. "We're not speaking technically. It'll be easier to go backwards, because it'll be easier to remember them."

There was another general nodding of heads around the room.

"Okay," said Booby. "Now let's get started, and I'm warning all of you—no more knock-down drag-outs. Just vote and keep your mouths shut. I've got to get back to work. Now for the last one first. . . ."

So awed were the Rotarians by their President's firm hand and decisiveness that they submitted without further discussion. They sat quietly and meekly while Booby and Ennis steered them backwards to Calvin's original motion to waive the provisions of the constitution requiring the president to vote in case of a tie.

"Okay—now we're ready to vote on Calvin's motion," Booby announced with pride. "But before you all get bent out of shape again like you did before, you might as well know that I've already decided what I'm gonna do. I'm gonna vote and break the tie. So if you waive the provisions of the constitution—or vote that we all have to have a meeting, or whatever it is we're voting on—if you do all that just to get me off the hook, you'll just be spinning your wheels. You ready to vote? And you might as well be, because I'm telling you right now, we're not gonna have any more discussions in this meeting today."

Calvin Turnbough stood up.

"Mr. President," he said meekly. "In view of your decision to break the tie, my original motion becomes pointless. Therefore, I withdraw my motion."

"Now, that's more like it," Booby said with a broad smile. "I don't see why you couldn't have done that in the first place, Calvin, and saved us all this trouble. Okay—now let's get this business out of the way and get back to work."

He stopped and rubbed the palm of his hand across his bald head. Then his manner softened.

"I don't feel right doing this," he apologized, "and I can assure you that I wouldn't do it, except that during our discussions, Willis came to me personally and urged me to vote in favor of his resignation. He assures me that he wants it this way, and I feel duty bound as a personal friend and as your President to honor the wishes of one of our most distinguished members and past presidents. Therefore, it is with a heavy heart that I vote 'Aye' on Willis Shumaker's letter of resignation. Announce the final vote, Lefty."

Lefty Aiken stood up.

"The final vote," he said, "is twelve *for* and eleven *against*. The *fors*—that is, the *ayes* have it."

At that precise moment, Willis Shumaker became an ex-Rotarian.

"You didn't count Townie's vote, did you?" Booby asked.

Lefty shook his head.

Booby looked to the rear of the room, where Townie Ledbetter still sat on the piano stool. He waved to him and smiled understandingly.

"Thank you, Townie," he said. "You can put your hand down now."

Townie grinned, raised his other hand and made a few hand signals at Booby.

"One other thing," Booby said. "I must apologize to our guest speaker for today." He nodded to Mr. Hightower, who had long since pocketed his manuscript and dismissed the speech from his mind. "It looks like we've used up all the time we ordinarily would have used for his speech. I sure hope you understand, Mr. Hightower, because I know you've prepared a fine speech." He turned to the membership at large. "Mr. Hightower has prepared a fine speech on 'Youth, Tomorrow's Leaders,' and I know that every Rotarian in this room would have profited from it. Who's the Program Chairman for next week?"

Dr. George Odom raised his hand.

"Is it all right with you, George, if we invite Mr. Hightower to come back next week and make his speech?"

George smiled broadly and nodded enthusiastically. He had not given the first thought to next week's program.

Mr. Hightower stirred. "I'm afraid that won't be possible, Booby," he said. "I've got another commitment and won't be able to make it. Thanks, though."

"Oh—that's too bad," Booby said. "Well—we're awfully sorry about it, believe me—but you saw what happened." He looked at Dr. Odom again. "Looks like you'll have to come up with a program anyway, George."

The smile faded from George's face.

"Any other business to come before the house?" Booby asked. His manner was threatening and his tone belligerent.

No one said a word. The Rotarians were dog-tired, anyway. The meeting adjourned. The time was two-thirty.

Meanwhile, Mrs. Boyd's telephone in the lobby had been on a jag with secretaries, clerks, stenographers and wives calling wanting to know when on earth Rotary was going to break up and what in the world were they doing for so long? Each member of the Rotary Club filed by and shook Willis' hand as though he were moving out of town. Despite himself, Willis got choked up and misty-eyed, wondering if, after all, he had done the right thing. But it was too late to worry about that. Willis Shumaker was an ex-Rotarian, and the only way he could ever be a member again would be to rejoin.

So that's how and why Willis Shumaker, past president and past everything else, resigned from Rotary Club. Lots of people were puzzled, but since he didn't volunteer any reasons, most of them were too polite to pick at him about it. They speculated among themselves, but none of their theories worked out. He wasn't mad at anybody. His health was good. His business didn't take up any more of his time than it ever had. He went right on working like a beaver on local committees, taking part in all drives, campaigns and worthwhile projects, never saying no to a request for assistance when and where he was needed. As a matter of fact, after he resigned from the Rotary Club, he struck some people as about the happiest and most contented man in town.

And he was.

3.

~❧

Purdy Robinson's Parade

If Purdy Robinson was a born worrier—and he was—his nature must have found complete release and fulfillment the year he was Chairman of the San Jacinto Day Parade. Even before he had lifted the first finger, his stature as a worrier had begun to soar, and by the time the parade had passed by he had become one of the great worriers of our time. From beginning to end, worries were stacked so high that he could hardly see around, over or under them.

Purdy had owned and operated Robinson's Hardware Store for twenty-six years in the same location on Main Street between Second and Third, directly across from Akers' Variety Store, between the Texas Gas Company and Howard Slaton's Ford Agency. It was an excellent vantage point from where he could keep abreast of daily happenings downtown—and worry about them. And worry he did. Indeed, he was inclined to worry about whatever happened to be handy—business, taxes, sin, his health, the weather, his grandchildren's newfangled education, high speed on the highways, and all the decisions, good and bad, from the City Council. The parade, then, was custom built for his own peculiar brand of brow-wrinkling. Especially if it was to be his personal responsibility. Frank Hudgins, druggist, said "Purdy's always worrying anyway, so he might as well be worrying about the parade as something else."

Purdy was in his mid-sixties, bony and chickenlike in appearance and build, which at first glance made him seem frail and undernourished, but he had stamina, ate like a horse, and was a worker. Too much the plodder, perhaps, he would get the job done if given enough time. He was a good citizen upon whom civic responsibility weighed heavily. To his everlasting glory, however, he recognized his own limitations and was not driven by the Head Man syndrome. He was a follower, not a leader, and was content with his customary view of life from the rear ranks. "If you didn't have any privates," he explained, "you wouldn't need any generals."

He was a good man, an honest man, a man with intense loyalties and an unshakable sense of right and wrong. In the morals department, nobody could lay a glove on him. He was not a good organizer, though, and in fairness to him, it should be noted that he pointed this out to those who named him Chairman of the San Jacinto Day Parade.

"I don't mind doing my part," he said to Booby Duckworth, cotton broker and High Commissioner of that year's San Jacinto Day Festival, the chosen one to inform Purdy of his elevation to high office, "but being head cheese of a big thing like this just ain't in my line, Booby, and you know it. I'm not the executive type."

"Aw, get out!" said Booby. "Who needs an executive? It's all a matter of getting your ducks lined up in a row, minding your p's and q's and following your nose. All you gotta do is set a deadline for registration of the floats and give everybody a copy of the rules. Then you figure out the assembly point and order of march. You don't have to map out the parade route. Just follow last year's. There's nothing to it. Make arrangements with the high-school band and pep squad, then go around to the car dealers and arrange for the Mayor's and Grand Marshal's cars—and Purdy, make sure one's a Ford and the other's a Chevrolet. We don't want Leroy Chambers and Howard Slaton getting mad at us again, so be sure that—"

"But Booby, that's the kind of thing—"

"Then you get somebody to build the reviewing stand. You can get anybody you want, but Cecil Poole usually does it, and he'll get mad as a hornet if you get anybody else. But like I said—it's up to you."

"I wouldn't let Cecil Poole build me a henhouse," said Purdy. "Not if I expected to keep the rain off the chickens. You must of forgot about the stand falling down once."

"Just one time!" said Booby. "And it was just one little corner—that's all. He put an extra two by four under that corner the next year, and it's been okay ever since."

"Yeah—but how about the other three corners?"

"They didn't need any braces. Now you want to make sure everybody's got two flags out front—Texas and American. Don't wait too long to check on that, so they can order them if they don't have any. And see if you can talk Dice Riley into buying a new flagpole. His broke several years ago, but he uses it anyway. The flag comes about to your shoulder. Then you get together with Artie Whelan and figure out when the 'No Parking' on Main Street goes into effect. It might not hurt for you to check on it yourself. You know how Artie is—he's a good sheriff and all that, but he gets sidetracked sometimes. Once we found a car locked tighter than a drum in front of the Little Gem and nobody knew whose it was. It stuck out like a sore thumb all during the parade. Now don't try to do all this yourself. Get yourself a committee and—"

"But Booby! That's what I'm talking about! I ain't no good at supervising committees."

"The Parade Judge has already been picked and you don't have to worry about that," Booby went on. "We got Representative Lee Devol this year—he's flying up from Austin, and he'd probably appreciate a nice little personal note from you, Purdy. Be sure and tell Willis Shumaker when Lee's arriving so he can meet him. Willis is the Official Escort this year. You don't have to do it yourself. Let Willis take care of that."

"They tell me that the high winds around here in April knocks them little airplanes around like they was box kites," said Purdy. "Seems kinda dangerous to—"

"Oh—before I forget it—one thing you want to impress on all entries is that they're responsible for their own floats. Don't get sucked into helping them individually, or you'll get accused of favoritism. You ought to take a look at the floats personally, though, Purdy, just to satisfy yourself that they follow the rules. No advertising allowed, you remember. They know that, but somebody might try to put one over on you, anyway, like the time Frank Hudgins posted price tags all over his float. Remember? Ennis Grissom had to make him take them off. It won't hurt for you to get in touch with Holly Ashcraft early in the game so he can start putting things in the *Courier* about the parade. Holly can be a big help, but you gotta tell him what you want."

"But Booby, I don't *know* what I want! That's what I'm trying to tell you."

"Good publicity is essential. *Very essential.* And the sooner, the better. Oh—before I forget it—be sure and get all your entries registered before you decide on the assembly point. Lefty Aiken did it the other way 'round once. He overestimated the length of the parade and assembled them out at the bypass. They had to march a whole mile before they got to where anybody was looking. By the time they got downtown, everybody was pooped. That's just a suggestion, you understand. You can use your own judgment in these matters, of course."

"Well, I never did any parade assembling to speak of—"

"I'm not telling you how to run your business, because this is your show from A to Z, but it wouldn't hurt for you to stop by the City Hall and check with Hershel Mansfield to make sure the Water Department's not planning any kind of work along Main Street on parade day. You remember that hole in front of the Texan Theatre and the parade had to detour around it? I just thought I'd mention it in case you hadn't thought about it."

"That place in front of the Eatmore Bakery gives them more trouble than all the others put together," Purdy said. "It spurts up like a geyser. Once it took three days to—*Booby!* I'm just not cut out for this kind of work. I—"

"Oh—if you don't mind one more little suggestion—I wouldn't try to U-turn the parade down by the depot, if I were you, Purdy. That was tried once, and it was the damnedest jam you ever saw in your life. The parade was meeting itself coming and going. The band had to break formation when it met the Home Demonstration Club float—they had a wide one that year. There wasn't room to pass. You oughta watch that, Purdy."

By now, Purdy's face had more lines in it than a road map. They were increasing with each word Booby uttered.

"I just don't know if I've got the experience for all this kind of—"

"Now, you're in complete charge, Purdy. I want you to understand that. You're the final authority."

"That's what I was afraid of."

"If anybody comes to me with a complaint, you know what I'm gonna do? I'm gonna send them right back to you, because you're in charge of the whole shebang. Do anything you like. You can decide which float comes first and which comes last, and I wouldn't listen to any arguments about it if I were you. Just put your foot down. Use your command authority."

"I'm not a commander, Booby!"

"Who said so? Why do you think the committee picked you out to chair the parade?"

"That's the next thing I was going to ask you."

"Listen. All you gotta do is mind your p's and q's, put your shoulder to the wheel and keep your eye on the ball. That's all. And *think ahead*. Stay one jump ahead of the pack. Maybe you ought to get a little notebook and make yourself a little checklist of things to do. Marvin Cross wrote them on the backs of envelopes one year, but Enid threw all the envelopes away when she was sending his pants to the cleaner's one day. Poor Marv got all messed up. Get a notebook, Purdy. *Get a notebook.* Just check off each little job as you complete it, and you won't forget anything."

By the time Booby had finished giving him pointers and moral support, Purdy was a wreck.

Nor was his wife much help. Eula Robinson was a large-chested woman who, even when seated in a chair, gave the unhappy impression that she was standing at full height glaring down at you. She wore a pince-nez, through which she apparently viewed everything with distaste and disapproval. She was one of those forbidding ladies who browbeat others into agreeing with her while at the same time daring them to do it.

"How come they picked *you?*" she hooted. "You never did anything like that in your life!"

"That's what I kept telling him, Eula!" he said miserably. "He wouldn't listen. He kept talking and telling me what to do."

"Why didn't you just say no, thank you?"

"He didn't ask me. He *told* me."

"Why didn't you just walk away from him and leave him talking?"

"I couldn't. We was standing in my own store."

She laughed, but she wasn't tickled. "All I can say is it's a funny way to run a parade," she said.

"Well—what would *you* do if you were in my shoes?"

"*Me?*" she screeched. "You got yourself into this mess, Purdy Robinson, and you can just get yourself out. Don't come running to me. If you've got any sense, you'll get back inside that store where you belong and quit trying to run things all up and down Main Street."

"I'm not trying to run anything, Eula! Booby just came in the store and started talking like I had already agreed, and I couldn't head him off. It was like talking to a Victrola."

"Hmpff! I don't see why you can't use your tongue. That's what it's in your mouth for, isn't it?"

"You just try talking to Booby Duckworth when he gets strung out like he does. You just try it!"

She shook her head in exasperation, adjusted her pince-nez with thumb and forefinger and fixed her husband with her most hopeless look.

"Purdy," she said, "I've never seen anybody like you. Never in all my life. You're always getting yourself tangled up in things, and you never know how to get loose. Nineteen years ago you led the singing in Rotary Club one day because Liles Greenwood had laryngitis, and you've been doing it ever since. I wouldn't be surprised if you're not permanent chairman of the parade every year from now on until you die. I'm telling you—you'd better get yourself out while the getting's good."

Her moral support, when added to Booby Duckworth's, was almost more than Purdy could bear.

San Jacinto Day, as every Texan was supposed to know,

was to commemorate the glorious day when Sam Houston and a small band of Texans captured Santa Anna, the Mexican dictator, and the favorite villain of all right-thinking Texans. It was not the occasion necessarily for the town's biggest bash. Aside from the parade itself, there was scarcely any tradition behind the day's activities. And even the parade itself could be a chancy proposition; one year, only three floats and the high-school band were entered, along with the Odd Fellows drill team, four members of which didn't have uniforms. Once there wasn't a parade at all—nobody would agree to take charge of it. Then, the parade coming in April as it did, sometimes the weather was still cold, and even if it wasn't, the rain, the dust, and the high winds were constant threats.

The other events of the day depended on the ingenuity and energy of the Festival Committee, and they varied from one year to the next: a rodeo, a street dance, a barbecue at the Fair Grounds, a carnival on the Court House lawn, or a pageant at the high-school auditorium. This last was generally unpopular, for no matter what the planning, Myrtle McAfee Dunlap somehow always ended up running the show, and she had a dozen tricks up her sleeve for sneaking her mother's patriotic poems into the performance, with Myrtle herself doing the reciting. Even so, no true-blue Texan could ignore San Jacinto Day altogether, not even those who weren't certain what it was for and confused it with Texas Independence Day. So the town usually managed to observe it one way or another. This year, a picnic was scheduled at the high-school football field for after the parade, but excitement didn't run high. A football field just didn't seem like the right kind of place for a picnic.

Purdy hadn't missed a San Jacinto Day parade in more than twenty years, but in all that time he had never been closer than the curb. His new vantage point made a difference. He followed Booby's advice and began to think ahead. Indeed, before Booby got out the door, he started thinking ahead and didn't sleep a wink for three nights. Suppose it rained? What if the high-school band couldn't participate? What should he do if a dust storm blew up? Stop the parade until the skies cleared? Call it off altogether? What if Lee Devol couldn't come? He saw Main Street as one vast gaping hole through the courtesy of the City Water Department. He had nightmares of a derailed locomotive at the railroad crossing, of a freak snowstorm in April, of a flu epidemic, of himself down with the grippe, of a parade with no floats in it. . . .

Purdy's wife saw what was happening.

"For goodness' sakes, Purdy!" she said. "You're worrying yourself sick, and you haven't done anything yet. Not one solitary thing. Why don't you at least start something—just anything—and worry about things *when* they happen? At the rate you're going, you won't have any worries left over when you might really need them."

He flubbed around for a week looking for a place to start. It was like trying to get a handhold on a whale. He did appoint a committee of three reluctant citizens, but he never got around to assigning jobs to them, and they were too shrewd to remind him of the oversight. Plans got off the ground anyway and somehow. Word got around and people began to swamp the Parade Chairman with suggestions, complaints and questions. At home, at the store, at Rotary Club, on the street, in church, in the barbershop, he had the feeling that they were following him, lying in wait, trying to trip him up. Main Street, to him, became one great ambush.

"They're driving me crazy," he told Holly Ashcraft one day at Rotary Club.

"Well, Purdy, I've been trying to get you to give me the stuff for the paper, and you won't do it," Holly reminded him.

"I just haven't had time, Holly. Every time I look up, somebody's standing there asking me about some durned fool thing or the other."

"*Put it in the paper, Purdy!* Give me the facts and let me write them up, and they'll stop bothering you. The reason they're asking you questions is because they don't know what's going on."

Actually, Purdy did not need Holly Ashcraft's publicity to the extent another chairman might. Eula Robinson had been doing *The Weekly Courier*'s job for Holly, and according to some tastes, doing it better. Eula Robinson was a walking newspaper, classified ads and all, and her progress reports on the parade included all controversies and disputes, along with thumbnail sketches of the participants and her own opinion of who was right and who was wrong. According to Miss Eunice Horton, telephone operator, and something of a reporter herself, Mrs. Robinson more than doubled her telephone time after Purdy was appointed Parade Chairman. Many parade discussions were kicked off with the opening statement, "Eula Robinson told me. . . ."

Even so, Holly pinned Purdy to the wall in the store one day and pulled enough information out of him for a story in the *Courier*. It wasn't a Pulitzer Prize job by any means, but at least the San Jacinto Day Parade was formally announced to the public, the rules were set out in black and white, and no one could claim ignorance as an excuse for not knowing.

Just the same, Purdy's telephone rang at all hours, night and day, at home and at work. People streamed in and out of Robinson's Hardware Store, not as customers, but as parade participants with problems to lay at the feet of the Parade Chairman. All of them were knotty, and some of them were impossible, but he worried about each in turn and some overlapping.

Junior Bird, his 6½-feet-tall, dismal, sixty-four-year-old

clerk with a bald head and oversized knuckles, who was about as big around as a chigger and was antiparade and, in many respects, anticustomer, threatened to quit and go back to his Watkins Products route if people didn't stop bothering him with parade business when his employer was away from the store. He didn't know anything about the parade, because he didn't want to know anything about it, and he was determined not to learn anything about it.

"Now, Purdy, I'm telling you for the last time," he warned him almost daily, "if you're gonna run this parade, you danged sure better stay in this store and run it and quit chasing around all over town!"

"Running the parade is what I'm out chasing around about, Junior," Purdy explained again and again.

"If that's what you're doing, then how come everybody traipses in here and asks *me* questions?"

"They're looking for me."

"Why don't they look for you wherever you are instead of in here, then?"

"Because they don't know where I am."

"That's what I'm talking about," Junior said, "and you'd better stay here and talk to them if you know what's good for you."

Mrs. Robinson, on the other hand, was delighted by her pseudo-official status as purveyor of parade information. Her knowledge was encyclopedic, or at least she gave that impression. She worked hard at the job. Sometimes after a lengthy telephone conversation, which most of hers were, she would flash Miss Eunice and ask if anyone had been trying to call her while the line was busy. If Miss Eunice's answer was negative, Mrs. Robinson would bless her out for not keeping a closer eye on the switchboard.

As March blew past and April lumbered in on clouds of dust, the parade began to take form with few surprises. Booby

Duckworth's briefing had been one great prophecy from first breath to last.

Purdy gave the lead-off position for floats to the Eastern Star, because they had requested it first. The Bronte Club demanded the lead-off position as its right, because it was the town's oldest organization (1904), so he gave the lead-off spot to the Bronte Club. The Eastern Star's founding date, as it turned out, however, proved to be somewhere between 1778 and 1851, an open-and-shut case for the lead spot, so he gave the lead-off position back to the Eastern Star. The Bronte Club ladies, on the other hand, had the distinct impression that *local* seniority had always been the criterion. Had that been changed?

Purdy didn't know, so he asked Booby. Booby didn't know, either, and he told him to use his own judgment.

His judgment was subject to influence by his wife.

"Purdy, what's this I hear about you not letting the Bronte Club have first place in the parade?" she asked threateningly.

"I didn't say they *couldn't*—not yet."

"What's holding you up?"

"The Eastern Star."

"What have they got to do with it?"

"They want to be first."

"Hmpff! Do you have any idea what the Bronte Club has done for this town?" she demanded.

He didn't, but he said he did.

"Then what's holding you up?" she asked again.

"The Eastern Star," he said again.

"Well, I'll just have you know that *I'm* a charter member of the Bronte Club," she said, becoming more belligerent with each syllable, "and I *know*—because I've been present all these years—what the Brontes have meant to this community. This is a more pleasant place to live because of what we have done. The Bronte Club has worked like slaves and raised money for one worthy project after another *all these years*. And do you have any idea—*any idea whatsoever*—of how many young talents have been brought to flower because of. . . ."

On and on she blew, breathing fire into her recapitulation of Bronte Club accomplishments, none of which, from where Purdy sat, seemed to bear directly on the relative position of the club's float in the San Jacinto Day Parade. But he got the message, anyway. The Bronte Club was awarded the lead-off spot, and the Eastern Star withdrew its float altogether. The club ladies on both sides of the dispute were angry with Purdy, but not with each other. Their memberships were too overlapping for that.

With that problem solved, or at least out of the way, Purdy got bent out of shape over Mr. Akers' request that the reviewing stand be built in front of his Variety Store.

"Whatcha want all that scaffolding blocking the front of your store for, Lon?" Purdy asked.

"So when they take a picture of the reviewing stand, my store will be in the picture, too. That's as good as an ad in the *Courier*."

"Gosh, I hadn't thought about that," said Purdy. "Maybe I oughta try to get it in front of my own store sometime."

"You're on the wrong side of the street. The sun would be in the judges' eyes. How about it, Purdy? Me and you has been friends a long time, and it looks like you could do just this one little thing. I want you to promise me right now."

"I can't exactly *promise* you, Lon, but I'll sure do my best to get it moved. Come to think about it, it's been in front of the *Courier* every year, and Holly gets all that free advertising in his own paper for nothing."

Purdy asked Cecil Poole to study Mr. Akers' request.

"I don't need to study it," Cecil said. "I been getting the same request from Lon Akers every year since they been having this parade, and I been giving him the same answer just as regular. How in blazes does he think I can build a reviewing stand in front of his store when there's a lamppost, a fire plug, and a big batch of power lines blocking the way? I must of told him a hundred times! Besides, I got last year's lumber sawed, stacked away and ready to bring out and assemble again this year. If I try to build the stand somewhere else, I'd have to remeasure and resaw, and I just don't feel like fooling with it. As a matter of fact, I'm thinking about taking a trip up to Sulphur, Oklahoma, to visit my second cousin, and I'm not sure I'll be on hand to fool with the reviewing stand at all, not even in front of the *Courier*."

Purdy was no match for all that. Mr. Akers lost again. The upshot of it all was that Purdy kept a close eye on Cecil Poole to stay abreast of his travel plans and almost got a double hernia getting back into the good graces of his long-time friend, Lon Akers.

Three merchants asked Purdy for the address of the company that sold Texas ceremonial flags. Five telephone calls, four personal visits, and two bum steers later, he supplied the information.

Junior Bird renewed his threats to quit.

Leroy Chambers agreed to furnish a Chevrolet convertible for the parade, provided the Mayor ride in it. The Mayor always led the parade. Howard Slaton agreed to furnish a Ford convertible under the identical conditions.

"I don't see what difference it makes whether the Mayor rides in a Ford or a Chevrolet," Purdy protested. "Whichever one he rides in, the Grand Marshal will be right behind him in the other."

Neither would budge. He asked them to toss a coin. They refused. Purdy dumped the problem into the lap of the High Commissioner. The High Commissioner dumped it back.

"Now, Purdy, I told you at the beginning you're the top dog in this parade," Booby reminded him. "You're the final authority which there is no higher than. So when you come right down to it, I don't actually have the power to solve this little problem for you. If I took any action, I'd be usurping your authority. You wouldn't respect me if I did that, would you?"

"I'd respect you more," Purdy said. "I wish we had a Buick dealer in town. I'd get two cars from him and tell Leroy and Howard to keep their Fords and Chevrolets."

"No, you wouldn't. If we had a Buick dealer, you'd have to think up a reason to have a *third* convertible at the head of the parade."

"Maybe the two cars could ride side by side."

"The street's too narrow."

"Maybe they could both ride in the same car, then?"

"Which one—Ford or Chevy?"

"Yeah—that's right. You know, Leroy Chambers ain't so hard to handle, but that Howard Slaton gets his nose out of joint over the least little thing. He said, 'There's no use talking about it, Purdy—the Ford goes first in the parade or they just ain't gonna be any Fords in the parade!' I wish I could get the Mayor and the Grand Marshal to walk."

Booby considered that. "As far as I know, that's never been tried," he said, "but neither was a milking machine until somebody put one of them little clamps on a cow's tits. It just might work."

Strangely, it did. Horace Cox, who was serving his first term as Mayor while campaigning for the office of County Attorney, fancied the image of himself marching in cadence to military music for all the town to see. It would be something pleasant for the voters to remember when they went to the polls in the July primary. Yes, he liked the idea very much.

So did Aubrey Clifton, President of the First National Bank, the Grand Marshal again that year. He was appointed Grand Marshal as often as the San Jacinto Day Festival Committee thought it could get away with it. J. Aubrey Clifton had done more parade marshaling than anybody in town. He saw in Purdy's proposal a patriotic and youthful opportunity to demonstrate to his depositors that he still remembered a thing or two from his doughboy days with the A.E.F. in France.

"Just tell the band not to play too fast," he admonished playfully.

Purdy wrote that in his notebook under his Parade Check-list of Things to Do.

He selected Seventh Street as the assembly point for the parade. Seventh Street intersected Main Street and was paved, whereas the next five or six cross streets were not. Artie Whelan threw a monkey wrench into the selection.

"Seventh Street is the Emergency Evacuation Route," he announced. "You can't use it. We gotta keep it clear."

"Whatcha gotta evacuate from, Artie? There ain't no war on right now."

"I know, but you can't never tell when one will start."

"If it does, it won't take long to clear the street."

"Maybe not," said Artie, "but the thing is, Purdy, you can't block that street in the first place. Understand?"

"No. I can't say I do."

"Well, that's too bad, ain't it?" said Artie, "Because the regulations say you can't block off Seventh Street, and that's that. I gotta enforce the regulations."

"You know as well as I do, we ain't gonna have a war on April the twenty-first!"

"I wouldn't be too sure about that. We had one on December seventh once."

"You're just being stubborn, Artie. I don't see any use in your acting like this. I picked Seventh Street because it's the last paved cross street until we get out to Eleventh. You know that."

"I'm doing my duty, and the answer is NO. Capital N, capital O. You might as well obey the law, Purdy, 'cause if you don't I'll hafta show you my badge. I don't want to hafta do that. Me and you have been friends too long for that."

Purdy moved the assembly point to unpaved Eighth Street and spread the word accordingly. Mrs. Charlie Bennett telephoned to ask if he would mind making that Ninth? Charlie, her husband, was laid up with a slipped disc, and it would be nice if he could watch the parade assemble in front of his house. Purdy had to say no, but it took a fifteen-minute telephone conversation to say it.

The beleaguered Chairman skipped church two consecutive Sundays to escape the many people who were certain to be waiting for him on the sidewalk out front ready to drive him crazy with parade questions and suggestions.

The thorniest of all Purdy's problems, hands down and running, took the human shape of Rhoda Fryer, a middle-aged, henna-haired, Kewpie-doll person with Betty Boop lips, a squeaky voice to match, mascaraed eyes, a beauty mark on her cheek, tight knee-length dresses, ankle-strap shoes and three-inch heels. Rhoda was proprietress of the Eat 'n Rest Inn, a two-story establishment out near the Cotton Compress, in which few people were known to have eaten and even fewer to have got much rest. She employed from three to six people, depending on the season, all female. She came into Robinson's Hardware Store one afternoon to enter a float in the parade.

Purdy had spent the morning in the City Hall and the Court House ransacking the buildings in search of the Lone Star bunting for the reviewing stand. No one knew where it was. It turned up in the broom closet outside Dr. George Odom's office on Second Street. No one knew how it got there. In the middle of the afternoon while Junior Bird was sulking in the storeroom and Purdy was puttering around the store wondering what to do if the water main in front of the

Eatmore Bakery *should* burst and they actually *couldn't* get it fixed in time for the parade, Rhoda Fryer walked through the front door.

She was wearing a perilously low-cut, sleeveless, slick, shining black dress that, to Purdy, seemed to shimmer and shake even when she wasn't moving. It was so tight on her body that anyone who was not myopic could have counted her heartbeats just by looking. She wore a black umbrella-sized hat, black fishnet stockings that couldn't have snared a perch, and black ankle-strap shoes on stilt heels. From her arm dangled a mammoth black purse in which she could have concealed a Goodrich tire. As she clicked-clicked into the store and down the aisle, Purdy looked up from a hodge-podge of wood screws that someone—probably Junior Bird in a fit of pique—had dumped haphazardly into the drawer. He was trying to sort them out. He stopped sorting and gulped twice.

The wood-screw problem faded into insignificance as he walked out into the aisle to meet a larger one.

"How're you, Rhoda?" he said.

"Just as fine as can be," she said. She smiled, and the beauty mark on her cheek moved slightly to the right. "Nice day, ain't it?"

"Yes, it is. What can I do for you?"

She held out a sheet of paper. Without looking twice or focusing once, he recognized it as an entry form for a float in the parade. It had been completely filled out, front and back. Signed, too.

He was aghast.

"*You* want to enter a *float* in the *parade?*"

"I was thinking about it."

He took the paper from her hand, but he didn't have the presence of mind to look at it.

"What kind of float did you have in mind, Rhoda?" he

asked, the back side of his eyeballs aching from the strain.

"Just a nice float covered in crepe paper—you know, like they cover 'em with," she replied.

Purdy pretended not to know that Junior Bird had come up from the rear of the store and was leaning against the turpentine shelf, both eyes bulging. Purdy glanced nervously at the front door, thinking perhaps he should take Rhoda into the cubbyhole office at the rear of the store, where they could talk privately and out of sight. He couldn't move. Junior Bird's stare had him nailed to the floor. He raised his voice to accommodate Junior's defective hearing and to keep his own life an Open Book.

"What I mean, Rhoda," he said in hog-calling tones, "is what—er—what kind of message was you thinking about? This is a patriotic parade, you gotta remember, and all floats ought to say a message of some kind, you see. You can't advertise anything."

"Oh, I wasn't thinking about advertising," she said hastily. "I got a refined place that serves first-class meals—everybody knows that, so I don't need to advertise. I wasn't meaning to, either."

She opened her black suitcase of a purse, took out a cigarette, fitted it into a long black holder and stuck the entire contraption into her mouth. She lighted it with a kitchen match which she struck with a flaming red thumbnail, blew a cloud of smoke toward the ceiling of Robinson's Hardware Store and added, "You oughta come out some time, Purdy, and see for yourself."

Purdy turned pale. Junior Bird knocked over a can of shellac thinner.

"I'll think up a real patriotic message," she went on. "You don't need to worry about that. I got a real feeling about the Alamo and Sam Houston and Davy Crockett and historic things like that. Why, I been through the Alamo myself *twice!* I'll get something real patriotic, you can bet your life. I got one or two employees that's real artistic."

They were standing in the aisle next to the screwdrivers, pliers, rasp files and wrenches, in full view of anyone who appeared in front of the store. And someone did appear. And she stopped. It was Letty Turnbough doing a bit of window-shopping. He stared through the window at her, transfixed, leaving the Rhoda-watching to Junior, who was doing a first-rate job. Purdy wrestled with an impulse to run outside and chase Letty away before she did something foolish, such as look through the front door. She moved past the window and hesitated at the door. His insides congealed. With concentration so intense that his head ached, he willed her on past the door, past the other display window and ultimately out of sight.

When he got all his organs to functioning again, he decided that, for better or worse, standing with Rhoda Fryer in the middle of the store for Junior Bird and all the town to see was a durned sight safer than sitting with Rhoda Fryer behind the closed door of an office for Junior Bird and all the town to wonder about. But since he saw no point in encouraging the public to look, he inched his way out of the aisle and around the back of the wallpaper sample rack which towered above his harried head. He hoped Rhoda would follow. She didn't.

He tried a stall. "You never had any floats in the San Jacinto Day Parade, did you, Rhoda?" he asked.

"Now that you mention it, I can't say that I have," she squeaked, "and I been thinking about that. Me and my employees was talking about San Jacinto Day just last week and how lots of people come from out of town to enjoy theirselfs, and we had this real uplifting discussion about how it would be real nice if the Eat 'n Rest Inn showed our appreciation for our freedom and our liberty by having a real nice patriotic float in the parade."

"Well, Rhoda, I reckon most people know how much you

appreciate your freedom and your liberty without you going to all the trouble of making a whole float. They're an awful lot of trouble to make. You have to spread chicken wire over the whole float and nail it down so you can put crepe paper on it. And that wire sticks in your fingers something awful! It can even cause blood poisoning if—"

"But I *want* to do it, Purdy!" she insisted. "One of my employees makes the prettiest crepe-paper jonquils you ever saw. Daisies, too. She makes carnations out of Kleenex that you can't tell from the real thing. She sprinkles talcum powder on them, and they even *smell* like carnations. Beats anything you ever saw! She's got her room decorated all over with 'em."

Purdy tried to take his eyes off Rhoda's face, but he couldn't. There was nowhere else to look. If he lowered his gaze too far, he could not avoid her chubby knees. If he didn't lower it far enough, he could not avoid her chubby bosom. In either case, the scenery was a scandal.

He made another stab. "We haven't got any business floats in the parade this year," he offered.

"You mean it's against the rules?"

"No—but none of the business merchants have turned in any applications yet, and it don't look like they will." He warmed to the potentials of the thought. "It's a funny thing about parades. Some years you get lots of business floats, and some years you don't hardly get any. This looks like one of them years when we ain't gonna get any. I thought maybe you wouldn't want to stand out and make yourself conspicuous."

He was wrong. She was delighted.

"Boy howdy!" she exclaimed. "Won't that be a real nice honor if I've got the only business float in the parade?"

He opened his mouth to reply. Nothing emerged but a dry whisper.

Someone came in the front door. He was afraid to look out

from behind the wallpaper rack to see who it was, and apparently Junior Bird didn't know anyone had come in at all. Junior was staring at Rhoda. His spectacles had slipped down on his nose, but not far enough for him to look over them. He was staring through the rims instead. His feet were set in concrete.

"There's a customer up front, Junior," Purdy informed him. He could have been telling him that $E=MC^2$.

"Junior?"

Junior came to.

"Go see who's up front," Purdy said.

"Where—oh—why, I didn't—"

He tore himself away from the turpentine and shellac thinner and with horse strides made his lanky way to the front of the store. His mind didn't seem to be on his work.

With the visual pressure eased somewhat, Purdy was more comfortable, but not much.

"One of my employees told me I oughta get a set of rules while I'm here," Rhoda was saying. "I wanna be sure we don't get thrown out on our cans."

Purdy bumped his head on the wallpaper rack.

He pulled himself back together and wished that either he or Rhoda were dead. He didn't care who, so long as he himself didn't have to make the selection. He heard Junior tell the customer—whoever it was—that Robinson's Hardware Store didn't sell nails. It didn't sound right, but he was too paralyzed in mind and body to figure out why.

He darted across the open aisle then to shelter again behind the wire, rope and clothesline counter.

"What kind of rules did you want, Rhoda?" he asked, wondering, but not wanting to know, who the customer was that Junior seemed to be in the midst of throwing out into the street.

"Some parade rules," she said. "One of my employees who

is always cracking jokes—you'd just die laughing at her, Purdy—said for me to get a list of 'Thou Shalt Nots.' She's always saying crazy things like that."

Purdy forced a sick smile while scratching about under the counter for a mimeographed sheet of rules. It was not where he kept them.

"I must of left them up by the cash register," he muttered.

Rhoda had stepped across the aisle and was now standing in front of the counter facing him. She waited. She hummed a little tune. She reached inside her bosom and adjusted the contents.

"Just a minute, Rhoda," he said hastily, racing behind the counters toward the front of the store and the cash register.

The humming ceased.

He rushed back with a mimeographed rule sheet in his hand. He shoved it across the counter where Rhoda could pick it up, then drew back to a safe distance. Instead of picking it up, though, she let it lie and leaned over the counter to study it. While she studied the rule sheet, he tried to study the entry form she had given him, but he couldn't. He was studying Rhoda Fryer's unladylike posture instead.

She was bent in half, resting comfortably with both elbows on the counter while the back end of her stuck out into the aisle perpendicular to the counter. She was mumbling the words on the mimeographed sheet, and as she mumbled, the perpendicular part of her was swaying from side to side. With her elbows as a fulcrum, the rest of her swung one way, then reversed directions and swung the other. Every so often, as if in tempo with her own mumbling, she halted abruptly as though there had been a collision—probably when she came to a period.

Purdy did his best to look over, around or beyond her—any way at all just so it was the other way. When he finally managed to unglue his gaze and turn it elsewhere, it came to rest on the horrified figure of long, tall Junior Bird standing at the front door staring down the aisle at the undulating Miss Fryer. He was a pillar of stone.

Purdy tried to focus his eyes and attention on Rhoda's entry form. It was no good. It was there in his own hand. He was looking at it. Yet, he couldn't see it. Even so, he felt that he had to say something about it to her.

"You understand this is just the application, don't you, Rhoda?" he heard himself say.

She looked up from her mumbling and swaying. "How do you mean?" she asked.

"I'll have to let you know later how it comes out."

He came from behind the counter and back into the open aisle.

She stood up straight, tugged at her shining black dress, which had worked its way up her thighs. She smoothed out some wrinkles that could not possibly have existed in such taut fabric, slapped her hips and looked at him keenly.

"Why can't you tell me now, Purdy?"

"Because I gotta act on it, you see."

"Act on it? Whaddya gotta do to it?"

"I gotta *act* on it, I told you. I gotta approve of it, or I gotta disapprove of it."

"Well, it ain't the rush hour at my place yet, so I don't mind waiting while you're acting."

"No, no! You don't understand! I've got to *study* it before I can act on it. That'll take a while."

Junior thawed himself out enough to return from the front of the store, too unsettled in mind and estate to notice that his route brought him squarely between his employer and the proprietress of the Eat 'n Rest Inn.

"Hidee-ya-do, Mr. Bird," said Rhoda. "Nice day, ain't it?"

Junior thought he nodded, but he didn't. He thought he looked at Rhoda, but he couldn't. His eyes were glassy, and they looked neither to the right nor to the left, but straight ahead. His bald head turned red. His Adam's apple moved down into his collar and stayed there. Stiff as a poker and getting stiffer with each long-legged stride, he walked on past—past the turpentine, past the house paint, past the nails, past the plumbing fixtures, past the screen wire—through the rear door and out into the alley before he could collect enough of his wits to figure out where he was and how he got there.

"Do you know any reason why you won't approve of my float?" Rhoda asked Purdy.

Purdy's face turned as red as the top of Junior's bald head.

"Well—it's just possible that—er—ah—"

"Possible what?"

Rhoda's eyes were making a sieve of him.

More than anything else, he needed a rest, a breather, an intermission, a respite, so he said, "No—I reckon I don't."

And he didn't. No legal reason, that is. He accepted her entry form, no matter how reluctantly, stuck it in a drawer, wished she would leave by the back door rather than the front, told Junior to mind the store for the rest of the day, and went home with an upset stomach, a ringing in his ears, and little dancing spots in front of his eyes. His wife, quite naturally, wanted to know what was wrong with him. He was afraid to tell her.

The following morning, when Booby Duckworth parked his car in front of his cotton-brokerage office, Purdy was waiting on the curb.

"You've *got* to usurp my authority on this one, Booby," he exclaimed, following him up the stairs to his office on the Third Street side of Court House Square. He outlined the situation as they climbed. "I didn't sleep a wink last night," he said in conclusion while Booby was fumbling with his keys to unlock the door. "You gotta get me out of this mess. I ain't asking you, either. I'm *telling* you!"

Booby sat down at his desk without removing his hat and motioned Purdy into a chair. Purdy ignored him. He was circling the office.

"Looks like you got your tit caught in the wringer, don't it, Purdy?" he said with a chuckle.

"You can talk dirty like that if you want to," said Purdy, "but it won't help matters. What we gotta do is figure out what to do about this terrible embarrassment."

Booby chuckled again. "You know what this town ought to do?" he said. "This town ought to erect a monument to Rhoda Fryer for durability. How long has she been out there doing business? Thirty years? Forty? Artie locks up the place and she opens it up again the next day like nothing had happened. They tell me that her house burned down once and she set up some folding cots in the barn and carried on her business without a hitch."

"That ain't what I came up here to talk about, Booby!"

"Okayokayokay—we'll figure out something. But you ought to calm down a little. Let's go down to the Little Gem, and I'll buy you a cup of coffee to settle your nerves. You can tell me all about it."

"I done told you all about it! Anyway, I already had a cup of coffee, and it wouldn't stay down. Besides, I don't want to go to the Little Gem, where people can hear us talking about it. Eula doesn't even know anything about it yet."

Booby threw his feet upon his desk and leaned back in his chair. "Now if you'll just quit wearing out my rug for a few minutes, maybe we can examine all the facts of the problem and see where we stand." He pushed his hat to the back of his head and fished a toothpick from his vest pocket. He picked his teeth on one side and then the other, then pointed the toothpick at Purdy. "The first thing we've got to consider is whether or not Rhoda Fryer is a bona fide citizen of this town. That's in the rules, you know. Is she?"

"Why, I guess so. You just got through talking about how long she's lived here. She was born and raised here—you know that. I never heard of her living anywhere else in all her forty-odd years—"

"Fifty-odd."

"Fifty-odd, then. Anyway, she lives here, so I reckon that makes her a citizen, don't it?"

"Okay—looks like we can't rule her out on that one," said Booby. "Now the second thing is whether or not she represents a duly constituted business or organization or society or institution. Does she?"

"I don't know how duly it is, but she—"

"But *is* it a business?"

"That's the problem, Booby!" Purdy exploded. "You know as well as I do what Rhoda Fryer does for a living! If it wasn't for that, there wouldn't be no problem!"

"Now just stick to the facts. *Is* Rhoda in business?"

"I'll say!"

"What kind of business?"

"Now lookie here, Booby, you're just trying to get me to say that word, and I won't—"

"Is her business listed under businesses in the telephone book?"

"I never did look."

"Then take a look." He tossed the telephone directory to him and added, "Check the yellow pages."

Purdy ran his fingers down the pages with no enthusiasm.

"It ain't under the W's," he announced.

"Aw, for crying out loud, Purdy! Look under restaurants! That's what she claims her business is, don't she?"

Purdy adjusted his spectacles and looked further.

"Here it is," he said, his face a study in sorrow. "Eat 'n Rest Inn, West Third Street. Phone two-one-two-J."

"Okay. Now does that satisfy you?"

"No, it don't. That ain't no restaurant no more than this office is a beauty parlor."

"Yeah—but can you prove it?"

"I ain't aiming to try."

"Maybe if you went out there and ordered something to eat and didn't get it, you could disqualify her for not running a restaurant as advertised."

Purdy looked at the High Commissioner as if he had sprouted a second head.

"Now, I ain't going out to Rhoda Fryer's and order *nothing!*" he shouted.

"Then why don't you go out and ask for a room? If she doesn't have any vacant room, you can—"

"Booby, you're plumb outa your head! Rooms is the one thing she *has* got—and none of them are vacant. She don't rent vacant rooms."

"Well, if she says she runs a restaurant and you can't prove she doesn't, it looks like we can't rule her out on that one, either."

Booby sat up straight, flicked his toothpick into the wastebasket, took another one from his vest pocket, and watched Purdy make a round trip from the filing cabinets to the water cooler.

"Aren't your legs getting tired?" he asked.

"All of me is getting tired," Purdy replied. "My head's getting tired, my stomach's getting tired, my eyes are getting tired, my liver's getting tired, and if I don't puke all over the place before this durned parade is over with, it'll be a wonder. Eula kept picking at me this morning about why I wouldn't eat breakfast and told me I oughta see the doctor. I said I'd of called him in the middle of the night if I thought he had any pills for what's ailing me. And she said, 'What *is* ailing you?' and I said, 'San Jacinto Day, that's what.' You know,

Booby, I wish Santa Anna had whipped us that day."

"Now, Purdy, you're taking all this too seriously. Why, you're as nervous as a pregnant nun, and—"

"Booby—I told you that dirty talk ain't gonna get you nowhere. You oughta be ashamed—"

"Okayokayokay—next time you pass my desk here, stop off for a minute and suggest something else we might catch Rhoda on. We've struck out so far."

On his next round, Purdy stopped by for a brief moment and said, "She's got a jail record a mile long."

"Maybe we can catch her on that. What do the rules say about jail records?"

"It don't mention jail records."

"Why did you bring up the subject, then?"

"Because it's *terrible!*"

"Well—if it's not in the rules, it looks like she's got us there, too."

"It sure as shootin' does," said Purdy.

"Looks like Rhoda's won."

"Stop talking like that!"

"You can't turn her down because of her big fat—"

"Watch out, Booby!" Purdy made another lap around the office.

"What are you going to do about it, then?" Booby asked.

"I don't know," he said wearily. "And when I say I don't know, I mean I don't know—unless we can turn her down on general principles."

"What kind of general principles?"

"General kinds."

"Name one."

"I don't know the names of all the general principles, Booby! I ain't a genius, you know."

"But what if she wants to know *which* general principle?"

"I'll just have to look one up, I reckon—or something."

[*127*]

"Which one?"

"*I don't know!* I already told you that! That's why I'm up here talking to you."

"When are you going to tell her?"

"Tell her what?"

"Use your head, Purdy! You've either got to let her have her float, or you've got to tell her she can't and why. She can't read your mind. So *when* are you going to tell her?"

"I haven't even been around to open up my own store yet," he said, "and you're asking me questions like that. Junior Bird's probably lost his key again, too. I'll bet everybody in town's got a key to my store—if they find all the keys he loses. Eula's going to get wind of this if I don't get it settled pretty soon, and when she does—*when she does*—nobody told me I'd have to worry about all these problems when I got this job, and if I'd of known about all this—"

"Take it easy, Purdy, *Take it easy!* Just calm down and take it easy, or you're gonna have a stroke."

"That'd be real nice, then I could just go to the hospital and not have all these worries to worry about." He reversed his direction and began to pace counterclockwise. "I'll tell you one thing for sure," he said. "I ain't gonna tell Eula that Rhoda Fryer's having a float in the parade. I just ain't gonna do it—I don't care what anybody says, *I just ain't gonna do it!* When she—"

"Okay—if you don't know any specific *general* principles to turn her down on, maybe you'll just have to approve her float."

"Well! Thank you kindly, Mr. Duckworth! That's certainly a mighty nice suggestion, ain't it? I could of thought that up in my own hardware store without your help. If that's the kind of stuff you're gonna tell me, I'd just as soon listen to Junior Bird, and he don't know anything about anything. If I wanted to know—"

"Suppose you do approve it? What'll be the harm?"

Purdy stopped cold and stared at the High Commissioner.

"Harm?" he croaked. "Booby, sometimes you talk like you haven't got a brain in your head! Every preacher and church in town will be down on top of me, that's what!"

"Maybe if you read the rules carefully, you can find something to get her on—a technicality or some piddling little clause that nobody ever noticed before—something like that. It's worth a try, isn't it?"

"I know them rules by heart," Purdy said, "and they don't say nothing about having harlot floats in the parade. They don't say you can, and they don't say you can't."

He resumed his pacing.

"That's too bad," Booby said sorrowfully. "I'd give anything if I could help you, but I guess you'll just have to use your own judgment about it."

"I haven't got any judgment—and besides, that's what you told me about everything else I asked you about so far."

"That's all I know to say. I do have one suggestion, though —but first, will you do me a favor and stand *still*—or sit down—or lie on the floor? You're giving me the heebie-jeebies."

Purdy moved to a window and looked out. He drew back abruptly.

"There's Reverend McWhorter!" he gasped. "He's going up the walk to the Court House!"

"Yeah? I'll bet lots of people go up that walk too, before they lock up the Court House for the night. As I was saying —suppose you do approve it? You don't have to broadcast it all over town, do you?"

Purdy stopped in front of Booby's desk and glared down at him. The veins stood out across his skinny forehead.

"For garden seed, Booby!" he yelled. "Do you think you can have a float full of—of—full of HUSSIES—going down the middle of Main Street with the whole town watching and keep it a secret? A parade is about the most public thing there is!"

"No—I mean, just don't mention it in advance."

"Eula asks me every night who's gonna be in the parade. What do you want me to tell her—nobody?"

"Just stall her off. Let it leak out on its own later. For the time being, though, you'll just be giving everybody something to yak about if you mention it now. And who knows, Purdy? This thing might work out better than you think. Rhoda might surprise you and come up with a lalapalooza that'll win the prize."

The parade chairman bolted for the door. That particular possibility had not entered his mind.

Several days passed, and if Eula had got wind of her husband's most distressing problem, she didn't let on. Meanwhile, Purdy assumed that Rhoda would stop in the store to inquire about the status of her application. He offered up daily prayers that she would not, and she answered his prayers personally. She stayed out of sight. He saw neither hide nor hair of her.

More days passed. One night at the supper table, Mrs. Robinson demanded that she be brought up to date on the parade. She was running short of information to pass along to the neighbors and assorted friends.

"Are the Business and Professional Women having a float this year?" she asked.

"Not like you're thinking about," Purdy replied.

"Who is, then? How come you haven't been telling me recently who's entering the parade?"

Purdy dropped his fork onto the floor and used an inordinate amount of time retrieving it.

"Purdy?"

"I don't know yet. They're not all in."

"I thought you set a deadline."

"I did."

"Then why don't you know?"

"Because the deadline's not up yet, and lots of people wait till the last minute."

She hung an ominous silence over his head. He knew what it meant, but he couldn't bring himself to do anything about it.

"*Well?*" she said after time was up. "Who have you got?"

"I can't remember," he said. "I left my list at the store."

"Seems funny to me," she said. "You can remember who's *not* having a float, but you can't remember who *is*. For somebody in charge, you don't seem to know much about what's going on. Why, when Frank Hudgins was in charge he told me himself how he wrote everything down ahead of time and how he went around personally and...."

Purdy tuned her out.

Another week went by, and Rhoda Fryer's unacted-upon application nagged at him like an unpaid bill. To be or not to be? Tell her or not tell her? Tell her what? When he could no longer tolerate the miserable limbo of his affairs, he amassed his courage, raked all his command prerogatives into a neat little pile and picked up the telephone to call Rhoda. Maybe she had changed her mind and he had been doing all this worrying for nothing.

Miss Eunice Horton's voice came on the line.

"Number, please?"

Purdy caught his breath and eased the receiver back into place. He had a sneaking idea that Miss Eunice listened in on Rhoda Fryer's conversations. He hadn't decided what he would have said to her, anyway.

The following week, he watched the door of his store as though it were booby-trapped. Time was creeping up, and somebody had to do something, didn't they? He inspected each day's mail with heart thumping and eyes half closed. He listened for the telephone and jumped two inches off the floor each time it rang. No Rhoda.

He drove out to the Eat 'n Rest Inn. Maybe she had lost interest in the whole business. If so, he could return her application to her and that would be that. He reached her house, got cold feet, and drove on past. His car parked out front for all the town to see? Once he imagined he saw her in front of Akers' Variety Store across the street. Without a word to Junior Bird, he raced out the back door, leaped into his car and drove around Old Loop Road, then crisscrossed the town until he figured Rhoda had already been into his store, if she was coming, or had gone on home, if she hadn't intended to come.

San Jacinto Day fell on Friday that year. On Monday of that week, Purdy figured that Rhoda Fryer had decided not to sponsor a float after all. By Tuesday, he didn't believe a word of it. Rhoda was operating on the assumption that no news is good news, he concluded, and was apparently at that very minute supervising her employees as they created what easily might develop into the fanciest float in the history of San Jacinto Day Parades. All day he wore his suede jacket (zipped up) against a chilly breeze that no one but himself seemed to feel.

On Wednesday morning his favorite water main in front of the Eatmore Bakery blew its top and spurted water all over that end of Main Street. Purdy had never seen so much water in all his life. As a consequence, he had no worries to spare that day for the Eat 'n Rest Inn float. He was too busy superintending the workmen as they struggled to stem the tide and repair the rupture. Nor did he have time to do any serious worrying on Thursday. About Rhoda, that is. He was too busy standing over the construction crew as they filled the gaping hole in the middle of Main Street. By Thursday afternoon he forgot Rhoda Fryer altogether; he was standing vigil over the newly patched concrete, all but blowing his breath on it to help it dry itself out.

On Friday morning—parade day—before the clock struck eight, he telephoned Hershel Mansfield, manager of the City Water Department, and threatened to have the law on him if the yellow barricade surrounding the patched concrete was not moved by noon. At eight-fifteen, he telephoned Artie Whelan and charged him with the responsibility of forcing Hershel to keep his word. At nine o'clock, he telephoned Horace Cox and demanded that he use his authority as Mayor to get the barricade removed as promised. At ten o'clock, he went out and moved it himself.

By noon, he was too nervous to eat dinner, so he stayed in the store and accommodated a team of short-change artists in town for the day. They took him for something like $17.50, but before he could bewail his loss properly, Lon Akers pushed it clean out of his mind with a chance remark that it was looking cloudy in the northeast and he sure hoped it didn't rain and ruin the parade.

But poor Purdy couldn't even keep his mind on that, for at twelve-thirty, Mattie Shumaker called to report that her husband, Willis, the Official Escort for Representative Devol, had sprained his ankle and was at that very minute soaking it in a pan of hot water and would be unable to meet Mr. Devol as planned. His plane was scheduled to arrive at the landing strip west of town at one o'clock.

Purdy moved away from the telephone, life closing in on him fast. He fought off a dizzy spell. How would he ever smooth it out if Representative Devol had to walk from the landing strip—alone? He stopped, leaned on the cash register and stared out into the street. The holiday crowd was gathering. Men, women and children were milling about, visiting, window-shopping and staking claims on sidewalk space from which they could enjoy the parade. He watched them absently, too numb to worry about what he should do. He had no Plan B for meeting Representative Devol.

Then J. D. Gribble, telephone repairman, walked by.

As if shot from a cannon, Purdy ran out and waylaid him. He grasped his right arm with both hands.

"How about you running out to the landing strip to meet Lee Dee-vol?" he asked. "Willis Shumaker sprained his ankle, and he's due in at one o'clock."

"Who—Willis?"

"No. Lee Dee-vol."

"Why me?" asked J. D., trying to overcome a seizure of indifference.

"Because you was passing the store," said Purdy.

"So was Townie Ledbetter," said J.D.

He pointed to the deaf-and-dumb Townie, who was standing at the curb, grinning from ear to ear, making hand signals at them.

"Now look, J.D.—somebody's got to meet Mr. Dee-vol. How about it?"

"Can't do it. I'm on duty."

"It won't take you long. All you gotta do is bring him down here to the reviewing stand, and then you can go back to work."

"You want me to go in my telephone truck?"

"It don't matter—no, wait! That might not look right. Go in your own car."

"It's at home leaking oil from here to hell and gone. It's got a busted gasket."

"Can't you borrow one?" Purdy pleaded. "Mine's out back."

"I can't go."

"Why not?"

"I told you—I'm on duty."

"And I told you—"

"You want me to go in my work clothes?"

He was wearing his olive-drab work shirt and pants. From his belt hung a bewildering array of screwdrivers, pliers, wire pinchers, drill punches and little leather pouches full of tools known only to God and telephone repairmen.

Purdy's face fell several inches.

"No, I reckon not," he said. He still held to J.D.'s right arm, though.

Anxiously, he surveyed the passing people for a familiar face. He recognized no one but Townie Ledbetter, who was still standing on the curb, grinning at them, rolling his eyes and making hand signals.

"Townie!" Purdy shouted. "You'd better stop making them cussword signs, or I'm gonna get Artie Whelan to pick you up!"

He turned his attention back to J.D., who was trying to free himself. He stared into his face for a moment, then threw in the sponge.

"Well—" he said with quiet resignation. "I reckon I could go myself if I have to."

"I'm sorry, Mr. Robinson, but you see—"

"Then how about you watching the store for me?"

"I'm on duty, Mr. Robinson, like I said. I was on my way out to old lady Cramer's. She claims she gets four telephone calls at once."

Purdy had about worn out all his red corpuscles straining to remain calm, but for all his exertion he could not keep down the excitement that was rushing up within him. Now it threatened to take the upper hand.

"Now you listen to me, J. D. Gribble," he said, a steely firmness coming into his voice and manner. "Junior Bird's due back from dinner any minute now, and it ain't gonna hurt you to mind the store till he gets here."

J.D. struggled to get free. "But I don't know where anything is!" he protested.

Purdy pulled him toward the door of the store.

J.D. pulled back. "I don't know how much anything costs, Mr. Robinson!"

"THEN DON'T SELL ANYTHING TO ANYBODY!" Purdy screamed.

He dragged J.D. into the store and stood him behind the cash register.

"Now I've just had about all the sassy talk I'm gonna listen to for one day," he raved. "I got forty dozen things to worry about and you're just diddling them up worse by being stubborn!"

"But Mr. Robinson, old lady Cramer said she—"

Purdy, however, was not listening. He was heading for the back door and his automobile parked in the alley.

Thus he left J. D. Gribble, telephone repairman, in complete charge of Robinson's Hardware Store while he himself went to meet Representative Lee Devol.

Had it not been for Willis Shumaker's sprained ankle and J. D. Gribble's telephone truck and work clothes, Purdy might have got around to inspecting the floats personally, including Rhoda Fryer's—if she had one—before the parade began. As a matter of fact, Item number 43 on his Parade Checklist of Things to Do was: "1:30 pm—go 8th St and insp flts."

He never made it.

For one thing, Lee Devol, who weighed 285 pounds and wore a wide-brimmed straw hat and string bow tie—despite the fact that such public officials exist only in Class B movies and bad novels—was in no hurry to leave the landing strip. He shook hands with everybody in sight, including a tourist who had wandered off the highway, a passing farmer, and a crop duster seated inside his plane ready for takeoff.

"Lee Devol, Sixth District!" he introduced himself affably and politically to each person whose hand he grasped. "Lee Devol, Sixth District, glad to see you glad to see you glad to see you a real pleasure!" Then without waiting for a reply, he would move on to another hand, another person. "Lee Devol, Sixth District, Democrat all my life like my daddy before me! Lee Devol, Sixth District. . . ."

For another thing, Lee Devol, with Purdy Robinson in trail, used up twenty valuable minutes downtown walking the twenty yards from Purdy's automobile behind his store to the reviewing stand. If he saw a hand with nothing in it, he shook it.

"Lee Devol, Sixth District," he hobnobbed in his best grass-roots manner. "Lee Devol, Sixth District, seventeen years in the Texas Legislature, thanks to you good people! Lee Devol Sixth District, just a poor Democrat country boy like my daddy before me! Lee Devol, Sixth District, seventeen years. . . ."

On the reviewing stand at last, Purdy looked at his watch. Even after the stiff overdose of affection and appreciation that was still flowing like blood from a cut artery, enough time remained for him to make a quick inspection of the floats. But there was a drawback. Lee Devol's Official Escort was at home with his foot in a pan of hot water. This meant that barring the appearance of an unscheduled, unappointed, unforeseen Samaritan, Purdy Robinson was, from that moment on, Willis Shumaker's replacement and Lee Devol's Official Escort by default.

Around and below them, people were packed three and four deep along the curb, and they were still gathering. Their faces were sticky with purple snow cones, pink cotton candy, yellow popcorn and red soda pop. They laughed, they shouted at one another, they waited happily and with patience.

Sizing up the situation, Purdy knew that he could not leave the Parade Judge on the reviewing stand unescorted while he himself inspected the floats. Not that the Parade Judge would have minded—he was too busy shaking hands. Nor would he dare take the Parade Judge along with him—there were too many unshaken hands waiting out on Eighth Street.

Purdy could do nothing but stand by and wait for parade time, and for Lee Devol to run out of hands to shake. He took off his hat, wiped out the sweatband with his handkerchief and wished that the battle of San Jacinto had been fought in Idaho.

Item number 43 was never crossed off the list.

Two o'clock arrived and departed with nary a sign of the parade. Purdy breathed on his spectacles, wiped them off, fitted them back onto his nose, shaded his eyes with his hand and peered out Main Street, thinking surely the first element of the parade would swing into view any second now. He saw nothing but a whirlwind or two and the other end of Main Street, which stretched out to nowhere and forever.

Around and below him, the people's patience was beginning to wear. They turned expectant faces up toward the reviewing stand. Purdy tried not to notice. Parents corralled their impatient youngsters and conned them with promises that the parade would be along at any minute now. Fathers grunted and perspired under the weight of tiny tots straddling their necks for a better view and nothing to look at. Harried mothers yanked their boisterous children out of the empty street and back onto the crowded curbs. They threw accusing glances up to the reviewing stand, shuffled impatiently and stood on first one foot then the other. None of which hurried the parade along.

To fill the gap, Purdy offered one humorous observation after another to Representative Devol about parades never starting on time. Each sally, however, came across more feeble than its predecessor. The rationalization was too weak to sustain him for long. Then he remembered.

His instructions had been explicit. The parade was not to move from the assembly point until the Chairman, Mr. Purdy

Robinson gave the signal in person. No deviation would be tolerated. In panic, he looked over the tiring crowd below, trying to ignore the carpet of irritable faces. He was searching for someone to deliver a message. He saw no one he recognized but Townie Ledbetter cussing in sign language. And Selma Dell Harvey, high-school student. She was wearing her pep squad uniform.

"SELMA DELL!" he yelled. "WHAT ARE YOU DOING DOWN HERE? You git on out to the assembly point this minute! Don't you know the time you're supposed to be there? Now git!"

"Oh—I got a blister on my heel, Mr. Robinson," she called back. "I can't march because...."

He didn't hear the rest of it, for his attention was interrupted by the sight of Sam Abernathy threading his way through the crowd. Purdy leaned over the bunting-draped railing and cupped his hands around his mouth.

"Hey, Sam! Come here a minute!"

Sam made his way to the foot of the reviewing stand.

"What's up, Purdy?"

"How about you running out to Eighth Street where the parade's assembled and tell them to move off?"

"What for?"

"Because it's past time to start, and I can't go. They can't start till I tell them they can."

"Eighth Street? My car's over at the Court House—probably blocked in."

"You can walk," Purdy suggested. "It won't take you long. Just run out and tell them to move off—that's all you've gotta do. Please, Sam? I got my hands full here."

"Look, Purdy—I can't go running out Main Street like I was thirteen years old. Why don't you call them on the telephone?"

"Because the parade hasn't got any telephones in it!"

"Then call somebody who lives on that street and tell them to go out and start the parade."

"I can't leave here, I told you!" He jerked a thumb in Lee Devol's direction.

"Where's Willis?"

"He sprained his ankle—please go call, Sam! This parade's got to get started *sometime* before San Jacinto Day's over with!"

"Who do you want me to call?"

"Whoever lives there—I can't think who—not right off."

"What do you want me to tell them?"

"Just tell them the Chairman of the parade, Mr. Purdy Robinson, says to move off."

"Is that all?"

"I guess so—oh, tell the band that Mr. Clifton said not to play too fast, because...."

Sam disappeared into the crowd.

He worked his way past the people and stepped inside *The Weekly Courier* office. He telephoned Coy Clisbee's house and received no answer. He tried Ennis Grissom's number, but before the telephone rang the second time, he recalled seeing Ennis and his wife, Pearl, a few minutes previously across the street in front of Pritchard's Furniture Store. He couldn't remember who else lived along their particular stretch of Eighth Street. He flashed the operator.

"Number, please?"

"Miss Eunice? This is Sam Abernathy. Who lives in the same block with Ennis Grissom and Coy Clisbee?"

"Several people, I imagine," she said. "What do you want to know for?"

"I got to telephone one of them to go out front and start the parade. Give me somebody's number."

"I thought Purdy Robinson was in charge of the parade."

"He is, but just give me somebody's number, will you please? I've got other things to do."

"Now let me see . . . don't Callie Davis and her mother live in that block?"

"I'm not sure—I think so."

"Or is it the next block down?"

"I don't know," said Sam irritably. "Look, Miss Eunice, I gotta go, so how about you calling Callie and tell her to go out front and tell the parade that Purdy Robinson said to move off?"

"Why can't Purdy call and do it himself?"

"He's tied up and can't get loose. Go on and call Callie, like I said. Okay?"

"It seems like a funny thing to tell somebody. What if Callie's not home?"

"THEN CALL SOMEBODY WHO IS!" Sam shouted and hung up the telephone.

Fortunately, Callie was at home.

"How come you're not at the parade, Callie?" Miss Eunice asked.

"They're assembling right in front of my house, you know," said Callie. "Mama and I are sitting on the front porch seeing more than we could ever see downtown, and we don't have to stand up, either. What did you want, Eunice? Maybe I can call you back after the parade leaves— did you know that Rhoda Fryer's in the parade?"

"*Rhoda Fryer?* What's she doing in the parade?"

"I don't know. That's what I'm trying to find out. What did you want, Eunice? I want to get back out front."

"Oh—I got this peculiar message from Sam Abernathy. He wanted me to tell you to go out front and tell the parade to start."

"*Me?* Why on earth does Sam Abernathy want *me* to start the parade?"

"I don't know. That's what he said tell you. I think he's been drinking."

"Well, drunk or sober, he ought to know better than that!

Purdy Robinson's in charge, isn't he?"

"That's what I told him, but he said Purdy's all tied up and can't come start it himself. He said Purdy told him to call. What's Rhoda got on?"

"A red satin evening dress," said Callie. "It's the loudest thing you ever saw in your life! Ora Rainwater's in it, too. She and Rhoda passed the house, laughing and talking to beat sixty. Ora had on this tight dress with big blue flowers all over it. Rhoda must have sewed her into it. You can see every wrinkle in her fat body. If she burps, she'll rip that dress apart."

"I wonder what they're going to do. Did you see them get on a float?"

"I couldn't see that far. Listen, Eunice, are you serious about me starting the parade?"

"I'm just delivering a message."

"Seems peculiar as all getout," said Callie. "Even if I did go out and tell them, nobody would listen to me."

"That's all I know about it," said Miss Eunice. "Are you *sure* it was Rhoda Fryer you saw, Callie?"

"Don't you think I know Rhoda Fryer when I see her? She spoke to me and Mama just as big as you please. And Ora waved and snickered, but she didn't actually speak. I've got to get back—"

"Go on—I've got a light on the switchboard, anyway. I'll talk to you later. Do what you think best about starting the parade, Callie."

As it turned out, Callie Davis did nothing. She didn't need to.

At two-forty, J. Aubrey Clifton, Grand Marshal with years of experience to his credit, grew tired of waiting.

"Let's go," he said to Horace Cox, the Mayor.

The two of them had been pacing the street, wandering up and down, visiting and chatting among the waiting units of the parade, members of which were by now sprawled over the lawns of nearby homes. Now the two men were up front again, still waiting, seated side by side on the curb.

"We're supposed to wait for Purdy to give the word," said Horace.

"True, true," said Mr. Clifton, "but where's Purdy?"

"Beats me," said the Mayor.

"Give the signal to the band, and let's go," said the Grand Marshal, getting to his feet. "I've had enough of this."

"Maybe you'd better do it, Aubrey. You've had more experience leading parades than I have. This is my first one."

"Okay, okay. I'm getting tired waiting around like this," said the Grand Marshal.

"Me, too," replied the Mayor. "Besides, I'm about to wet my pants."

Mr. Clifton stepped back a few paces and instructed Grady Dilbert, high-school band director, to sound off and move off. Grady had read the rules, too, and he knew that his instructions were coming from an unauthorized person, who it so happened was holding a ninety-day note with Grady Dilbert's signature on it.

The parade moved off.

Meanwhile, Purdy had long since run out of topics to discuss with Representative Lee Devol. Not that much discussion was necessary, for Lee, ever interested in keeping his fingers on the pulse of his constituents, was leaning over the railing—all 285 pounds of him—shaking hands with the voters below.

"Lee Devol, Sixth District, it's a real pleasure to be with you folks, yes it is! Lee Devol, Sixth District, just a poor country boy who loves the Lone Star State! Lee Devol, Sixth District, a Democrat all my life like my daddy. . . ."

With what little apprehension he had left in him, Purdy watched the legislator, praying that Cecil Poole's flimsy carpentry was dependable enough—just this one time—to keep Representative Devol from crashing through the railing and flattening two acres of citizens below.

He took three deep breaths to quiet his churning, growling stomach and to head off an eruption. He looked out Main Street for the umpteenth time. There were not even any whirlwinds to look at now. What was he supposed to do with the Parade Judge if it turned out that there was no parade to judge? He looked about for Sam Abernathy to inquire into the fate of his message. He saw J. D. Gribble instead.

"Did Junior get back to the store okay?" Purdy shouted.

J.D. cupped a hand behind his ear. "What did you say?" he yelled .

"I said look around and see if you can find Sam Abernathy—"

A shout went up from the crowd. The first element of the parade had turned onto Main Street and was headed for downtown. Purdy began to breathe again. But not permanently.

At about Fifth Street—he couldn't tell exactly—the parade stopped. He strained his eyes, adjusted his spectacles and tried to determine the cause of the delay. He could see a float turning out of the line and pulling over to the curb, but since he had not inspected the floats personally, he hadn't the foggiest notion which float it was. All he could make out were white-clad figures climbing down off the float and scurrying back into the line of march. Above their heads they struggled with something large and white.

The parade moved again.

Lee Devol suspended the handshaking and took his place alongside Purdy Robinson to watch the parade approach.

First marched His Honor, Mayor Horace Cox. He was stepping lively, smiling broadly, bowing deeply and waving grandly to his constituents, who lined the curbs from the Texan Theatre to the Fort Worth & Denver depot. He was followed by J. Aubrey Clifton, also marching but not quite so lively. He was out of breath and out of sorts, scowling at the back of the exuberant candidate for County Attorney, who somehow didn't seem to mind the senseless march from out in the middle of nowhere. The band set a brisk rhythm to the tune of "The Washington Post March," but the Mayor and the Grand Marshal kept apace with a peculiar languor that suggested an irreverent disregard for the music if not a total inability to hear it.

The high-school pep squad followed the band, marching under the shade of a billowing Lone Star flag held suspended above their collective heads like a giant canopy.

The combined choirs of the elementary schools, oblivious of the stirring music of the band a few yards ahead, came next, raising their tiny assorted voices in a medley of "Beautiful, Beautiful Texas," "The Eyes of Texas," "Deep In The Heart of Texas," and with no guile whatsoever, "The Yellow Rose of Texas."

Mr. Devol turned to Purdy as the choirs moved past and complimented him on his cleverness and originality in not placing the color guard at the head of the parade.

"I saw only one parade in my whole life where they put the color guard at the end," he said. "It was out in Deaf Smith County, as I recall—and this is the second. Originality is what I like! I certainly do! Yes, yes, yes, I like that! Shows imagination!"

Purdy stared at him and attempted no reply. A color guard had not crossed his mind, not for the beginning, the middle nor the end of the parade.

The Bronte Club's float, as expected, depicted the Alamo with two young men out front, one in the uniform of Santa Anna's Mexican Army, the other in buckskins. They stood like statues pointing rifles at one another.

The County Cooperative Cotton Ginners Association (CCCGA) presented a bale of cotton wrapped in Lone Star bunting at one end of their float, while at the other, three youths with faces blackened and cotton sacks slung from their shoulders, were bending low, apparently vying with one another for the single stalk of cotton blossoms that sprouted from the floor.

The exhibit of the Latin American Friendship League featured a fancy grillwork, behind which stood Ida Bell Clifton in Spanish flamenco costume, blinking coyly over the top of a lace fan at Waldo McWhorter in serape and sombrero, guitar under one arm, and his skin darkened to a rich brown by pancake makeup. In the cab of the truck, wearing his gray, wide-striped, double-breasted Sunday suit, red necktie, red socks, and new Panama hat purchased especially for the occasion, sat the driver, Jesus Muniz, the only full-blooded Mexican in town.

The Volunteer Fire Department simply piled all its volunteers aboard its new fire engine and inched along with the rest of the parade.

Next came the Daughters of the Texas Republic, Bessie Beal Beardsley Chapter, all nine members present and accounted for but, for some reason not readily apparent to the spectators, on foot. Theirs was the float that had broken down at Fifth Street. Huffing and blowing, their makeup streaked and their hair stringy with perspiration, they were attired in long, flowing white chiffon and struggling among themselves to keep aloft in a stiff wind a billboard-sized streamer emblazoned with the words, "VALOR, TRADITION AND GLORY." Their formation was ragged, but the crowd forgave them and applauded enthusiastically.

The high-school Chemistry Club's float was swarming with half-naked youths painted to resemble Indians. They slapped their mouths while emitting war whoops and bouncing about the truck bed as though it were covered with a layer of hot coals.

The Odd Fellows Drill Team marched three abreast and three deep. Every so often, they sidestepped to display their virtuosity; then to clinch it, they parted ranks and closed them again three times in one short block.

The Kiwanians followed in a multicolored, stripped-down Model T touring car spilling over with clowns in baggy pants and a bird dog wearing a dunce cap.

The Ethelbert Nevin Music Society decorated its float with a huge cardboard cutout of the State of Texas, in front of which sat three strapless-gowned maidens with violins simulating a recording of "The Rosary," "Narcissus," and "Mighty Lak a Rose."

The Brownies, Cub Scouts, Girl Scouts, Boy Scouts, and the DeMolays filed past in that order.

The last float in the parade was the entry of the Eat 'n Rest Inn, Rhoda Fryer, proprietress. A mass of crepe-paper jonquils and daisies and Kleenex carnations, its focal point was a lunch counter at the rear of the exhibit. Behind the counter stood Rhoda Fryer, red dress and all, serving delicacies from a silver tray to her employees, Babe Pruitt, May Bingham, and Ora Rainwater respectively. Almost as conspicuous as the hysterical colors of their ball gowns were the jeweled pinkies they displayed as they acted out their roles of grand ladies dining in the grand manner. Above the counter, printed in red, white and blue block letters was the single word, "PEACE."

Immediately following the Misses Fryer, Bingham, Pruitt and Rainwater and bringing up the rear were several members of the Future Farmers of America leading their prize-winning bull, which had sired more offspring than any other such animal in recent memory. Unfortunately—for that time and place—the beast wore a red felt coverlet containing his name: APPASSIONATA.

As Appassionata lumbered off toward the depot, trailing

Rhoda Fryer and her employees, Representative Devol turned to his Official Escort and allowed as to how that was the finest parade he had ever seen in all his years of public service. What's more, he declared, he didn't see how he would ever be able to pick a winner from so many beautiful, imaginative and original floats.

"Just between you and me," he said, "I thought that dining-room scene was about as pretty a float as I ever saw in all my twenty years of parade attending. I'm telling you, Purlie—you don't mind my calling you Purlie, do you? We certainly know each other well enough by now for first names! As I was saying—you've got the flower of Texas maidenhood right here in your fair city. That was evident in that dining-room scene—quite evident. Yes, yes, yes, it was evident all right. No doubt about it—now tell me what to do about turning in my decision."

Purdy was uneasy. And nervous. And suspicious.

"Well, you see, Mr. Dee-vol—"

"Just call me Lee—that's what my friends call me, and that includes you. Just call me Lee."

"Oh—well, thank you. That's right nice of you, Mr. Dee-vol. All you got to do—er—ah—Lee—is write the name of the winning float on a little slip of paper, and I'll take it to the Grand Marshal. But there ain't no hurry, because they won't announce the winner until the picnic, anyway. You can think it over a while," he added. "As a matter of fact, I think maybe you *ought* to think it over a while."

"If I could just follow the dictates of my own heart," said Lee, "I'd just declare a tie among all of them, including that magnificent bull at the end. Never saw anything like it in my life. By the way, Purlie, *who* was that lady in the red dress on that float that—"

"But that float didn't have no Texas theme, Mr. Dee-vol!"

"*Lee*—call me Lee! So it didn't—no Texas theme. I suppose for a glorious occasion such as San Jacinto Day, it's all-important to depict a Texas theme. Yes, yes, yes . . . I wasn't going to overlook that. Not at all. You're right to remind me of that, too. I see why they made you the head man, Purlie. That's not hard to see at all!"

With his heart in his mouth, his fingers crossed and his mind ajumble, Purdy asked Representative Devol if he cared to go ahead and make his decision now, or wait until later.

"I think I'll do it now," he said. "If you'll just permit me a moment or two of deliberation, I'll just take care of that difficult little task right this minute."

He deliberated while he took his pen and paper from his pocket, a matter of three seconds, four at the most. He bent his head over the paper while Purdy tried not to die. Mr. Devol looked up from the paper.

"What's the name of the organization that sponsored those valiant ladies marching and carrying that big sign?" he asked.

"You mean the float that broke down?"

"Tha-a-a-a-t's the one! Valorous ladies all—just like their sign said. Pure valor and courage. What's their name?"

Purdy's heart overflowed. "Daughters of the Texas Republic," he said, choked to the teeth with gratitude. Then he added, "Bessie Beal Beardsley Chapter."

"Wonderful lady, Bessie Beal Beardsley—wonderful families, the Beals and the Beardsleys—wonderful patriots—wonderful ladies. . . ."

Representative Devol handed his decision to Purdy, shook his hand, said he had been the perfect host, and if he didn't mind, he wanted to have a few words with Horace Cox and some of the other city and county officials.

"Don't worry about me any more," he said. "I'm right at home among all these good people. I'll find my way around. I just want to wander around and *mix* in with them all I can. I'll see you at the picnic, Purlie, and we'll have some more of our wonderful talk together. . . ."

So saying, he wrung Purdy's hand again, stepped down

from the reviewing stand and began handshaking his way through the dispersing crowd, laughing, visiting, complimenting, back-slapping and vote-getting all the way.

As for Purdy himself, he had no intention of going to the picnic. His job had ended with the parade. He went home with a view toward collapsing. But he had one remaining obstacle before he could clear the decks for a complete, and perhaps final, breakdown: his wife.

With mouth wide open and tongue flapping, she took her husband to task for not being more choosy about who wasn't in the parade and who was. Particularly the latter.

"I've never been so embarrassed in my life!" Eula Robinson ranted. "You ought to have heard what people said! I'll tell you right now, it was a shame and a disgrace the way you let Rhoda Fryer and all those—those—all those—those *persons* prance and twist around in front of the whole town! And that Ora Rainwater didn't have on a stitch—*not a stitch*—under that floozy dress she had on—and all those trifling no-account hussies making like they were eating dinner and that Rhoda twitching and squirming around! I can't imagine what got into you, Purdy Robinson! What was going on in your mind? Can you tell me that? The *very idea* of you allowing that kind of carrying on in the middle of Main Street in front of decent men, women and children! I don't know how I can ever show my face around town again. I *just don't know* if I can look Reverend McWhorter in the eye Sunday or not. . . ."

On and on she sputtered and raged. Purdy tuned her out every few paragraphs or so, but not really. That would have been no more simple than turning off the wind. He was paradesick, San Jacinto Day-sick, Lee Devol-sick, Rhoda Fryer-sick, and now he was getting wifesick.

The entire experience had been nerve-shattering. Strange, too. He could think of nothing in his past—and, he hoped, future—to which he could compare it.

While his wife continued to blast him, he let go with a big sigh and decided that inasmuch as life seemed to have become an uninterrupted string of Firsts, he might as well add one more to the list before the little men in white coats showed up to take him away. And add another he did. A real trailblazer.

"SHUT UP!" he screamed at his wife.

Then Mrs. Purdy Robinson added a First of her own.

She didn't say another word.

4.

⤞

Myrtle McAfee Dunlap's
Concern with Culture

Myrtle McAfee Dunlap was cultured, and the worst thing anybody could do to her was not to think so. Those who tried it learned the hard way not to ever think so again, especially to her face. Watching her prove them wrong was scarcely worth the wear and tear. She considered herself the town's cultural leader with a capital C, and she worked hard to keep her leadership in good running order. But leaders come and they go, and one terrible day, with an audience in attendance, Myrtle went. It happened on her mother's birthday. At last report, she had taken up the ukulele and five-card solitaire.

As she saw it, culture was a trust, an article of faith handed down by her dear, dead mother, Bertha Horton McAfee, poetess, whose reputation was not entirely local. She had published one verse in *Grit*, one in the Amarillo *Globe Dispatch*, and one in *Bluebonnet*, a Texas magazine that folded after only two issues and hasn't been revived yet. Locally, she had published three poems in *The Weekly Courier*, four on the bottom of funeral notices, and a whole passel of them on back pages of church bulletins. But that was not her total output. Far from it.

Whereas some ladies piece quilts, put up peach preserves or go to Ladies Aid, Bertha Horton McAfee wrote poems. She wrote them for breakfast, dinner and supper, for summer, winter and fall, to celebrate, to commiserate and to inaugurate. She claimed she couldn't help it. There they were, poems buzzing around in her head like little bees, and the only way she could quiet them was to commit them to paper. In other words, Bertha Horton would write a poem at the drop of a hat, on any subject, of any length, in any mood. You name it, and she'd rhyme it. All you had to do was give her a topic and stand back; you'd get a poem every time. The cardboard cartons bulging with her manuscripts, handwritten in flowery script and decorated around the edges with curlicues, certainly seemed to bear that out. The Miscellaneous section of her subject index read like an almanac.

While Myrtle herself did not inherit her mother's compulsion for writing, she did inherit her appreciation for the arts, and she used it as she would a weapon to stir up the community's interest in the finer things and, above all, to elevate its artistic sensibilities. It wasn't easy, but she tried. She was forever trying to organize something—a literary discussion group, an art exhibit, a book-review series, a music-appreciation class, a poetry-reading workshop, and on occasion, a bell-ringing society. Sometimes she succeeded, and sometimes she did not; it depended on local enthusiasm, which frequently was less than hysterical. She directed plays and revues, too. Once for the San Jacinto Day Festival, she field-commanded a historical pageant that was so big and had such a large cast that virtually nobody came. The bulk of the ticket-buying public was onstage.

She was aghast at the number of mothers who were allowing their children to grow up into cultural knotheads. With apparent disregard for the consequences, they ignored Miss Addie Barker's piano classes, Mozelle Bishop's toe-dancing instruction, Mrs. Grady Dilbert's Voice Studio, and Mrs. Winnie Cox's Workshop for Expression and Dramatic Reading.

"I can't *imagine* what they must be thinking of," she said, "to let those poor children grow up in a cultural desert when there's an oasis in plain sight."

While Miss Addie and her counterparts were not ungrateful for Myrtle's recruiting drives in their behalf, they had to tell her every now and then to take it easy. Their classes usually ran at capacity; most of the time they couldn't take on an additional pupil, even if Myrtle handcuffed him and brought him in on a tether.

"You shouldn't have got that Chism boy all charged up to take voice lessons, Myrtle," Mrs. Grady Dilbert complained. "I'm running full up, and I just can't take him."

Myrtle was sophisticatedly cool.

"You mean you *can't* or you *won't?*" she asked.

"Both," replied Mrs. Dilbert. "He couldn't carry a tune if it was tied up in a paper sack."

Myrtle was the County Library's most persistent and nagging critic, particularly if she spotted a book that was misfiled or not catalogued accurately. She berated Velma Agnew, librarian, up one side and down the other for her insensitivity toward her intellectual responsibilities.

"Suppose someone came in searching for this book," she said, taking a volume from the P's and putting it in the B's where it belonged. "Would you want to be personally responsible for depriving their minds of its contents?"

Velma peered over the top of her spectacles at the book.

"Look, Myrtle," she said wearily. "Nobody would check out that book if I put it in the front door where they'd have to step over it to get inside the building."

The book had to do with the granular structure of the calcereous subsoil in Erath County.

Once when Velma saw Myrtle cruise past the library looking for a parking place, she got up, locked the door and pulled down the shades.

Eagerly and aggressively, Myrtle volunteered her services for judging flower shows, speech competitions, music auditions and essay contests. Fortunately, the supply often exceeded the demand, and her talents went a-begging more often than not. Mr. Taylor, the debate and dramatic coach at the high school, said he wished he could keep the Interscholastic League competitions a deep, dark secret—at least, from Myrtle.

"She thinks she's a qualified judge of *everything*," he said, "and she gets offended when I don't let her judge *anything*. If she'd only judge the events, maybe I could put up with her, but she takes over and tries to *instruct* my students as well! 'Myrtle,' I said to her, '*I'm* the teacher, not you. Besides, this is a contest, not a class.' And she said, 'Any occasion is a class if there is knowledge to be imparted.'"

Myrtle had other outlets for her talents. She was a performer in her own rights, ever alert for an opportunity to give one of her musical readings, a book review, a lecture, or a public recital of her mother's poetry. Mr. Taylor's problem was a pushover as compared to a play director who tried to leave her out of the cast of a play. Or to include her. It wasn't that her acting talents were any weaker than the average amateur's. It was just that she too often felt that the play couldn't possibly limp through to the final curtain without her taking a hand in its direction.

She owned a set of the Harvard Classics and claimed not to have missed a Book of the Month Club selection in twelve years. She read *The New Yorker* and *Harper's Bazaar* and all the Reader's Digest Condensed Books. Her record collection included Gershwin and Grieg and all the known recordings of Jeanette MacDonald and Nelson Eddy. She kept a length of polished driftwood on her coffee table, an oil painting of Texas bluebonnets over her mantel, and a silver card tray by her front door. She drank iced coffee and ate watercress sandwiches. She answered the telephone with a "Yes?" rather than a "Hello." She smoked cigarettes in long jeweled holders, wore dark glasses, draped her coat over her shoulders, painted her toenails, drank tea with the most elegant pinkie in town, served coffee in demitasse cups and sugar in lumps. With tongs.

There were no two ways about it, Myrtle McAfee Dunlap was cultured. Doggedly, determinedly, militantly and belligerently, she was cultured, and there was hell to pay for those who doubted it. Slim Bobo could testify to that, for he got it with both barrels when he took his hillbilly string band to Wichita Falls to play on the radio and made the mistake of asking Myrtle to go along and read a piece of corn-pone doggerel midway in the program. The upbraiding he got for a reply was so eloquent that it may even yet find its way into anthologies. She allowed for no such detours on her road to culture.

Two obstacles, however, did slow her down. Eventually, they stopped her dead in her tracks. One was her husband, Elmo, and the other was Ada Gossett, her hired woman. Neither was culture-prone.

On the face of it, Elmo would appear to have been easy pickings, for he was a musician. That is to say, he played trombone—the only trombone—in the Municipal Band. He played by ear, though, which was a handicap. The black notes on a sheet of music were as mysterious to him as the assembly directions on a mechanical toy. Consequently, his musical sights were restricted by low visibility. He loved music, but he loved it indiscriminately and, according to Myrtle, the wrong kind. He had nothing against classical and operatic music. It was just that if he couldn't hum it, whistle it, or play it on his trombone, he didn't know if he liked it or not. That, and his inability to read the notes, were constant embarrassments to his wife. She thought his musical leanings were lacking in direction and needed shaping, but she could do little to help him, for when she mentioned it, he didn't know what she was talking about.

When the Municipal Band received a new arrangement and ran through it the first time, Elmo sat by and listened to fix the tune in his head. On the second time around, he played the trombone part as he heard it in his mind, which frequently was not what the composer heard when he wrote it. If the band played the arrangement wrong, Elmo learned it wrong. When the band corrected its mistakes, Elmo had one hell of a time correcting his. Sometimes he never corrected them at all. Tootie Perkins, director and cornetist, who occupied the next chair, steered Elmo through complex passages when he felt like it and kicked him in the shins when he didn't.

The Municipal Band was a volunteer organization composed of local citizens who loved music and needed an outlet to express it. It performed only in the summers. This meant that because of individual members' vacation plans, the composition of the band was a sometimes thing. If Marcella Overton, tuba, took her vacation the first two weeks in August, say, the Municipal Band played its concerts on the Court House lawn for two weeks minus tuba, and Tootie could do nothing about it but gnash his teeth. He cried real tears, though, the summer Oscar Jenkins and Alvin Bennett, snare and bass drum respectively, went on separate vacations at the same time. There went the entire percussion section. Fortunately, Tootie knew how to cope with an understrength organization, although it wasn't much fun. He had learned it from adapting fifty-part arrangements to a twelve-piece band, which wasn't as difficult as it might appear. He simply distributed the music sheets to whoever was present, and the band played on.

The only 100 percent available member of the band, the only member who never seemed to leave town, the only member who never seemed to have any plans of his own, was Elmo Dunlap, who, when you came right down to it, was beyond question the most dispensable member of all. There was not one musical arrangement in the band's catalogue that didn't sound better without him. Tootie and the other musicians, however, were too kind and considerate to explain these matters to him, and he interpreted their silence as critical approval.

Consequently, no adversity was great enough to keep him away from rehearsals and actual performances. He played one concert with fever of 102 degrees and another with an abscessed tooth. He got two speeding tickets coming home from Childress once, such was his determination not to miss the band concert that evening. His fellow musicians still shudder when they recall the concert on the Court House lawn with Elmo sporting the great white father of all summer colds. Unless they happened to be looking straight at him, they couldn't tell if he was blowing his trombone or his nose.

Myrtle seldom attended the concerts. She couldn't afford to. Her presence might be construed as endorsement of the music, which was appallingly lowbrow, and that, of course, would have been at cross purposes with her crusade to improve the quality of the town's cultural output. Neither did she want to risk overhearing another critical judgment like Sam Abernathy's one night when the band got lost mid-tune and had to start in again from the beginning.

"The Municipal Band," said Sam, "couldn't play 'Come to Jesus' in whole notes."

None of this is to mention the awful humiliation of watching her husband turn beet-red in the face and behind the ears while blowing his brains out to produce those clinkers. So she stayed away.

But she couldn't stay away from Elmo's trombone-playing. He practiced at home during his free time, which he seemed to have more of than the ordinary business man. His business was insurance—all types—and he did well with it. His office on Main Street between the Marvella Beauty Shop and *The Weekly Courier* was pleasant, easily accessible from the street, and up-to-date, with all the latest office equipment and furniture, but he was no slave to office routine. Without Jessie Atwater, he might have been, but the point is academic, for he did have Jessie; she had been operating his office for twenty-two years and knew more about his business than he did. And that was handy, for sometimes she didn't lay eyes on her employer from morning till night, though she knew how to track him down if and when she needed him. If the arrangement looked peculiar to some people, they could not criticize the results. Dunlap Insurance Company prospered. So, whether Elmo was goofing off or out beating the bushes for new clients, he had plenty of free time to devote to his trombone-practicing.

In fairness to his wife, it should be said that she would not have objected to his trombone-practicing around the house if somewhere along the line it had improved his playing. But it didn't. The entire operation was roughly similar to blowing up a balloon with a hole in it.

"Why don't you take up golf, dear?" she asked him one day during a trombone-practicing session, thinking that a spot of conversation might be a welcome diversion from climbing the walls.

He claimed that golf required too much time. "I can practice my trombone-playing at odd times—fifteen minutes here or a half hour there," he explained. "Golf takes all afternoon or all day."

"Yes, it does, doesn't it?" she said hopefully, but he never caught on.

Elmo practiced in their bedroom upstairs, in the garage, and even on the front porch unless Myrtle was present to shoo him back inside.

"I do wish Elmo would raise his musical sights," she said to her friends who dropped in for a cup of tea with trombone background. It was her device for heading off critical observations about her husband's tin ear. Or beat them to the punch, as it were.

Her friends were too polite to mention that Elmo's musical sights were already miles above his ability, and they managed to steer clear of talk about his talents. Everybody except Ada Gossett, the Dunlaps' hired woman. She thought Elmo was a genius.

She attended all the band concerts on the Court House lawn and sat where she had an unobstructed view of the trombone section (Elmo). Her critiques afterwards were almost more than her employer could endure.

"You oughto of been there, Miz Dunlap," she said once. "They was playing 'The old gray mare, she ain't what she useta be,' and when they come to this part where Oscar Jenkins beats on the drums like horses' hoofs, Mr. Dunlap he slid that trombone clean down to the bottom and went WAAH-AAAH-WAAAH!"

With one hand spread across her mouth and the other pumping the air in imitation of a trombone, she pranced across the kitchen and back again.

Myrtle flinched.

"*Please*, Ada!"

"I'm telling you it sounded just like a real mule, Miz Dunlap. Honest!"

"Yes. Those light, amusing selections do seem to go well in the summer outdoor series, don't they?"

"When Mr. Dunlap comes home to dinner, I'll ast him to play that WAAH-AAAH-WAAH part for you, Miz Dunlap."

"Perhaps," said Myrtle. "And speaking of *lunch*, Ada, I think we'll use the blue cloth today."

"Why can't you eat in the kitchen?"

"It's more pleasant in the dining room."

"But I just got through washing and ironing that blue cloth," Ada grumbled. "Why can't you eat on that white cloth we used at supper last night?"

"That's a *dinner* cloth, Ada, not a *luncheon* cloth."

"It's a *table*cloth, ain't it? You oughta use regular oilcloth, anyway, like everybody else does. I was telling Flossie Jenkins the other day about how you use all them linen tablecloths when they ain't nobody here but us, and she said she'd quit if she was me."

Ada was not insubordinate. She wasn't even sassy. She had an independent spirit, though, and in that respect, she was akin to every other hired woman in town, any one of whom would set you straight in a flash if you called her a servant or, worst of all, a maid. It wasn't that they were touchy about their social status. Indeed, their social status was not the easiest thing in the world to pin down. Mrs. Charlie Bennett and her hired woman, Flossie Jenkins—Ada's friend—had been members of the same Sunday-school class for twenty years, and when the class had a social at the Bennetts', Flossie's status might seem fuzzy. At refreshment time, Mrs. Bennett served a plate to Flossie as though she were a bona fide guest, which in true fact she was, even though she might be required to remain and clean up after her classmates had gone home.

The real problem was that none of the hired women around

town thought of domestic work as a full-time career. They worked by the hour, by the day, or by the job, always with an eye peeled for some other kind of work that would pay more money. Some housewives had been rehiring the same woman every week for years, each week as though it were the first, only because the women were unwilling to commit themselves to a permanent arrangement that would keep them off the open labor market.

It was not unusual, therefore, for Della Hubbard to do Mrs. Willis Shumaker's washing one day and sell her a pound of weenies at Riley's Grocery & Market the next, which meant that some poor housewife was left holding the bag and it full of dirty laundry. Isobel Higgins worked in the school cafeteria, the Alamo Rooming House, Akers' Variety Store and, when she felt like it, for a few families around town, none of whom were stupid enough to believe they had first claim on her services. Carrie Metcalf worked at the hospital during epidemics, at Mrs. Boyd's Hotel during banquets, at Mr. Winbury's slaughter pen during hog-killing and hired out for domestic work only on rainy days—sometimes.

Ada Gossett was more dependable than most, but not enough to give her employer a full feeling of confidence and a well-rounded sense of security. Even after seventeen years, Myrtle Dunlap couldn't feel that their working relationship was entirely out of the woods. She dealt with Ada accordingly—as though she were a short-fused stick of dynamite.

Whereas some people have nervous stomachs and some people have freckles, Myrtle had an uncultured husband and an uncultured hired woman. She endured them both with grace, gameness and a heart of oak. She could do no less short of divorcing one and firing the other, unthinkable alternatives, for in her own fashion she loved them both. Instead, she plugged away at them with a courage born of ignorance. She dragged Elmo to programs and recitals, nudging him throughout to keep him awake, confident that eventually a cultural osmosis would take place. She "helped" Ada to rise above her lowly background, thinking that somewhere in that ugly swamp a beautiful lily might some day bloom.

Beforehand she briefed Elmo on what to expect from whatever program she was forcing him to attend. Afterwards, she filled him in on those portions that had escaped his appreciation, i.e., all of it. She tried to titillate his interest in literature with character sketches and plot synopses from whatever book she happened to be reading. She urged him to keep his elbows off the table when eating, to keep his shoes on when in church, and to keep his hands out of his pockets when walking down the street. She chided him for wasting his time in the Blue Moon Domino Parlor and for hanging around the depot with Avery Massey to watch the trains come in. She pleaded with him to become more active in civic affairs, to be a leader and not so much a follower.

"If you'd only put your mind to it, you could do big things, dear," she reminded him. "There's no reason why you couldn't be president of the Rotary Club, for example."

"But Myrt—Ennis Grissom is President of Rotary," he said.

"I wasn't speaking of this particular year, dear," she replied. "And I do wish you wouldn't insist on calling me *Myrt*."

She taught and retaught Ada how to set the table properly, how to serve a meal, how to answer the telephone, how to greet callers at the door. Ada listened and watched and didn't learn a thing. She persuaded Ada to switch her days off to be available when Myrtle entertained her literary discussion group and learn a ladylike thing or two in the process. It was a mistake.

In the first place, Ada had been personally acquainted with most of the guests since childhood and reminisced freely with them about matters they had been working years to forget. In the second, it was difficult to tell who was the hostess, what with Ada dominating conversations even when she was out in the kitchen three rooms away.

"Ada, my pet, you must remember that ladies don't raise their voices and shout from room to room," Myrtle admonished her afterwards.

"That's what *you* think!" Ada hooted. "You oughta hear Mrs. Whelan yelling upstairs in the jail when the prisoners get to raising a ruckus and Artie ain't home!"

Myrtle delivered subtle little lectures to both her husband and her hired woman about their morals, the language they used, the company they kept, the places they went, the clothes they wore, the attitudes they affected. She tried to be patient, for she knew that Rome wasn't built in a day. What she didn't seem to know was that these two particular Romes might never get built at all.

But she chipped away at them, apparently unaware that she was getting nowhere. And that was peculiar, for all she had to do was stop occasionally to total the score, and she would have seen that Elmo and Ada were racking them up while she herself was collecting nothing but big round goose eggs.

And so the score was standing at 279–0 in their favor when several years ago, to commemorate her mother's birthday, Myrtle presented herself in "Dramatic Recital of Selections from the Notebooks of Bertha Horton McAfee." This was her second such presentation—she called it the "Second Edition"—and the second year she had staged it in her own home. She envisioned the affair as an annual event that would some day come to be mellowed by time, hallowed by tradition and flocked to by crowds. So far, none of those things had happened. The previous year's turnout had not been a stampede exactly, and this year's enthusiasm had not yet been wild enough to send her out shopping for a church auditorium or to hire a hall. So, as she had done the year before, she lined her living room with folding chairs borrowed from

L. T. Ditmore's Funeral Home and made ready for another cultural assault on the town.

Although attendance was by invitation only, she spread the word that it would not be considered gauche for the unfavored to request permission to attend.

"After all," she explained, "we don't want to deprive one single, precious soul of this cultural refreshment."

On the morning of the recital, two unrelated events took place, neither of which she could have foreseen and planned for. Her husband landed his biggest client of the year, and her hired woman became a grandmother.

At eleven o'clock in the morning, after depositing the juicy new policy in the capable hands of Jessie Atwater, Elmo knocked off work for the day and celebrated his way home via Smokey Rainwater's Tavern, an establishment on a road west of town that wasn't on the way to anywhere but had the heaviest traffic in the county. Several bottles of beer and two hours later, he appeared at the back door of his own home. Ada was in the kitchen making cookies to serve at intermission.

Elmo handed her a shopping bag knobby with frosty brown bottles of beer.

"Here—stick these in the refrigerator," he said.

She took the bag from him and peeked inside.

"I oughta drink one of these myself," she said unhappily. "Tessie went out and had herself a baby yesterday. She called me from Amarillo."

"Well, congratulations!" Elmo said. "Have a beer to celebrate!"

"But Tessie ain't married, Mr. Dunlap!"

"Then have *two!*" he urged.

She opened the oven and looked inside at a pan of cookies.

"Miz Dunlap, she might not like it—her having all that poem-reading and carrying on in the house today." She closed the oven door. "She's upstairs now painting her fingernails and curling her hair. Last time I looked, she was putting black stuff around her eyes. It was making her look like a hussy, so I says—"

"You don't need to worry about ole Myrt," said Elmo. He took a bottle of beer from the shopping bag and held it out to her. "Who's the proud papa?"

She studied the beer with apprehension for a moment. Then, apparently settling whatever conflict might have been raging within her, she took a stout gulp.

"Durned if I know," she said. "I ast her, and she said, 'Aw, it ain't nobody you know, Mama,' and I said, 'Looks to me like if I'm gonna be the grandmaw, I oughta know the daddy's name,' and she said, 'What for? It ain't the baby's name nohow.'"

She drank to the bottom of the label.

Elmo opened a bottle for himself.

"Here's to Grandmaw Gossett!" he said, following his toast with a long drink.

"Now ain't that a fine come-off?" she said. She emptied her bottle. "Now don't let me forget them cookies in the oven," she went on. "That batch oughta be about done."

Elmo opened her a fresh beer.

"I ought not to drink no more, Mr. Dunlap," she said. "I got a weak bladder."

"Beer's good for weak bladders," he said. He thrust the bottle at her. "It's the best thing in the world. You know what beer does? It puts a *lining* in your bladder, that's what. I'll bet people with the thickest bladder linings are the people who drink the most beer. Drink up—*Grandmaw!*"

He poked her in the ribs. She let go with a guffaw and poked him a good one in return.

"*Grandmaw!*" she echoed. "Don't that beat all? I guess I'm as much a grandmaw as anybody else—even if it ain't legal."

[*166*]

"I heard recently that there are more illegal grandmaws in Texas than long-horned steers. What do you think about that?"

She glanced at the beer. Her eyes lighted up. "Maybe a little snort to cool me off won't hurt none," she said. "Cooking cookies is hot work." She took a snort—king-sized. "You know, Tessie ain't really a bad girl," she said. "She ain't what you'd call bad—if she'd just learn to keep her pants on when—"

"Oh—Adaah?"

It was the voice of Mrs. Elmo Dunlap at its most tinkling and charming. It came from upstairs.

"I'd better go see what she wants," Ada said uneasily. She hurried to the door and peered through the dining room toward the stairs at the front of the house. "I wish I had some Sen-Sen," she added.

"Finish your beer," Elmo urged. "She can wait."

Ada studied the bottle in her hand.

"Well—one more slurp ain't gonna change the price of potatoes, I don't guess," she said.

She drank deep from the bottle and moved back into the kitchen, where Elmo was now seated at the table.

"As I was saying, Tessie might get hot pants sometimes when she ought—"

"A-daaaah? Where—who's that you're talking to down there?"

Elmo placed a finger against his lips and shook his head.

"Don't let her know I'm here," he whispered. "She'll make me go to the recital, and as I recall, that wasn't in the wedding vows—was it?"

"It mighta been," said Ada. "But don't worry about it, 'cause if it was, we'll just take it out."

She stuck her head through the dining-room door.

"It ain't nobody, Miz Dunlap," she yelled. "I was just memorizing some Scripture verses."

"I need you up here, Ada, my dear," Myrtle called out.

Ada turned the bottle up and drained its contents in one gulp. Elmo looked on in awe.

"I gotta see about. . . ." Her voice trailed off as she looked about the room with eyes that were slipping further out of focus with each successive blink. "Now what was it I was gonna see about?"

"A-daaaaaaaah!"

The music had drained from Myrtle's voice. Ada pulled herself together and remembered.

"Oh yeah—the cookies," she mumbled. She did not go near the oven. "Don't let me forgit them cookies now—"

"*A-daaaaaaaaah!*"

"One thing you gotta remember, Ada," Elmo said helpfully. "Tessie ain't exactly built like a packing crate, you know— and when you got a shape like hers, well you gotta expect—"

"That's what I tried to tell her, Mr. Dunlap—exactly! I said, 'Tessie, if you don't quit twitching your bottom all over Main Street, I'm gonna make you wear a Mother Hubbard and—' "

"ADA GOSSETT! PLEASE show me the courtesy of replying when I call!" Myrtle's tones were devoid of all culture and charm now. "I'm trying to preserve my voice, you know. . . ."

Ada tugged at her dress, wiped off her mouth with the back of her hand and burped.

"OKAY, MYRTLE!" she bellowed. "JUST HOLD YOUR HORSES, WILLYA?"

She started for the door.

"Hey—the cookies are burning!" Elmo cried.

"Well—git 'em out!" she called over her shoulder as she took off through the house in a slow trot.

Elmo looked in the oven at two dozen blackened, smoking

cookies. He grabbed a potholder, set the pan in the sink, doused the sorry batch from the cold-water tap and watched it sizzle for a moment. Then, leaving the sink smoking and steaming, he escaped through the back door with a bottle of beer under each arm and one in each hand.

The recital was scheduled for two-thirty. Seven ladies and a ten-year-old girl chewing bubble gum showed up. Myrtle announced a short delay for the benefit of others who might have been unavoidably detained. Ten minutes later, Mrs. Nellie Wilcox Perkins, Tootie's mother and a lifelong friend of Bertha Horton, appeared and took her seat. She was ninety-three, a widow, hard of hearing and bothered with gas pains. Her vision was poor, her memory faulty, and she walked with a cane. Apparently, she was the sum total of "the others."

Myrtle wore a floor-length gown of pearl gray with flowing sleeves and a silk rope of royal purple tied around her waist. Ada likened it to a fancy bathrobe. Elmo said it resembled a shroud. Myrtle thought it looked classical. She struck a pose behind a lectern in the double door leading to the dining room, and the recital began.

> "Oh come all ye
> With fancies free
> Who wouldst dream with me
> And welcome be!"

She smiled theatrically, bowed deeply with a wide sweep of both hands, and waited for the initial enchantment to wear off her listeners.

The little girl blew a giant-sized bubble.

"Thus the poetess called to the ages," declaimed Myrtle. "And so I call you to dream through these Selections from the Notebook of Bertha Horton McAfee, Second Edition. Lift your hearts and let your spirits soar as we roam through the lush green meadows of language, romance and beauty.

> "Oh sun and sky
> Please tell me why
> You are so high.
> Wish you were low,
> So I could know
> You per-son-ally.
> And
> I
> Do."

Mrs. Perkins leaned forward on her cane, squinted her eyes and cupped a hand behind her ear. The little girl got up and went to the bathroom.

> "Flower and tree
> Please tell me
> Your mys-ter-eee
> So I will be
> Your friend."

The recital was under way.

Meanwhile, Ada sat at the kitchen table and waited for intermission, her cue to serve the tea and cookies. She shelled a mess of black-eyed peas for supper, ate a half dozen of her own cookies, repaired the ripped hem of her dress, then dozed in her chair. When she came to, the recital was still under way. She drank another bottle of beer to keep awake. Then Elmo appeared at the back door.

"How's it going in there, ole *Grandmaw?*" he whispered in a whisper that would qualify as a whisper only in a football stadium. He came on inside.

"*Not so loud!*" she cautioned him. "They'll all hear you."

"How's it going?" he repeated. "She put 'em to sleep yet?"

"Durned if I know," she replied. "I ain't been listening."

She cracked the door to the dining room, and they both listened in silence for a moment.

> "From dawn's early light
> Till midnight late,
> We'll give our might
> To the Lone Star State."

Ada closed the door.

"It took me a whole hour to git that burnt smell outta the house," she said, returning to the table. "Miz Dunlap, she gassed around something awful and got in an uproar like I burnt the house down. It wasn't nothing but a pan of cookies, and we still got enough cookies for a church social. Lookit all them cookies!"

Elmo fixed an unsteady gaze on the kitchen cabinet. It was covered from one end to the other with towering heaps of cookies. Or so it seemed.

"Mygawd! Who's she expecting—Coxey's Army?"

"Durned if I know—but if they show up, we can feed 'em, can't we?"

They enjoyed a hearty laugh.

"I ran outa beer," Elmo said. "I was out in the garage sitting on the bumper of the car watching a horned frog chasing a spider, and something happened to all the beer. Gimme a coupla bottles, and I'll go upstairs and see about my own bladder. It's getting weak like yours."

She fished two bottles from the shopping bag and handed them to him.

"You can't go through the dining room," she reminded him. "They'll see you."

"Then I'll go outside and come in through the front door and the hall."

"But they'll see you from the living room when you go up the stairs!"

"Myrt won't," he said. "She can't see the stairs from her pulpit in the dining room. Get yourself a bottle and come on up."

"Naw—I better stay here. You be quiet when you go upstairs now. Miz Dunlap, she won't like it if you stumble around and drown out her poem-reading."

"Better give me the opener."

"Before you get away with it," she said, "I might as well open up another one for myself. It might help my bladder lining while I'm waiting for Intermission."

She opened a bottle and drank half its contents nonstop.

"You want some cookies to eat with your beer?" she asked. Her stomach rumbled mightily.

"I guess not. You'd probably make me eat the burned ones."

Ada let go with a horse laugh. "We ain't got any more burnt ones—you washed them in the—"

She was cut short by a body-rattling burp.

"We burnt the hell outta that batch, didn't we, ole buddy?" she said. She clapped him on the back. The blow threw him off balance. She drank the rest of her beer.

"You know, Ada, you got a real fine sense of humor," he said, recovering and steadying himself against the refrigerator. "Here you are a grandmaw without any son-in-law . . . and you burned up . . . burned . . . burned up—the cookies, wasn't it? Yeah—the cookies. Then you have to listen to my mother-in-law's poems. That's what killed her, you know. The doctor said it was her heart, but it wasn't. It was all those poems. You know what she did? She wrote a poem once about garbage cans! It was full of stuff about the poor forgotten chicken bones and corncobs and orange peels that nobody was interested in now that they had served their purpose. Can you imagine that?"

"I don't know much about poems," she said. "Tessie used to know some little dirty verses—"

[*172*]

"See what I mean? You got a fine sense of—you know what? Let's me and you drink these two beers."

They did.

"I gotta go," he said. "Gimme two beers, and that's all I want. Even if I ask you for any more, I don't want them. See? I'll just hafta give one of 'em back to you—me with that bladder disease and all. I think I caught it from you, Ada."

She laughed. "Bladders ain't contagious, Mr. Dunlap!"

"That's what I think happened, anyway," he said. "I never did have a weak bladder until today—so you just tell me where else I could have got it. And you sure better go easy on that beer-drinking if you're gonna serve cookies in the living room—*Grandmaw!* What if you spill 'em in ole lady Perkins' lap?"

"Wouldn't that be a sight?" she whooped. "She's wearing her best Sunday dress, and if it ain't at least fifty years old, I'll kiss your foot and bark like a fox."

At the thought, she started to laugh again and couldn't stop. Elmo hit her on the back once or twice, but it helped her none.

"Well—while you're laughing, I guess I'll go up—"

He departed.

Ada sat down at the kitchen table. again, got her laughter under control, and went to sleep once again.

In the living room, the recital droned on with one minor distraction. Aside from the poetry itself, that is. The audience turned to watch someone come through the hall and go up the stairs.

Myrtle assumed it to be Ada. She suppressed a frown, turned on an additional batch of charm, raised her voice to regain her audience's attention and made a silent vow to give Ada a piece of her mind after the recital was over. Maybe at intermission. She had given her explicit instructions to stay in the kitchen and not go rattling around all over the house.

[*173*]

"Crockett and Bowie, where'er you go,
Your glorious names, we'll always know,
Ye brave men of the Al-a-mo
Your spirits shine on—"

She pulled up short and froze.

From above her head came the dreadfully familiar sounds of Elmo's trombone.

"WAAH-AAAH-WAAAH!"

Myrtle turned pale. Mrs. Nellie Wilcox Perkins dropped her cane.

"—us all
In winter, spring,
Summer and fall. . . ."

From behind her, Myrtle heard the back door swing open and slam shut.

"For freedom you died,
Ye brave men true,
Davy Crockett and Jim Bowie, too. . . ."

The front door burst open. Myrtle could hear the sound of rushing feet. Her audience turned its collective head and watched someone run up the stairs. Myrtle could not see who it was, but if Elmo was already upstairs—and she hadn't even known he was at home—*that* had to be Ada. . . .

"Into our lives you'll e'er bring
The inspiration for which we'll sing
Your eternal praises."

"WAAH-AAAH-WAAH!"

Myrtle considered the possibility of calling an intermission —emergency type. She had a few verses yet to go, else there would be no transition into her first-half wind-up, "Ode to a Homeless Dust Storm." Maybe if she stopped with "The Glory That was Sam Houston's," the intermission wouldn't be—

"WAAH-AAAH-WAAH!"

Myrtle took a deep breath and raised her voice.

"As long as mesquite trees grow
We'll remember the A-la-mo. . . ."

She was drowned out by boisterous chattering from upstairs, followed by the bleary laughter of Mrs. Ada Gossett,
hired woman and grandmother.

"Do it agin, Elmo!" she shouted. "You do the horse part,
an' I'll sing it this time. Okay?"

Daintily, Myrtle tapped the lectern with a forefinger and
forced a smile. It was strained, but under the circumstances, it
would have to do.

When that didn't beguile her audience as she had hoped,
she made a decision, and to hell with the transition into her
first-half wind-up, homeless dust storm and all.

"And now, dear friends, she called out. "Shall we have a cup
of tea?"

"WAAH-AAAH-WAAAH—SHE AIN'T WHAT SHE
USETA BEEEE!"

Mrs. Perkins leaned on her cane, this time in the direction
of the stairs. She cupped a hand behind her ear and strained
her eardrums.

"AIN'T WHAT SHE USETA BEEEE—AIN'T WHAT
SHE USETA BEEEEEEE!"

Mrs. Perkins rapped the floor with her cane in appreciation.

"Hee-hee-hee," she chuckled. "Tootie ought to have heard
that one!"

Myrtle's smile had turned grim and was now being executed
through teeth that were grinding energetically.

"Dear *friends*—shall we—"

"WHAT SHE USETA—whatsa matter, Elmo? You run-
nin' outta wind?"

"WAAH-AAAaaaa. . . ."

The old gray mare was cut short by a clang and a clatter. Elmo's trombone fell to the floor. The noise was followed by a heavy thud and the creak of bedsprings. Elmo had thrown in the towel.

Silence. But not for long.

Ada Gossett appeared on the stairs, her hair disarrayed, her hem ripped out once more, the front of her dress twisted to one side, her eyes bloodshot and unfocused, her steps anything but certain. She clutched the railing to steady herself.

"Y'all ready for the tea and cookies?" she shouted as she reached the bottom step. Myrtle's audience watched her, mesmerized. "We burnt up one batch," she went on, "but they's plenty more where they came from. We got more cookies than the Girl Scouts and the Eatmore Bakery put together—we got cookies running out your—"

"ADA!" Myrtle screamed.

Otherwise, no one said a word. Myrtle leaned on the lectern, eyes fixed on a flower design in the carpet. Ada lurched into the living room.

"Ole Elmo, he went sound asleep smack dab in the middle of that horse part," she said. "He blowed hisself out, I reckon." She stumbled over a folding chair. "He never did have enough wind for a decent-sized poot, nohow."

So saying, she threaded her unsteady way past the row of chairs, past her employer, through the dining room and disappeared through the kitchen door.

Myrtle didn't watch her go. She had buried her face in her arms on the lectern, and in that position she remained until her audience—all nine of them—had filed out the front door, leaving her to cope with her domestic and cultural problems unassisted.

For the three days following, she did not speak to Elmo and Ada. Not the first syllable. They tiptoed around the house, speaking in whispers or not at all, watching her with worried eyes, sweating her out with anxious hearts, handling her with kid gloves, waiting for the lid to blow off. It never blew.

Part of Myrtle had died.

On the fourth day, she bundled up her mother's manuscripts and presented them, along with an assortment of books, to the County Library. She didn't even hang around or go back later to see if Velma Agnew had catalogued them correctly or if she shelved them properly. Culturewise, she has not been particularly active since.

Nowadays, she works the crossword puzzle and the rebus picture in the newspaper each morning and listens to the soap operas on the radio in the afternoons—if the characters get in enough trouble to make things interesting. Mrs. Virgil Fuller reports that she stopped by one morning and found Myrtle on the back porch in a rocking chair tatting a doily, while Elmo sat on the bottom step practicing his trombone. Ada was out in the back yard bringing in the washing off the line and telling Myrtle about her new grandchild, her third.

"But I still ain't got no son-in-law to speak of," she was saying as Mrs. Fuller let herself through the back gate.

"All three of them seemed to be enjoying themselves and having the time of their lives," said Mrs. Fuller. "Myrtle was even chewing gum. Smelled like Juicy Fruit."

5.

~e

The Natural Talents of Merlin Hancock

Merlin Hancock's schoolmates might not remember him for his horn-rimmed spectacles, for his wild unruly hair, or for his six-foot, overgrown, flabby figure, on which he wore his mismatched clothes with complete abandon. They might have forgotten his casual way with all things educational, his irreverence towards progress, and his slaphappy view of life in general. But one thing they do remember, and that's how once during the great Depression, while they were standing around with flat pocketbooks, poor-mouthing and feeling sorry for themselves, Merlin took the bull by the horns and did something about it. It's no trouble for them to think back to the time he tried to lick the Depression with nothing but his natural talents. And he won, too—for one day, at least.

It all happened on a spring morning in front of the high school, where all the kids were milling about with sluggish spirits and academic apathy, waiting for the first bell to ring and hoping that Mr. Jenkins, the janitor, had lost the keys to the building again. Everybody, that is, except Merlin.

He was passing in and out among the student body trying to raise money, for he had a date with Imogene Clements that night and no funds. He claimed he needed a dollar, which for an ordinary date in the middle of the week with nowhere to go was too extravagant for the other kids to consider seriously. It did elevate Imogene's social status, though. Her social rating zoomed sky-high, even topping Bernice Pipkin's. Bernice had moved to town from Archer City in the fall and was naturally expected to maintain her New Girl's stranglehold on the dates at least for the balance of the school year.

Still, no one was willing to invest in such a risky venture as somebody else's date, especially Merlin's. He was a poor credit risk, even with his own daddy, who had refused to finance any more romances until his son got his clarinet back. Several weeks previously, Merlin had hocked it for $3.75 and still had not the remotest prospect for redeeming it. You might say that he sold it. His daddy knew nothing about it until he and Mrs. Hancock went to the Spring Band Concert and noticed that their son was not in the clarinet section. How could he be? He had no clarinet.

"Maybe I could stand on my head or dance in the street for tips," Merlin suggested playfully after three passes around the school yard had yielded only thirteen cents, which it was rumored came from Imogene Clements herself.

All the kids got caught up in the spirit of Merlin's suggestion and offered alternate proposals in the same whimsical vein: smoking a cigarette in study hall, hiding Miss Craig's lecture notes, goosing Mr. Taylor, or locking Mr. Jenkins in the boiler room (again). One wild proposal set off another, any one of which might have been worth watching but not necessarily paying money to see.

It was almost time for the bell to ring, and Merlin was getting desperate. If his schoolmates had any money in their pockets, he knew he had to get his hands on it then and there before they squandered it on club dues, school supplies and foolish lunches. He brushed his hair out of his eyes, shoved his horn-rimmed spectacles upon his nose, looked over his unconcerned schoolmates and made a quick estimate of his chances. At best, they were shaky. His schoolmates, he decided, were a sorry lot. He sighed.

"For a whole dollar, I'd run around the block in my B.V.D.'s," he said half jokingly, but only half.

He struck sparks.

"When?"

"Now."

"You mean right here in front of God and everybody?"

"—and Tilly May Foster," he added. Tilly May was easily shocked. She blushed more over less than any other girl in the school.

Merlin's proposition caught on. But a dollar? Few spectacles were worth that much.

"Pass the hat," he urged, warming to his own idea now that he saw it might contain money. "You ought to be able to get a dollar out of this many kids."

But they couldn't. Ninety-seven cents cleaned them out. Merlin preferred to hold out for the other three cents, but he didn't have time. The bell would be ringing any minute now, and he had to act fast. Making a quick assessment of the situation, therefore, he reduced his fee accordingly, verified the count, gave the money to a trusted friend for safekeeping and, without further ado, peeled down to his B.V.D.'s, stepped out into the street and began to run.

A great shout went up from the school yard. The entire student body came alive. As though someone had tilted the campus on its side and poured the kids out into the street, they spilled over the curb and took in after Merlin. They were a trampling, squealing, surging mob, covering every square inch of the pavement without regard to local laws, safety regulations and oncoming automobiles. Traffic stopped. Marooned motorists sat helplessly, mesmerized by the onrush of wild, excited kids.

Old Man Bartlett was coming down the street in his vegetable wagon cussing at Raymond, his horse. But Raymond couldn't hear him, for like his master and the stranded motorists, he too was caught up by the stampede and immobilized. The crowd split around both sides of the creaky old wagon and stormed past, leaving it lighter by goodness knows how many carrots, turnips and green onions.

Old Man Bartlett stood up on his wagon seat and shook his fist at tomorrow's citizens, screeching holes in his lungs, threatening to tell their daddies and to have the law on every blooming one of them. Roland Abernathy, who made straight A's and won the County Meet in Declamation each year, became conscience-stricken and returned a turnip to the wagon, but Old Man Bartlett's threats didn't worry anybody else. They were too fascinated by Merlin Hancock running down the street like crazy in nothing but his B.V.D.'s.

With hair flying and body shaking like jelly, he made for the corner as if chasing his hat. His horn-rimmed spectacles bobbed up and down on his nose. His mouth was spread across his face in a jubilant grin. He lifted his knees high and hugged his elbows close to his sides as he had seen the other boys do in track meets. His heavy low-quarter shoes (size 12) slapped loudly against the pavement, but their sounds were lost among the wild cheers of his investors, who stayed on his heels to make certain that he did not cut the corner or otherwise cheat.

"Atta boy, Merlin!" the boys shouted. "Come on, Merlin! You can do it, babe-eeee!"

Joe Ben Wagner, county winner of the 440 dash, took the practical view. "Pace it, Hancock," he urged gravely. "You've gotta pace yourself, or you won't make it."

The girls were scandalized, but not enough to keep them from following Merlin.

"Oh, Merlin, how can you *dooooooooooo* it!" they squealed.

All but Imogene Clements, who remained properly and modestly silent. But she didn't miss a step. She stayed in there with the best of them, running with energy she did not know she possessed.

The most energetic of all, though, was Merlin Hancock himself. After all, he was being paid to run.

"Easiest dollar I ever made!" he shouted happily.

"Ninety-seven cents!" corrected his followers.

"I'll sell a milk bottle to make up the difference," Merlin yelled. He parted the hair from in front of his eyes and steadied his spectacles on his nose.

"You haven't made it yet," yelled someone. "You've still got nearly four blocks to go!"

"But I'm getting paid!" cried Merlin, "and you're running for NOTHING!"

Everybody laughed, shouted and cheered him on.

So much approval and encouragement went to his head; it was more than he could cope with. As partial payment therefor, he decided to give his followers something extra for their money, unaware, of course, that the rhythmic opening and closing of his seat flaps had already provided a more scandalous bonus than any of them had bargained for. But never mind.

As he neared the first corner, he slowed his pace and shifted into a high-stepping strut in a lame imitation of Elwood Spears, the school drum major who could drop his baton and retrieve it with more grace than any other drum major in the Texas Panhandle.

"How's that?" Merlin shouted as he zigzagged his way around the corner.

His schoolmates were delighted.

"Atta boy!" they cried. "You're the one, Merlin, babe-eeee!"

"You're not pacing it, Hancock," Joe Ben said.

Merlin responded with a loud whoop and a holler and resumed his full ninety-seven-cent speed. One of his black socks had worked its way down to his ankle and was bunched into wrinkles around his shoe top. The other remained in place, which for onlookers created a peg-legged effect as he chugged one knee in front of the other. So with one sock up and one sock down, Merlin dashed past the side entrance of the school.

Across the street, housewives rushed out onto their front porches to see what was going on. Some joined in and ran the course. Mrs. Booby Duckworth turned her ankle following Merlin around the second corner and had to limp home. When Booby came home at noon and found her soaking her foot in hot Epsom salts water, she explained that she had hurt it crossing the ditch around back of the school. Certainly that was not untrue.

No one had ever seen such running—or such a runner. Merlin was a mess, and he was magnificent. He ran without form, his gait was uneven, he breathed in rugged gasps, and his hair was shaking up and down in his face like a dry mop. Over all, he ran with the grace of a cement mixer, but no member of the track team ever topped his performance, before or after. He knew where he was going and why, and as the saying goes, he gave his customers a run for their money. No one ever got a bigger ninety-seven cents' worth.

Mr. Taylor, the debate and dramatic coach, looked out a side window barely in time to see Merlin go chugging past. He dropped the flowers he was arranging on his desk and ran to a rear window for a better view. Finding that unsatisfactory, he climbed to the bell tower, where it was probably safer, anyway.

"Goodness gracious!" he was heard to exclaim afterwards, "I never *dreamed* that Merlin Hancock had such big legs!"

Tilly May Foster was hurrying down the sidewalk from

[*183*]

her home, but at the sight of her classmate in his B.V.D.'s with the seat flapping open and shut, she turned red and fled. She did not come back to school for two days, thereby spoiling a perfect attendance record of six years' standing.

Mr. Hightower, the school principal, had just parked his automobile back of the school but was afraid to get out of it, what with the entire student body rushing around the corner and coming at him hell-bent-for-leather, chasing Merlin Hancock, who looked wilder than usual and, for some yet-to-be-determined reason, had on no clothes. He sat in stupefied silence as the mob roared past; then when it looked safe, he went into the building to find it deserted and the entire faculty and staff out front on the curb. All except Mr. Whittle, the elderly science teacher, who was alone and oblivious in his classroom on the second floor in the far corner of the building, poring over some new professional literature he had received in plain wrappers two days previously.

Miss Weathersby, the history teacher, grew impatient out front waiting for Merlin to complete the circuit and ran inside to telephone his mother.

"Merlin's running around the block this very minute in his B.V.D.'s!" she screamed breathlessly into the mouth piece.

"Merlin who?" asked his mother, a slow starter in the mornings.

"His *underwear!*" replied Miss Weathersby.

"Oh, dear," said Mrs. Hancock. "I do hope he didn't forget to put on clean ones."

Merlin ran past the rear of the school, and his other sock joined its mate at shoe-top level. He took off his spectacles and handed them to Buster Clark. Having no safe place to carry them, with so much running and all, Buster put them on himself and went totally blind until he could take them off again.

Meanwhile, Merlin's other followers had run into problems

of their own. Melba Dean Shumaker broke the heel off her left shoe. Fatty Huffman ran out of breath and stopped. Dolly Meek's purse flew open, and the contents spilled out onto the pavement. Waldo McWhorter stumbled and found himself at the bottom of a seven-student pileup. Curley Murphy's right shoe came untied and rubbed a quick blister on his heel. Selma Dell Harvey contended that she was having a heart attack and had to be pulled along by Claudine Alverson. Willard Osborne stepped on Dolly Meek's mirror and broke it. Joe Ben Wagner didn't pace himself properly and sprung a charley horse in his right leg.

As Merlin drew abreast of the study-hall windows, he wiped the sweat from his face, brushed his hair from his eyes and threw in another extra. This time, he turned around and ran backwards.

That also got over big.

"Yea—Hancock!" shouted the kids. "That's the way to do it, babe-eeeeee!"

Merlin lifted his arms above his head, gave his admirers a figurative handshake, let go with a wild yell, then righted himself and ran on down the street.

Mrs. Lottie Easley, a widow who lived back of the school and raised flowers when there wasn't a water shortage, telephoned Artie Whelan, the Sheriff, to complain about the high-school kids trampling over her flowers.

"You mean they're standing around stomping on them?" Artie asked, trying to get the picture.

"No—they're running through my yard trying to catch some boy without any clothes on."

"Well—they'll all be past by the time I could get there," Artie said and hung up the phone.

Merlin rounded the third corner.

By now he had lost whatever form he had had to begin with, but he still retained his spirit. All of it. He slowed down, tired and out of breath, but his backers spurred him on with threats to withdraw their money if he didn't make it back around to the starting point.

"I'll make it," he panted. "I got muscles and power I haven't used yet."

Then to prove it, to reassure them, and to make it clear that there would be absolutely no refunds that day, he let go with an Indian war whoop and broke into a feeble facsimile of a Hopi rain dance.

It didn't make much of a hit. The kids were getting tired, too.

Merlin pushed on with his eyes fixed on corner number 4 and the home stretch.

Mrs. Luther Hoyt, who lived on that corner, was sitting on her front porch in a rocking chair with one leg doubled under her reading a magazine. This had been her favorite posture for so many years that she had mashed her left foot out of shape and had to walk with a medium-sized limp. She looked up from a Faith Baldwin serial to see what appeared to be the entire township storming up the street, apparently heading straight for her house. Thinking that her neighbor, Mrs. Virgil Fuller, who lived behind her across the alley, might enjoy the excitement, she got up and limped through the house and out the back door to fetch her.

Attracted by the noise, it so happened that Mrs. Fuller, not having found any new complications in her favorite soap opera to engage her attention, was hurrying along the side of Mrs. Hoyt's house toward the school to see what was going on. Finding the rocking chair empty, she ran into the house to see why her neighbor wasn't in her customary place on the front porch. Thus, while they searched for each other in each other's houses, they each missed the very thing they were searching for each other to come out and see.

And Merlin staggered on.

Old Man Bartlett had made it past the front of the school and was crossing the next intersection when all those crazy kids swooped down on him and lightened his load once again. He jumped down from his wagon and took in after them.

"I'm gonna get your hides for this!" he screamed, his face the color of his freshly dug beets. "The whole kit and caboodle of you is gonna hear about this—you jes' wait and see!"

He snatched a turnip from Harley Meadows' hand and, finding it half chewed, threw it back at him and hit Raymond squarely in the tail. Raymond reared up. His owner socked him a good one with his fist and jarred his arm all the way up to his neck.

Merlin steamed around the last corner and chugged for home.

During the run, a formal reception committee had formed itself and was now waiting in front of the building. Composed of Mr. Hightower and three lady faculty members who were enjoying the excitement more than they should, they watched with unteacherly interest as Merlin puffed into the stretch, blowing like the Fort Worth & Denver switch engine. It has always been a point of controversy whether Miss Craig, the English teacher, was a member of the committee or if she ran the course with Merlin. Her presence at the finish line has been established beyond question, and it is a well-known fact that she was short of breath, but whether from excitement or from running has never been cleared up once and for all.

Merlin crossed the finish line to the greatest ovation in the school's history. His followers collapsed onto the grass, some onto the curb, and a few onto the pavement itself. It was a bedraggled student body.

Merlin collected his ninety-seven cents, counted it to make certain it was all there, got his spectacles from Buster Clark, put them on and counted the money again, this time so he could see it. He picked up his clothes and presented himself to the reception committee. But that's misleading. The reception committee presented itself to him.

"All right, Merlin," said Mr. Hightower in his most official and authoritative tones. "Let's go inside."

"Don't you want me to put on my clothes first?" Merlin asked between gasps.

"You can dress inside," said the principal.

"It don't seem right to go in the school like this," Merlin said.

The lady members of the faculty nodded their heads in agreement. Mr. Hightower lost some of his official poise.

"Well—I'll admit that it *does* seem rather peculiar."

In silence, he studied the situation for a moment. While he studied, the entire reception committee broke into open discussion. The nearby students plus Old Man Bartlett, who had been swept along in the rush to the finish line, chimed in. To dress in public did seem indelicate, they agreed. Not to dress at all, however, seemed even more so. Yet, their views on what was proper and improper under the circumstances were not based on any known precedent. They argued and discussed while Merlin withdrew from the conference to catch his breath and pull his socks up out of his shoes.

"I *would* like to cool off and comb my hair before I put on my clothes," Merlin said after a time.

"*Comb your hair?*" Mr. Hightower was startled.

"Well, I'm dripping wet with sweat."

"I can see that," said Mr. Hightower. "Still. . . ."

He studied the situation further. He could not, in good conscience, permit Merlin to lounge around in public taking his ease in his B.V.D.'s. On the other hand, Merlin was a wreck. Perspiration streamed down from his forehead and across his eyes. His cheeks were wet, his tongue was hanging out. His B.V.D.'s were clinging to his body, bringing out in sharp relief more of his huge anatomy than the lady teachers and young girl students felt free to look at. And all of it was shaking like an old Model T with the engine idling. Finally, Mr. Hightower reached a decision. He adapted Merlin's needs to his own sense of decorum.

"All right, Merlin," he said, his official poise regained. "Bring your clothes with you, and you can put them on inside and in private."

While the entire student body and Old Man Bartlett looked on, Mr. Hightower and his committee formed a screen around the school's newest celebrity and led him up the sidewalk to the main entrance of the building. Just before they passed from sight, Merlin squeezed the last drop from his ninety-seven cents' worth of entertainment. With the gallantry of a royal courtier, he stepped aside, bowed deeply and held the door open wide for the lady teachers to enter first. Then, with his big body quivering like jelly and the seat flaps of his B.V.D.'s opening and closing with each stride, he followed them through the door and out of sight. Just before he disappeared, he looked back at the assembled students and gave them the finger—with a big grin. Ronald Colman was never more elegant. Errol Flynn was never more charming.

Classes were late starting that day, and not even the teachers seemed to mind. The students were hot and excited anyway and in no immediate mood to absorb much in the way of knowledge. With so much excitement to distract him, Mr. Jenkins forgot to unlock the science laboratory and the library; nor had he remembered to flip the power switch for the lights in the auditorium, where the Choral Club was scheduled for a first-period rehearsal. Someone went searching for him and found him sweeping the floor immediately outside Mr. Hightower's office, where Merlin was being interrogated behind a closed door. He yielded his key ring on the spot and said he could not attend to the auditorium lights until he had finished sweeping the office floor, which incidentally turned out to be only after Mr. Hightower had finished grilling Merlin.

Mr. Hightower finished soon enough and expelled Merlin from school for three days.

When Merlin returned to school, his was an exalted status. He was the school's central attraction for several days, the boy everyone clustered around out front while waiting for the bell to ring, the student everybody wanted to be seen with, the boy they wanted to walk down the hall with between classes.

"Yeah, Merlin!" they greeted him.

"How're the old legs today, Merlin, ole buddy?"

"Hey, Hancock! Doing much running lately?"

Miss Craig kept him after school five days to make up three days' work. Mr. Taylor did everything but bribe him to recruit him for the debate team. Boys swamped Imogene Clements with notes asking her for dates and proposing marriage. Tilly May Foster couldn't bring herself to look Merlin in the face for two weeks, something of a negative accomplishment inasmuch as she sat squarely across the table from him in biology lab. Old Man Bartlett changed his vegetable route and was never again seen in the vicinity of the high school.

All in all, it was a great day, at least on a par with the day Judge Crawford addressed the Student Assembly and talked straight through two periods, which somehow never got made up. Even today, there are people in town who do not know that Merlin Hancock is the Road Commissioner for the State of Texas, with offices in the capitol building in Austin. Yet, they know that Merlin Hancock is the name of the boy who ran around the block in his B.V.D.'s for ninety-seven cents on that outstanding, ever-vivid day.

The saddest thing about Merlin's using his natural talents

to lick the Depression, however temporarily, was not that Mr. Hightower expelled him from school for three days. Indeed, he was rather envied on that score. No. The worst part of it was that for all his efforts, Imogene Clements' mother forbade her to keep her date with Merlin that evening. To her way of thinking, Merlin had revealed a side of himself that was unbecoming, and Imogene would be better off if she never went out with him again.

Even so, the kids actually regretted that they had not been able to pay Merlin the full dollar that he requested. He deserved it, although as it turned out, he really didn't need the money.

6.

~~

Henry Atkins' Black Folder

Henry Atkins was a bill collector whose specialty was overdue and hard-to-collect accounts. But perhaps it is misleading to call it a specialty, for he worked on no other kind; business establishments didn't need his services for accounts that were not overdue or for those they could collect themselves. They needed his talents only for recalcitrant debtors, some of whom might be dead beats who sneaked in when the creditors weren't looking, some of whom might have overextended themselves and were making no effort to pull in their horns, and some of whom might parcel out their cash each month but not necessarily into the right places. So, it is not too far-fetched to say that Henry Atkins dealt in trouble with a capital T.

Each month he called on the commercial firms in town to ask if they had any overdue accounts that he might collect for them. If they did, he would accept them on a commission, file them alphabetically in a black, accordion-style, leatherette folder that fitted snugly under his left arm and go out to call on the offenders in person.

He was a familiar sight on the streets, and everybody in town knew what was inside that folder. They might not know the names exactly, but they did know why they were in the folder. Consequently, when that folder was under his arm, he had a hard time striking up a friendly conversation in public. No one liked to be seen talking to him for fear onlookers might get a wrong impression. Artie Whelan, the sheriff, was the only other person in town who generated such concern among people he met on the street, some of whom made it a point to laugh like crazy at everything Artie said so no one would get the idea they were being arrested or otherwise having trouble. People didn't snub Henry. They merely managed to be in a hurry to get somewhere else if he seemed inclined to stop and pass the time of day. His own father-in-law ducked into White's Auto Store once when he saw Henry coming down the sidewalk with that black folder under his arm.

When empty-handed, however, Henry had no distinguishing characteristics to set him apart from the next two or three hundred people you might see. He fitted in somewhere between young manhood and middle age, in those indeterminate years when people on both sides more or less considered him a contemporary. Slight in build, mild in manner, soft in speech and reeking with insignificance, he was acceptable without being sought after, respected without being admired, and well liked without being popular. In other words, he wasn't anybody you would notice in a bus station even when it wasn't crowded. Neither was his wife, Birdie, a rather plain, almost severe lady who wore owlish spectacles with black rims and a tight bun of mouse-colored hair on her neck. If she was several years older than her husband, no one would have been surprised to hear it, but that was probably because no one would have worried about it one way or the other. Henry and Birdie Atkins were two of those people who could be present, or they could be absent, and you'd never consider it long enough to question it yes or no. Frequently they went to things, then afterwards had to convince those present that they had been there.

Birdie was a practical nurse whose business fortunes, like her husband's, were on-again-off-again propositions. She worked only when people had money, and he worked only when they didn't. Between them, however, they earned a decent living, no matter how chancy it might be from one month to the next. They had no children and lived in a modest bungalow on Sixth Street with a swing on the front porch, two metal lawn chairs and a portable barbecue grill in the back yard, and wooden awnings cut out with crescents over the west windows on the driveway. They moved an oscillating electric fan from room to room in the summers and closed off the living room and one bedroom in the winters. They drove a secondhand Plymouth in good condition, made time payments on the refrigerator, the washing machine and the vacuum cleaner, subscribed to *Reader's Digest* and the Wichita Falls *Record News*, and saved green trading stamps, with which they had acquired an automatic percolator and a croquet set.

They attended church in fits and spurts, played dominoes occasionally with the people next door, went to softball games and picture shows, tried their luck at fishing when the river had any water in it, spent Saturday afternoons downtown, and ate Sunday dinner sometimes at the Little Gem Cafe. Henry might have spent more time at Smokey Rainwater's Tavern than people thought he should, but so did everybody else, and he was never taken to task for that. Birdie liked to dance and sometimes persuaded Henry to take her to the Elks Club public dances on the second Friday of the month. He didn't enjoy the dances, for frankly, Birdie was an atrocious dancer; pushing her around the floor for an entire evening almost wore him to a frazzle, but he went. All in all, it can be said that they appeared to be contented, adjusted and reasonably busy. If they were not real dynamos in the community, at least they were there, they paid their taxes, they voted, they mowed their lawn, and without them the town's population would certainly have been less by two.

One of the most serious drawbacks to Henry's line of work was that certain people he called on were not hospitable toward him. They resented him, were offended by his presence and took a dim view of his mission, however legal, necessary and justified it might be in the eyes of Henry and his long-suffering clients. It was a built-in peril. For that reason, he was forever coming home at night with a knot on his head, a little cut on his cheek or perhaps the corner of a tooth missing. Fortunately, Birdie had the equipment and the know-how to patch him up and send him out again almost as good as new. At the sight of Henry on the streets dressed in a new bandage or wearing a Band-Aid, people knew what had happened to him without knowing who was responsible. They speculated on it, though, and sometimes hit the nail squarely on the head without ever knowing what good marksmen they actually had been.

And Henry wasn't about to tell them. He had his hands full as it was, dealing with irate debtors at close range, and he knew better than to increase their displeasure by blabbing their business all over town. One knot for one overdue account was sufficient, and he saw no profit in making it two. So he kept his mouth shut.

Even so, word leaked out occasionally. One of the Newberry boys over on Northside—and it isn't clear which one, for there wasn't one among the four brothers who could get a nickel's worth of credit anywhere in town—one of them spread it around that he was responsible for Henry's broken rib that made it difficult for Henry to inhale and exhale properly.

"He come up on the front porch and ast me how about

paying a little on this bill I had at the cleaners'," said which-ever Newberry it was. "My own mother was rocking in a rocking chair on the other end of the porch, and she heard what he said. Now they ain't nobody that can come up on the porch and talk like that in front of my own mother. It ain't respectful. So I tole him to git offa the porch, and he says, 'I thought maybe you could pay a little bit this month—somethin' on account.' So I says, 'Listen, Henry Atkins, I don't owe *you* that money. So I don't know what call you got to come up here asting me for it.' He said, 'I'm collecting for the cleaners—this bill is eight months overdue.' *Right in front of my own mother!* So I jes' hauled off and let him have it—right in the middle of his breadbasket. He oughta know better than saying all them things right in front of people's own mothers."

Such were the risks that Henry took when he went out to meet the foe. A lady turned the garden hose on him once. Another shooed him off the sidewalk with her broom. One cranky debtor untied his mongrel hound and shouted "Sic 'im!," but he couldn't get the animal awake and on his feet long enough to obey. Another time Henry went around to the back porch of a home where the lady of the house was doing the family washing. When she had had enough of him, she ran a bath towel through the wringer of the Maytag and hit him in the face with it. An itinerant farmer east of town took in after him with a shotgun, but he didn't fire it. Henry returned that particular bill to Cletus Pritchard at Pritchard's Furniture Store on Main Street and told him what he could do with it. He knew the difference between acceptable and unacceptable risks.

Nobody could understand why Henry engaged in such a hazardous occupation. He certainly didn't look nor act like a person who would earn his living going around upsetting people.

"It's a living," was his only explanation.

"So is making dynamite," J. D. Gribble said.

Henry didn't argue about it. He listened to such talk with a slight smile and the kindly expression he always seemed to wear on his face. Sam Abernathy told him that was his problem.

"You look too easy to beat up on, Henry," he said. "You don't look fierce enough. If you'd put on about fifty pounds and frown at people instead of smile at them, maybe they'd leave you alone."

Maybe. But he let Sam's advice go unheeded. He got into enough trouble when he used his own system; he had no intention of increasing it by using Sam's. The thing was, Henry considered himself a businessman, and while he was not unappreciative of advice on how to run his business, he did not feel that he needed it, any more than Purdy Robinson needed advice on how to run his hardware store. He relied upon his own professional experience and know-how, which, after all, he had more of than anyone else around. He was the only professional bill collector in town.

He was courteous and tactful in his work. He had to be, for the work was extremely personal and highly sensitive. It was not unlike that of a process server in that it required face-to-face confrontation for it to be effective. He couldn't leave messages for people to get in touch with him or to call him on the telephone, for they would not do it. He had to see them in person, but to do that, he had to find them first. Some of the debtors whose names were in the black folder were experts at making themselves scarce.

Henry was accustomed to knocking on doors and receiving no answers. The abruptly silenced radio and suddenly stilled household were not novelties to him. It was not unusual for him to enter a place of business and discover that the person he had come to see had been present all day until just before Henry walked in the door.

"Why, he was sitting right there just a minute ago," somebody in the office would say.

"Do you know when he'll be back?" Henry might inquire.

"Well—no, because I don't know where he went."

Aside from Dr. Beasley, Henry probably ran up against more sickness than anyone in town. During the course of a week or a month, a number of people were always too ill to see him. Enough, if all of them had had the same ailments, to make an epidemic. Rufus Cook's wife told Henry that Rufus was in terrible condition and couldn't be disturbed.

"But I just saw him over the back fence mowing the lawn," Henry said.

"It was one of those sudden attacks he has all the time," she said as she closed the door.

Henry was an old hand at recognizing disguised voices on the telephone, not that uncovering the deception helped matters, necessarily. Once he telephoned Herman Crowder, who often covered the mouthpiece of the telephone with a handkerchief before he answered it. Henry didn't need to ask who it was on the other end of the wire.

"Hello, Herman? This is Henry Atkins."

"Herman's not here," said Herman. "This is Dale."

Dale was Herman's brother.

"When do you expect Herman back?"

"Gee, I don't know, Henry," said Herman. "I just got here myself. I think Herman's out of town."

"You certainly sound a lot like Herman," said Henry.

"Yeah?" Herman said with a laugh. "People are always getting me mixed up with Herman."

When he was lucky, Henry could catch people unawares, but that didn't always get him anywhere, either. He telephoned Edna Buckley as Phase One of a six months' campaign to collect $7.50 for the Marvella Beauty Shop.

"Hello?" Edna said in her normal, cheerful manner.

"Is this Edna Buckley?"

"Yes. Who is this?"

"This is Henry Atkins. I—"

"I'm sorry," she said with no change of inflection. "There's no one here by that name."

She hung up the telephone.

Birdie thought that Henry didn't take advantage of some of the opportunities open to him. As they were coming out of the Texan Theatre one evening, she spotted Barney Tidwell a few steps ahead of them. Barney's name was so permanent in Henry's black folder that Henry often toyed with the idea of taking him out of the T's and filing him in a special, private section labeled "Tidwell."

"Didn't you tell me that Barney Tidwell was sick in bed and couldn't have company?" Birdie whispered.

"Yes. For over a year now, I've been told that he's too sick to recognize his own children."

"There he is now with that wife of his. Why don't you catch him while you can?"

"I can't—not now," said Henry.

"Why not? Don't you remember the amounts?"

"Oh, yes, I remember the amounts all right. There's seventeen ninety-five for Delsey Jacobs, twelve thirty-six for the City Drug Store, five seventy-eight for White's Auto Store, eleven seventeen for the Model Garage, and twenty-three sixty-nine for Riley's Grocery and Market."

"Then why can't you catch him now and ask him about it?"

"Because I'm off duty," Henry replied.

He felt that his business, like any other, should operate on a set schedule with regular working hours.

Birdie was sympathetic toward the troublesome and unpleasant aspects of Henry's work, and she made it a rule to interfere as little as possible. She violated her own rule, though, when she was nursing Mrs. Fannie Traxler on the day shift.

"Buford asked me to wait until next week for my pay," she said one Friday night. Buford Reagan was Mrs. Traxler's son-in-law and her sole source of support.

"Buford ought to know that two weeks' pay will be twice as hard to pay next week."

"That's what I told him. He said you came around to the shop and pressured him into paying that old bill at Simpson's Lumber Yard, and he didn't have any money left over for me. I hope you know, Henry, that you cut your own throat on that one—and mine, too. We'd have got along lots better on my week's pay than your piddling little commission that knocked me out of it."

Henry said he had only been doing his duty, and Birdie said it would behoove him, then, to get out and do some more, for she had a sneaking idea that when the Big Total appeared on the Board, a week's pay would be missing. How to square that with the payments on the washing machine, the refrigerator, and the vacuum cleaner was something he might be thinking about in the meantime.

"The next time you have to collect from one of my patients, I wish you'd let me know," she said. "Maybe we can work out some kind of arrangement between us."

"That would not be ethical," Henry said. As a businessman, he had certain standards to maintain.

However, that was the only time they ever had a conflict of interests to deal with.

East side, west side, all around the town—that was where Henry's work took him. He was as familiar-looking as a mesquite tree down in the Addition, a random assembly of houses and half houses to the west side of Mr. Winbury's slaughter pen and north of the Cotton Compress, where many of the town's colored people lived. Considering the normal number of overdue accounts to be collected in the Addition, it would seem to be a profitable lode for Henry to have mined. But it was not. The accounts were, for the most part, small; people doled out their payments in fractional sums, fifty cents this week, twenty-five the next, and sometimes as little as a thin dime. It was slow and paltry going. Once they started, though, many of them paid regularly and without default. For stretches during his career, Henry followed collection routes through the Addition with regular stops along the way in the manner of the rent collector or the newspaper boy. Certain debtors expected to see him before noon on Tuesday, say, and Henry was never known to let them down.

After paying for more than half of an overstuffed chair from Pritchard's Furniture Store, Clinnie Bell Tucker fell behind in her payments, then eventually stopped them altogether. Henry Atkins was called in on the case. After much cajoling, he managed to steer her back onto the payment road once again. She became one of Henry's regulars, but her weekly payments were so small that it seemed that they might go on forever. Henry called on her for so long and with such regularity that a friendship grew up between them. If Clinnie Bell should be occupied about the house or in the yard when Henry arrived, he didn't mind waiting, sometimes inside the house, sometimes on the front porch, sometimes following her up and down the clothesline while she hung out the washing. It was not unusual for him to remain a while after their business was transacted to inquire into her health if she should be pregnant, which she frequently was, or how things were going at the church, where she was the noisiest singer in the choir, or into the whereabouts of some of her husbands, of which she lived in total ignorance.

One morning when Henry arrived, Clinnie Bell was seated on the front porch with her newest baby in her arms. She looked up as Henry approached.

"I cain't git him to do no nursin', Mr. Atkins," she complained.

Quickly and modestly, Henry looked the other way. In the interests of propriety, he felt that he should not look directly at Clinnie Bell's bosom, which lay bare, big and black—the more exposed since her baby was manifesting no interest in it whatsoever.

"I'll just wait," said Henry politely, gazing at the Cotton Compress a half mile to the south and studying its architecture with exaggerated interest.

"I jes' don' know what I'm gonna do," said Clinnie Bell. "He ain't had nothin' to eat all mawnin'." She looked down at the baby and drew its head to her bosom. "Git it!" she pleaded. The baby turned its head away.

"Git it!" she repeated, this time with impatience.

The baby would have no part of "it."

Henry walked up onto the porch and sat down on the top step.

"He sure do get contrary," said Clinnie Bell. She shook the baby semigently. Again she drew the baby's head to her bosom. "Git it!" she commanded. "Now you go on and git it!"

Again the baby turned away.

Against his will, Henry looked around to find Clinnie Bell looking at him with half apology and half embarrassment.

"Maybe he's not hungry," Henry suggested.

"He oughta be!" said Clinnie Bell, glaring down at her reluctant infant with wrinkled forehead. "Git it!" she shouted. "Git it like I tole you!"

She shook her head in exasperation and looked at Henry, who was still sitting on the top step, now staring openly at Clinnie Bell and her unhungry baby. Suddenly, Clinnie Bell's eyes brightened with inspiration.

"Do like *you* gonna git it, Mr. Atkins, and see what he do!"

Henry departed that day without collecting one red cent.

In general, Henry's work fell into a pattern of sorts, and while it was anything but monotonous, it had its predictable aspects. One particular overdue account, however, did not fit the mold. It bore the name of Grover Hicks, Welder—Electric and Acetylene—whose shop was located north of town just beyond the cemetery turnoff. The bill was from L. T. Ditmore's Funeral Home, of all places, and was for Grover's wife's funeral, of all things.

Henry did not, as a routine matter, call on Mr. Ditmore to ask if he had any overdue accounts to collect. It did not occur to him that he might. He assumed that everybody paid their funeral bills when due, especially since they didn't have many, nor did they have them often. But apparently, he did not figure it out correctly. Mr. Ditmore telephoned Henry and asked him to stop by and see him.

Ever since most people could remember, L. T. Ditmore's Funeral Home had stood at the corner of Second and Goode Streets, across the alley from Chambers Chevrolet and one block this side of the County Jail. Although Mr. Ditmore had modernized the building and his equipment through the years, the exterior retained its original and unique appearance—fieldstone with a tin roof and a cupola on top. It was one of the town's landmarks. Mr. Ditmore himself was one of the town's institutions.

L. T. Ditmore had a fine reputation throughout the county as the undertaker who smiled at funerals. People said they could not imagine dying without Mr. Ditmore in attendance smiling down at them. Theories about his smiling, however, were not in accord. Some said it wasn't a smile at all but a public reflection of his kind heart and sympathetic nature. Others said it was a smile all right but a professional smile acquired from years of experience in the undertaking business. Still others said the smile was acquired from wine bottles which, according to rumor, he kept in a storeroom at the rear of his establishment and smashed to smithereens when empty so the trash-pickup man wouldn't recognize them and blab it all over town.

Whatever the origins of the smile, he turned it on Henry Atkins and brought him up to date on the status of Grover Hicks' delinquent funeral bill. They were seated in Mr. Ditmore's office.

"I don't check people's credit rating before I provide my services—not as a general rule," said Mr. Ditmore. "You just can't always do that in this business, you know. Anyway, most people have a burial policy of some kind to cover at least part of the expenses, and I don't even investigate that—not at the very beginning. So I treated Grover just like I treat everybody else."

He smoothed his hair with the palm of his hand. Mr. Ditmore's hair was his most distinguishing feature—aside from his smile, of course. It was brown, straight as a two-by-four, parted low on the side, and plastered tightly across his skull and low across his forehead like an extra layer of skin. At first glance, you might think his face had been painted two-toned, but if you looked again, the overall effect was that of a stocking cap that had been pulled down too close to his eyes. His hair was never disarranged. Not one strand. And it was all his. No one suspected a wig, for nobody in his right mind would buy a wig that resembled Mr. Ditmore's hair. He could walk bareheaded through a whirlwind and not need to comb his hair afterwards. How he managed it was his secret. Perhaps he used Vaseline or Stacomb. Some people thought he used starch.

"Didn't Grover have a burial policy on Blanche?" Henry asked, trying to assemble all the facts.

"Yes, he did," said Mr. Ditmore, "and that's what's peculiar. Some people have the insurance company pay me direct, and some get the checks themselves and pay me themselves.

Grover didn't do either. He said he'd pay me when the check came in, but he didn't."

"Was the policy large enough to cover the funeral and all expenses?" asked Henry.

"Yes, it was," replied Mr. Ditmore.

"Was it large enough to leave him a few dollars to spare after he paid the expenses?"

"No, it wasn't. It just so happened that the expenses and the amount of the burial policy came out to the same amount."

"The *exact* amount?"

"Yes, it was. Right to the penny. Wasn't that a coincidence?"

"Yes," said Henry.

"But Grover didn't pay me, and I didn't push him, with him being so bereaved and all. So I waited and waited to give his bereavement time to wear off. Well—I'd see him every now and then coming in off that road from Smokey Rainwater's Tavern. Do you know the one I mean?"

Henry nodded.

"Well, when I saw him coming in from that direction, I thought maybe he was feeling better," Mr. Ditmore went on. "I saw him riding down the street with Velma Agnew a few times. She works right across the street there at the library, you know. They were laughing and carrying on, and it looked like Grover might be getting on his feet again. Then I saw them eating dinner together in the Little Gem Cafe one Sunday when my wife's aunt from Tulia was visiting us and we took her to Sunday dinner at the Little Gem. We always like to do that, you see. Velma and Grover seemed to be enjoying themselves, and it looked like he was coming right along."

"Pardon me, Mr. Ditmore, but how long was all this after Blanche died?" asked Henry.

"Oh, I'd say a month or six weeks. Then I noticed his car

over in front of the library several times, and sometimes he picked Velma up to drive her home, and sometimes he'd drive her to work early in the morning. Always looked pleasant, too. So I thought maybe his bereavement was in good enough shape for me to have a talk with him."

"How long do bereavements usually last?"

"It varies. For some people it might go on for a year or two. And I've seen people who have trouble staying bereaved until the funeral's over. It's hard to say. Anyway, I called Grover on the phone. He said my bill had plumb skipped his mind, and he'd come right down and take care of it, but he never did. Excuse me a minute, will you, Henry? I've got to look after something in the back. Just take a second."

He got up and disappeared through the double swinging doors into the rear of the building, leaving Henry alone in the office. When he returned, smoothing his hair with the palm of his hand, his professional smile seemed to be broader and, somehow, more profound.

"Now, where were we?" he said. "That's a fine-looking necktie you've got on, Henry."

"Thank you, Mr. Ditmore."

"You'd be surprised how many people bring razzle-dazzle neckties in here for me to put on their loved ones, and I have to tell them it's not in good taste for the services. One lady got her dander up about it. 'You're a fine one to be talking about good taste, L. T. Ditmore!' she said. 'Anybody who's got the nerve to drive up to a drive-in hamburger stand in a hearse and sit there eating hamburgers in it hasn't got any business talking about good taste!' Oh, she was mad at me, Henry. Yes, she was. What she didn't realize was that I had had three services that day, and I didn't hardly have time to get out of that hearse, much less to sit down and eat a square meal. So I just stopped by the Trade Winds for a hamburger and a Coke on the way back from the cemetery. I wasn't there more than fifteen minutes. Now maybe it did look peculiar for me to be eating hamburgers in the hearse, but gee whiz, Henry! I don't see why—"

"That's interesting," said Henry. "Now you were telling me how Grover Hicks told you he was going to come down and—"

"Oh, yes—so I mailed him bills every month, one after the other, and nothing ever happened."

"How long ago was this?"

"Eleven months this month."

"Didn't he pay you anything on account?" asked Henry. "Anything at all?"

"No, he didn't. Not one red cent. Some people have to pay these things a little at a time, and I'm prepared for that. It's pretty slow for both of us, but they at least show their good intentions by paying what they can each month. But not Grover Hicks. If he's got any good intentions, he's keeping them a deep dark secret. So I had a few talks with him— personal-like, you know—and told him just to give me a few dollars all along to whittle the bill down some, and he said he'd certainly do it if it killed him, but he never did. You just don't know, Henry, how it hurts me real deep to have to hound people about a thing like services for their loved ones, them being so bereaved and all. I'd give anything if—oh, there's that bell again—excuse me, Henry, if you don't mind. Just take a second."

Mr. Ditmore got up and disappeared through the double swinging doors again.

Henry hadn't heard a thing.

Mr. Ditmore returned to the office, his smile more professional than ever. Even his hair seemed to be more plastered.

"So I was wondering if maybe you'd take Grover's account and see what you can do with it," he went on. He rubbed his right cheek to still a twitch. "I certainly am not doing any

[*207*]

good with the bill on my ledger like it is, and I—oh, I don't want you to think I'm winking at you, Henry." He giggled. "It's a little twitch I seem to get when I'm under a strain, you see." He giggled again and rubbed his cheek again. "It's been almost a year now," he continued, "and if you want my honest opinion—just between the two of us—I think Grover Hicks is trying to put one over on me."

"I certainly hope that's not true," said Henry in businesslike tones.

"Well, I don't know what else to think. He spends lots of time in the County Library—you can look out that window there and see the front door. Velma Agnew told me the other day that Grover has taken up reading to ease his grief. I don't mean to sound hardhearted, but you would think his grief would be pretty well eased by now, wouldn't you?"

Mr. Ditmore waited for Henry to agree.

"You see, Mr. Ditmore, I don't know all the circumstances of Grover's grief, so I'm in no position to say."

"Well, I think so, anyway," Mr. Ditmore said. "One day I was out front when he came out of the library, and I went across the street to have a word with him. I just came right out and asked him what he did with the money from the burial policy, and he said there's an awful lot of expenses connected with people dying, and he had used it up. Now, you remember that Blanche Hicks dropped dead sudden-like. Wasn't sick a minute. So Grover didn't have any hospital and doctor bills that I know of. The only expense he had was my bill, which he hasn't paid any money on, so I don't know what expenses he was talking about. Do you know what I think?"

Henry sat passively and waited for Mr. Ditmore to continue. A business tactic of his was not to reply to rhetorical questions.

"I think Grover's fibbing to me," said Mr. Ditmore.

"That's your considered opinion?"

"Yes, it is. And do you know what else?"

Henry waited passively again.

"I think he spent Blanche's whole burial policy on a certain lady in this town whose name I'm too discreet to mention."

"You have sifted the evidence and come to that conclusion?"

"Yes, I have. That's why I called you. Would you like to take the account?"

"Why, yes, Mr. Ditmore. I'll be glad to take the account," Henry said. "If you'll just give me a copy for my files, I'll be most happy to see what I can do."

"I'll have to go in the back and get it," said Mr. Ditmore with more pleasure than such a small errand would seem to warrant. "That's where I keep my accounts, you see. It'll only take a second. Excuse me, Henry, if you don't mind."

He disappeared through the swinging doors before Henry had the opportunity to reply. While he was gone, Henry occupied himself by wondering what kind of records Mr. Ditmore kept in three four-drawer filing cabinets that stood against the opposite wall.

Mr. Ditmore returned empty-handed from the rear of the building. He was raking the flat of his hand across his hair as though he were ironing it. His professional smile now bordered on outright laughter.

"What do you know about that?" he said cheerfully. "I haven't transferred Grover Hicks from this filing cabinet to the file in the back where I keep them!"

He scratched around in the second drawer of the middle cabinet while humming "Abide with Me." At long last, the humming ceased.

"Oh, there you are, you little dickens!" he said to a long sheet of blue paper he had fished from the cabinet.

"How do you like this color, Henry?" he asked.

"Very nice."

"Used to have all my statements on gray paper, but they looked too sad." He examined the blue paper for a moment. "At the same time, you can't have paper that's too happy. Not in this business. That's why I decided on this shade of blue. And blue it is! You ought to see all the blue paper I've got in the back. Stacked halfway to the ceiling! That paper salesman was a whiz! Why, when your great-grandchildren get their funeral bills, they'll be on this blue—"

"May I see it, please?" said Henry, extending his hand.

Mr. Ditmore handed the paper to Henry.

Henry looked at the paper, then at Mr. Ditmore. He was puzzled.

"This has Wiley Hancock's name on the top of it," he said.

Mr. Ditmore leaned over Henry's shoulder, looked at the blue statement, took it from him and laughed merrily.

"So it does! I came close, though, didn't I? I looked in the Ha's instead of the Hi's. Not bad, eh, Henry?"

He turned back to the file cabinet still laughing.

"Old Wiley Hancock's folks paid that one right on time," he snickered. "Hee-hee-hee! Right on time and right on the nose. Easy as sneezing. Didn't even have to ask them for it!" He ruffled the file folders. "I sure didn't have to worry about that one. No sireeee! Wheeeeee!"

"I just happened to notice that Mr. Hancock's bill was paid with a check from an insurance company," Henry said. "I suppose that was a burial policy, too?"

"Yes, it was," said Mr. Ditmore. "That's the easiest way to handle these things. Saves the family lots of trouble."

"The amount seems so large, though."

"Well, you see, old man Hancock had two policies there, actually. The other one was for his wife. When she died, the children didn't know about the policy, so they paid the bill themselves and never used the policy. I don't know why

Wiley didn't mention it to them."

"So Mr. Hancock's funeral was larger than usual?"

"Yes, it was. A fine service. One of my finest."

"Was his bill equal to the amount of the two policies combined?"

"Yes, it was. Imagine that! Two coincidences in one day, eh, Henry?"

"Yes," said Henry.

Mr. Ditmore thumbed all the way through the H's and back again until he found Grover Hicks' overdue account. He handed it to Henry and leaned against the filing cabinet. His eyes were beginning to cross.

"I hope you can collect it, Henry, because if there's anything I hate, it's a dead beat, and I'm beginning to think that's what Grover Hicks is."

Henry did not reply. He did not consider it good business practice to make personal judgments about recalcitrant debtors. He took the itemized statement and in a businesslike manner filed it under the H's in his black leatherette folder, and got to his feet to tell Mr. Ditmore good-bye. The undertaker, however, was disappearing once again through the double swinging doors to the rear of the building, smoothing his hair, this time with both hands. Henry departed without saying anything further.

Grover Hicks' Welding Company—Electric and Acetylene —occupied a rusty, tin, barnlike building with double doors at each end and no windows anywhere. It sat back from the highway amid a growth of brush, mesquite trees and tumbleweeds, strewn among which were the remnants of a plow, the cab of a Mack truck, a few steam radiators, and a huge rusty boiler that might have powered the *S.S. America* unassisted. It was the most uninviting piece of real estate between the Fort Worth & Denver Railroad tracks and the river eight miles to the north, the kind of place that no one would enter unless they had urgent business to transact, and nowhere else to transact it.

Grover Hicks himself was welding when Henry Atkins appeared in the door of the shop and didn't see him come in. Grover was big and beefy. Not fat. Just full to the top and bulging in spots like a barracks bag tied up and ready for shipment. His face was fat, his jaws were puffy, and fat creases around his eyes gave them a jolly, twinkling expression that really wasn't there at all if you looked the second time. He had hands like a catcher's mitt and a stomach that was not entirely contained within his belt, and even though he was not a woman, he would have been well advised to wear a brassiere. He was pleasant enough, but a booming voice, when added to his bulk, made him a mite too overwhelming for some people's taste.

Henry stood in the doorway, wondering how the owner could make heads from tails in what looked like an indoor junkyard. Junk was piled in the corners, along the walls, scattered at random over the dirt floor, and all of it was metal, including some additional steam radiators, the remains of a motorcycle and the frame of a baby buggy. In the semidarkness, he waited for Grover to finish welding a little metal doodad onto a larger one.

Grover finished his task, flipped a switch that turned off the blue sparks, looked around, saw Henry, and shoved his heavy goggles to the top of his head.

"Why, hello there, Henry!" he greeted him affably. He laid his tools on the table, took off his gloves and climbed over piles of assorted junk to where Henry stood in the doorway. As he approached, his eyes moved to the black folder. There they stayed.

"How's it going with you, fellow?" he boomed heartily. Apparently he was addressing Henry's black folder rather than Henry's pleasant face.

"Very fine," said Henry. "Very fine and dandy."

"You won't believe this," said Grover, "but I was just thinking about you the other day. You don't seem to come around here much any more."

"No, I guess I don't," Henry replied.

It was an understatement. Until that moment, Henry Atkins had never set foot inside Grover Hicks' Welding Company.

"You oughta come around more often! I got a lotta interesting things here that you probably don't know anything about. Why don't you stop by more often?"

"Maybe I will," said Henry.

"I'll betcha don't know what that is," said Grover, kicking a long, thick length of angle iron.

He was right. Henry hadn't even wondered about it.

"Well, I'll tell you. That's a piece of the leg off Orville Shrader's windmill. His boy—that wild one that's always getting kicked out of college—run his daddy's pickup truck smack dab into the corner of the windmill and sliced off the leg like it was butter. Look at that, would you? Cut just as smooth as if it was sawed! He was gonna buy a whole new leg, and I said, 'What're you talking about? I can weld that thing back together so you can't tell it was ever cut off!' I'm going out and fix it for him as soon as I get time. I get lots of interesting jobs like that—all the time."

Somehow he was unable to take his eyes off Henry's folder.

"Yes, that is interesting work, Grover," said Henry. "I hope I'm not keeping you from your work, but—"

"Keeping me from my work? Are you kidding? Any day I don't have time to stop and chew the fat with ole Henry Atkins, that's the day I'll be ready to close up shop, I'll tell you right now! Come in here and let me show you a job I did on Joe Cranston's sump pump. If you can show me where I welded it together, I'll buy you a cuppa coffee with cream and sugar in it. Come on and let me show—"

"I really haven't got time, Grover. I wanted to talk with

you a minute about a little matter that's kind of embarrassing—"

"Embarrassing? Listen, Henry, I certainly don't know what could be embarrassing between a coupla ole buddies like you and me." His eyes darted to Henry's face for an instant, then back to the black folder. "I wish I had time to run down to the Little Gem with you. It's been a long time since you and me had a cuppa coffee together."

"It certainly has," said Henry, and that, too, was an understatement. Henry had never drunk a cup of coffee or anything else with Grover Hicks. "But as I was saying, Grover—"

"You know, Calvin Turnbough does pretty well with that cafe, don't he? He started out with nothing and learned that business from the ground up. Runs a mighty fine place—clean and sanitary like a hospital operating room. Yes, sirree! I'm always kidding ole Calvin about all the money he's making. Just the other day, I said, 'Calvin, next time you go to the bank with all that money—' "

"It's about Mr. Ditmore's bill, Grover," Henry said abruptly.

Grover's manner changed. As though a light had been extinguished, his jovial and affable manner became sad and grave. His eyes reflected great pain. He bowed his head, stared at his feet and was silent.

"It's a long time overdue," Henry said. "Mr. Ditmore's been waiting for his money over eleven months now, and I was wondering if maybe you could pay a little on account and get yourself started on a plan to reduce this outstanding obligation."

"I been bereaved," Grover said. He did not look up.

"Yes. Mr. Ditmore told me."

"You just don't know how hard it is to think about money and material things when you get all bereaved like I been."

"I'm sure that's true," said Henry. "That's what makes it embarrassing to bring up matters like this. Blanche was a fine woman."

"She was a saint," said Grover. He brushed a big knuckle across the corner of a fat eye.

"Mr. Ditmore realizes how hard it's been for you, Grover, and I do, too. He doesn't expect a check for the entire amount —not now. He just thinks maybe you could start paying a little each month and reduce the total as you go along."

"It's hard to talk about these everyday matters in connection with a saint like Blanche." Grover's voice was husky. His big bosom heaved mightily. "She always handled the money and paid all the bills. Wouldn't let me worry myself about it. To tell the truth, I can't hardly stand to look at the checkbook no more, because it reminds me of her. It just stirs up my heart something awful, Henry. It's mighty hard on me."

"It's hard on me, too, Grover, and I hate to bother you about it, but life must go on, as they say."

"Yes, I heard that before, and it's a mighty fine saying. I been thinking maybe I oughta memorize it for myself."

"Yes, I suppose you could do that," said Henry, unimpressed. "Now if you pay me a few dollars today, let's say, and then a few dollars each month—regular payments on a regular basis, like rent—you'll find that it's not too hard to do. The thing, Grover, is to get into the *habit* of paying. Put it in your regular budget."

Grover shook his head slowly and sadly. "I know how this looks to L. T. Ditmore—a fine gentleman if there ever was one. If I gotta owe money I'd rather owe it to L. T. Ditmore than anybody in town. Blanche thought the world of him. That's one of the reasons I haven't been back around to see him. It makes me think of Blanche and tears me up something awful. He didn't mention that bill to me for the longest time. I guess he understood how bereaved I was. I still am, for that matter. I been thinking maybe I oughta start going to church every Sunday and see if that'll help any."

"Yes, that might do you good, Grover," Henry said with no emotion. He recognized such tactics and was not easily taken in by them. He hadn't been a bill collector all these years without learning a thing or two about human nature in the process.

"In the meantime, Grover, what can I tell Mr. Ditmore? Two or three dollars right now would be a decent start. Once you take the first big step, you'll find it easier to train your mind on it. You'll have a definite goal to work toward."

"You know, Henry, I can't think of anything I'd rather do —for your sake as well as Mr. Ditmore's, because I realize you gotta make your living, too. But the truth of the matter is that you caught me at a pretty bad time. But I'll tell you one thing for sure. If I had any cash in my pocket, you'd be the first person to get it. The abso-lute-ally first! But I had so many expenses when Blanche passed away—"

His voice broke. He paused and stood in respectful silence for a moment. Henry looked on and waited for him to get over it.

"It's been taking me a long time to pull myself back together again," he went on. "But I want you to tell Mr. Ditmore that I'm gonna start paying on that bill right away."

"But not this month?"

"Gosh, I wish I could, Henry. I really do. But it looks like I'll just have to wait and start next month instead."

"Then I guess I'll have to come back around the first."

"I hate for you to go to all that trouble on my account."

"*Mr. Ditmore*'s account," Henry corrected. He smiled.

His little whimsy brightened Grover's mood. He chuckled.

"Just the same, I'm gonna look *you* up," he said. "It's a long way over here to my shop, and I won't want to put you out any. I'll track you down on the first of the month. How's that for a switch? I guess not many people track *you* down, do they, Henry?"

"No," said Henry.

Grover laughed openly. A tube of overhanging stomach shook in disproportion to the amount of humor contained in his little sally.

"Are you sure you don't have time to take me up on that cuppa coffee?" Grover asked, cheered visibly. He was smiling and jovial once again.

"You said *you* didn't have time."

"Well, what do you know about that?" Grover whooped. "That's a good one on me, isn't it?" He threw back his head and laughed loudly. Suddenly he stopped and became grave again. "That just shows you the state of mind I've been in since my great loss," he said. "I just can't seem to remember things."

"I see," said Henry, still unwilling to be moved. "Well— I'll see you next month, Grover. And I sincerely hope you will work out a systematic plan to reduce this obligation. You'll feel better about it yourself once you've started."

"I sure hope so," said Grover. "I need something to take my mind offa my grief. It's an awful heavy burden to carry."

Henry departed, leaving Grover Hicks standing in the doorway of his welding shop. As he backed his car out through the weeds and onto the highway, he waved. Grover waved back and managed a brave smile.

On the first of the following month, Henry waited all day for Grover Hicks to track him down. He waited all day the second, and all day the third. On the fourth day of the month, he returned to Grover Hicks' Welding Company and again found the owner making blue sparks.

"Wouldn't you know it?" he said when Henry walked through the door. "I've been knocking myself out to finish Hal Murdock's tailgate here so I could go out and collect some of the money that's owed me so I could come see you. And you beat me to it! You sure look after your business, Henry! I guess that's the reason you're so successful."

Henry Atkins was not susceptible to flattery. In his business, he could not afford to be.

"You promised to look me up, Grover," he said, not unpleasantly but not pleasantly, either. "I took your word."

"Don't you think that's been on my conscience? But you see Hal Murdock's got a load of hogs he wants to move over to his brother-in-law's place at Shradersburg, and he's been on my back to get through with his tailgate."

Henry moved closer and looked at a messy clutter of metal, none of which seemed to be a tailgate. "What are you doing?" he asked. "Making him a new one?"

"No—but you don't know Hal Murdock! As finicky as an old maid! Everything's gotta be just right. But as I was saying, I've been hurrying so I could go out and do some collecting and pay some on that L. T. Ditmore bill. It just looks like I can't never get away from this shop." He sighed deeply.

"Maybe you should restudy your priorities with a view to rearranging them," Henry said.

Grover stared at him blankly. "How's that?"

"Put first things first," Henry explained.

"That's what my customers ought to do. Some of them just won't pay up like they ought to. You know what I mean?"

"Yes," said Henry.

"Gee, I'm sorry you had to come all the way over here for nothing, Henry. I'll tell you what I'll do. I'll go out and see what I can collect this very day. Old Minnie Chiles' fence will just have to wait. She says her chickens are running loose all over the county—but she'll just have to let 'em run. I'll see what I can scare up, and I'll come around and see you, Henry, so you won't have to do all that driving and make a special trip."

"That's what you told me before."

"What? Yeah—I *was* gonna track you down the other day, but I just couldn't shake any money out of my customers. But don't you worry about it none."

"I'll try not to," Henry said.

The month passed, and Henry did not see hide nor hair of Grover Hicks except driving down Main Street with Velma Agnew, at the Little Gem Cafe with Velma Agnew, turning off onto Old Loop Road with Velma Agnew, in front of the County Library with Velma Agnew, pulling away from Smokey Rainwater's Tavern with Velma Agnew, speeding out Eleventh Street with Velma Agnew, coming out of the Texan Theatre with Velma Agnew. It seemed that everywhere he looked, Henry saw Grover Hicks with Velma Agnew. Somehow, though, Grover never saw Henry. Velma did, but not Grover. Henry waited for Grover to track him down. Nothing happened.

On the first of the month, Henry returned to the welding shop.

"They just wouldn't pay me," Grover said sadly. "I started to track you down, but I knew how disappointed you'd be, so I just didn't say anything about it."

"I'm accustomed to disappointments, Grover."

"You were right about one thing, Henry. Thinking about a systematic plan for paying that bill has made me feel a lot better. Just thinking about it has been helping my feelings. I've been getting out and around a little more."

"Yes. I saw you a few times with Velma Agnew."

"Who? Oh—*Mrs.* Agnew!" He laughed. "Why, yes— Mrs. Agnew works at the Library and has been encouraging me to read books."

Henry could be firm when the occasion demanded it.

"Now see here, Grover," he said firmly. "We've got to get down to brass tacks on this Ditmore matter. Suppose I come around on the fifteenth of the month? Some people get paid on the fifteenth, you know, and that might be a better time for you—and for me."

"Well, you've been so nice to me, Henry, I'll just have to say yes. I told Mrs. Agnew one day during one of our conferences that there wasn't a nicer couple in town than Henry and Birdie Atkins, and that if I was bad sick, I'd call Birdie Atkins before I'd call a doctor. You sure are lucky to be married to such a fine lady."

He contemplated the ground in silence for a moment.

"Well, I'll come back on the fifteenth, Grover," Henry said when the moment was over. "Maybe we can work something out."

"That'll be real nice of you, Henry, and I'll be on the lookout for you."

"Yes, I guess you will," said Henry.

On the fifteenth of the month, Grover Hicks' Welding Company—Electric and Acetylene—was closed. On the sixteenth, its owner told Henry that he had been at home flat on his back with a terrible case of the shingles. Henry prescribed some ointment that he himself had once used for a skin rash but that would probably work as well for shingles.

"This Ditmore account has been lying dormant and inactive over thirteen months now, Grover," Henry said authoritatively.

"How's that?"

"It's getting pretty old for an unpaid bill."

"You think I don't know that?" Grover said. "If you think it's easy to have that burden along with the shingles—on top of my great bereavement, you just don't know."

A faraway, lonesome expression came into his eyes. He gazed through the big double doors and out across the junk-filled weeds, the mesquite trees and a passing whirlwind beyond.

Henry returned on the first day of the month.

"Well, Henry, it looks like trouble runs in bunches, don't it?" said Grover, not a trace of cheer in his voice and manner. "I just never saw anything to beat it! I collected some money that was owed to me, and I put it aside for you. Then I got this call from the bank. The check bounced, and I had to give the money to the bank! That left me holding the bag."

He threw two ham-sized hands into the air in a gesture of defeat.

"Now what can you do?" he went on. "Will you tell me that, for Pete's sake? When I collected this money, I said ole Henry Atkins is gonna get this money even if it means I don't get any food to put in my mouth."

He paused a moment and his manner became philosophical.

"I know how to cut corners, Henry. You might not know that, but I do. I *know*, because I had to do it—with all my expenses when Blanche passed on to her reward, you know."

"Mr. Ditmore said he didn't think you had any expenses except his bill."

"He said that?" Grover was pained. "I guess he forgot about the telegrams and phone calls I had to make."

"Well. What are we going to do now, Grover?"

"First of all, I gotta get this certain party to make that check good—wish I could tell you his name, Henry, so you could watch out for him. I don't want to poison your feelings —you know that. But I'll get him—don't you worry about it. I'll get him."

"When should I come back, then? Tomorrow?"

"No—save your gas and tires. That's been bothering me, too, the way you're running the wheels offa your car and spending your own money. I'll look you up. You've got my word."

Another two weeks went by and Henry heard nothing from Grover. He saw him, though, with Velma Agnew parked in front of the Trade Winds Hamburger Stand, going in and out of the County Library, making U-turns down by the depot, turning in off the road from Smokey Rainwater's Tavern, driving out Third Street. Usually they were so engrossed in conversation that Grover never saw Henry. Velma saw him twice and nodded to him, but Grover didn't.

Henry went back to the welding company on the fifteenth of the month.

"It's getting close to fifteen months on this delinquent account, Grover," Henry reminded him.

"You're not gonna believe a word of this, Henry, but this guy's got this bill with me—not much, and it wasn't overdue. Just due. I saw him in front of the Eatmore Bakery the other day, and he tried to pay me. I said, 'Oh, no, you don't! No, sirree! You just take that money and give it to ole Henry Atkins and tell him it come from me!' Now I just found out this very day that he didn't do it. I wish I could tell you his name, so you'd know the kind of people I have to deal with. It's getting to where you can't trust hardly anybody, isn't it?"

"Yes," said Henry.

"Of course, you don't have to worry about trust and things like that—not like I do, being alone in the world and all. You've got Birdie, and I'm telling you that any man that's married to Birdie Atkins is sure ahead in this world."

Henry agreed that Birdie was a fine wife. They discussed her work, her loyalty to Henry, her pay, how often she worked, and her cool head in a crisis.

"Well, Grover, I think it might be better if I drop around on Saturdays from now on," Henry said decisively. "Lots of people get paid on Saturdays, you know. Maybe your collections will come in weekly better than they've been coming in monthly."

They both agreed that the Saturday visits would be a splendid idea, and it was—in theory. In practice, however, Grover's pocketbook was no fatter on Saturdays than it was on any other day of the month.

"How're you coming with Grover Hicks, Henry?" Mr. Ditmore asked him every now and then, sometimes on the telephone and sometimes in person when he ran across him on the street.

"Nothing yet, Mr. Ditmore," Henry was always forced to report.

One day during a lull in his activities, he dropped into L. T. Ditmore's Funeral Home to give the undertaker a full-scale progress report which, alas, didn't amount to much.

He found Mr. Ditmore in the process of removing a basket of magnificent white mums and pink gladioli from his office. Distaste was written over his face.

"Too much, too much, *just too much*," he was muttering. "A family gave me these in appreciation. You know what I'd like to see just once? I'd like to see an ugly, skinny stalk with the leaves falling off and no blooms, in an old coffee can—just once! You want to take these to Birdie?"

"I'm afraid not," said Henry. "She'd think I've been out fornicating."

"Hee-hee-hee! That's pretty good, Henry! Excuse me while I take these in the back. Just take a second."

When he returned, the distaste on his face had been replaced by his beloved professional smile, or whatever kind it was.

"You don't know how it is, Henry," he said. "People are always giving me flowers to show their appreciation. Now I appreciate their appreciation, but gee whiz! I wish they'd think up something besides flowers—like a hamburger with onions at the Trade Winds. I work around flowers all day every day—beautiful flowers, expensive flowers, flowers tied up in ribbons and bows, flowers that'll put your eyes out. That's why I don't have any flowers in my yard at home—

except an old diseased cactus plant that I keep thinking will die, but it hasn't yet." He sighed.

Henry listened sympathetically and tried to tell Mr. Ditmore that he was beginning to understand, but Mr. Ditmore had not finished complaining.

"You remember Woodrow Bridges? Had fourteen children, all married and scattered every which way. They all came back when their daddy died. Well, at least eleven of them gave me a bouquet before they left town. I thought those flowers would live forever. They like to have never died! I sneaked in a couple of arrangements on another service, but that's all I could get away with. About a week later, while we were having a service—I can't remember whose it was—some lady came in the front door and walked into my office and started bawling like a calf. I said 'Wrong room, lady. If you'll go through that door there, you'll find the loved one.' She saw all the flowers in my office, you see, and she thought—"

"That's interesting," Henry interrupted. "I wanted to tell you about Grover Hicks. He's a tough one. He always puts me off with tales of his own troubles, but I'm onto him. I learned long ago in this business not to let myself get hoodwinked."

"Well, I should certainly hope not! I don't know how it is in your business, Henry, but I know how it is in mine. I can't be too outspoken about money matters. I have to take it easy with people and not be straightforward at all. I have to spend more time with them on a personal basis than maybe Frank Hudgins does when he sells somebody a bottle of Doan's Kidney Pills—Whoops! I'll bet you think I'm winking at you again, Henry. It's that twitch."

He giggled.

"I see," said Henry wisely.

"So I was thinking maybe you might spend more time with Grover on a social and personal basis," explained Mr. Ditmore.

"But I make it a practice not to mix pleasure with business," Henry said professionally. "It can lead to difficulties."

"Pshaw! All I'm talking about is for you to get away from money matters sometime and *visit* with Grover about other things—like a friend, you know. It might work wonders. I had to go out to Earl Snodgrass' place and wait around and watch him milk that old spavined cow of his before he would pay me a red cent for his daddy's funeral. I almost tore up the bill when he tried to make me taste the milk. Just between you and me, it was my economy service—the lowest-priced service I had all year long. You might want to try the friendly approach sometime, Henry."

As the only bill collector in town, therefore the first and final authority in his field, Henry tried not to be affronted by L. T. Ditmore's presumptuousness in telling him how to run his business, but at the same time, he recognized the potential in his suggestion.

"I can assure you it wouldn't be difficult," Henry said. "Grover Hicks talks all the time. He's talking when I walk into his place and he's talking when I walk out. I'll consider your suggestion, Mr. Ditmore, and if I find that it has merit, I'll arrange my schedule so that I can spend more time with Grover on a personal basis."

He did.

He continued to call at the welding shop each Saturday without fail, except once when he was at Dr. Beasley's seeing about his jaw, which he feared might be broken. Each week he stayed longer than it took him to determine that Grover Hicks wouldn't be parting with any money that week. The two of them visited, laughed, talked, told jokes, discussed local events of mutual interest, allowing their conversations to roam far beyond Grover's finances and attendant difficulties.

They discussed Birdie Atkins' practical nursing; Grover said he would have given anything in the world to have had her on hand during Blanche's final illness. They discussed Henry's secondhand Plymouth; Grover examined the radiator for any spots that might need welding. They discussed fishing in Pease River when it had water in it; Grover gave Henry a paper bag full of metal scraps from which he could make sinkers. They discussed the Atkins' need for new plumbing fixtures in their modest bungalow; Grover took Henry out behind the shop and showed him an old bathtub half hidden by the weeds and gave it to him outright—if he didn't mind hauling it away.

They discussed Henry's health and well-kept appearance; Grover attributed it to Birdie's cooking and her slick way with an ironing board. They discussed the many handyman tasks around the home; Grover gave Henry a cardboard box filled with nuts, bolts, screws, nails and wires, all good as new if Henry didn't mind scrubbing off the grease and rust. They discussed Henry's portable barbecue grill; Grover welded on a broken leg free of charge. They discussed fences; Grover gave Henry a used hasp for his back gate. That was one gift, however, that Henry couldn't use, for he didn't have a gate. He didn't even have a fence.

As a business relationship, it was first-rate. As a personal relationship, it was a fine one. Henry was pleased with himself that he had so shrewdly combined the two. But always the businessman, he was careful to maintain the proper balance between them. He saw to it that Grover did not lose sight of the financial aspect of their association, which after all was the foundation on which it rested. And Grover cooperated to the utmost. He borrowed five dollars from Henry one Saturday morning.

He promised to repay it the following week.

Henry didn't mention the loan to Birdie. He knew he could never make her understand how it had come about. Indeed, he didn't understand it himself. All he knew for certain was that one morning he departed the Grover Hicks Welding Company five dollars lighter than he had arrived. His feelings were not unlike those of an almsgiver whose pockets had been picked while dispensing alms.

Nor did he mention the loan to L. T. Ditmore. The transaction smacked of poorer business practices than he cared for his client to know about. Besides, he didn't want the undertaker to entertain the possibility that Henry's collection labors might be split in a two-way struggle for Grover's money.

And therein lay a moral dilemma that tied Henry in knots. Which should he collect first—his own, or L. T. Ditmore's money? The question, as it turned out, was purely academic. On the following Saturday, he collected no money for either.

Nor did he collect any money the next week, the next, or the next.

But that did not ease the dilemma. Not in the least. Which should come first if, some fine day and through some odd combination of circumstances, Grover actually should hand him some cash? On the face of it, Mr. Ditmore's account had priority, certainly. Not only because of its age and size, but because it was the root from which his own overdue account had sprouted. On the other hand, his five-dollar loan to Grover Hicks had been an incidental transaction, a small deal on the side, personal, short-term, and in no legal sense related to Grover Hicks' bill for the funeral of his wife, Blanche. Yet, he needed the five dollars; he was in no financial position to allow the debt to become rusty with age. L. T. Ditmore or Henry Atkins? Funeral bill or personal loan? From week to week, Henry did battle with his conscience and struggled to find an answer to the untidy question of who should get Grover's money first. All this on the assumption, of course, that *someday somebody* would receive *some* money from Grover Hicks. Academic or not, it was a tough question. Henry began to lose weight.

In the meantime, the fine business relationship continued.

On the personal front, however, a slight tension developed; at least, from Henry's side of the alliance. Grover appeared to be as free, easy, relaxed and friendly as ever. Each Saturday he gave Henry coffee from his thermos bottle. He made him a key ring from some scraps of brass. He replaced an old Band-Aid on Henry's cheek with a new one. He gave Henry a spare pair of welding goggles. He brought him a recommended list of books from Mrs. Agnew's library. He squirted grease in the lock of the trunk on the Plymouth and opened it for the first time in four months.

Atkins or Ditmore? Five dollars or a hundred times five dollars? Collector or client?

On a Saturday morning at the height of the season's first dust storm, when the entire world was dirty brown from top to bottom and the boisterous wind was slapping the second-hand Plymouth around the road as though it were a kite, Henry pulled up in front of the welding shop, put on Grover's spare pair of welding goggles to keep the dust from his eyes, and fought his way across the weeds and into the shop.

"Well, well, Henry ole buddy!" Grover shouted as the two of them struggled to close the big door against the gusty wind. "I was afraid you wouldn't come today with the dust blowing and all. I was gonna call you to be sure and come."

Henry turned loose of the door and sprang back as though it had bitten him.

"You were going to *ask* me to come?"

Grover was now fighting the door alone.

"Yeah. I got a big surprise for you today."

He leaned against the door, panting.

"Shove that bar across there, will you, Henry?" he gasped.

Henry shoved the bar into place and followed Grover across the dirt floor with no enthusiasm. He had long since become accustomed to Grover's surprises. As a matter of fact, he was benumbed by Grover Hicks' surprises. His anticipation lay dormant.

"The only thing you could do to surprise me, Grover, would be to pay me some money," he said wearily.

"*That's it!*" Grover shouted.

"What's it?"

"Money!" Grover boomed. "I'm gonna give you some money!"

Thereupon he handed Henry a ten-dollar bill.

Henry stared at it as if it were a live hand grenade. The academic question had become real. It had become practical and immediate; it demanded an answer.

"Well, now, Grover—what's this for?" he asked, unable to stop staring at the green bill in his hand. "Is this all for Mr. Ditmore or is part of it for me?"

"You can do what you like, Henry!" Grover said, excited and pleased with himself. He slapped Henry on the back. "I'm not gonna tell ole Henry Atkins what to do! No, sirree! You got a good business head on your shoulders, and you can do what you want with that money. You can take your five out of it, or you can put it all on L. T. Ditmore's bill."

"That's not fair, Grover!"

"What's not fair about it?"

"You should tell me what the money's for. I need to know if you're paying me back or not."

"But Henry—you don't understand! I'm gonna let you decide that for yourself! I figure since you and me have become such good friends, I don't need to dictate to you what to do."

Henry put the ten dollars in his wallet, fought back the tears, told Grover good-bye, got into his Plymouth, backed out onto the highway and allowed the murderous wind to hurtle him all the way out to Smokey Rainwater's Tavern, where he stayed until closing time, socializing with Smokey and his wife, Juanita, who sometimes filled in as bouncer on

Saturday nights. When he pulled into his driveway, Henry almost ran over the paper boy.

On Monday he returned L. T. Ditmore's bill to him and told him what he could do with it—in a businesslike manner, of course. At last account, Henry was still calling on Grover Hicks regularly, so it must be assumed that he applied the entire ten dollars on L. T. Ditmore's funeral bill. If that's assumed, it must also be assumed that Henry's regular visits to the Grover Hicks Welding Company are for the purpose of collecting his own five dollars. Otherwise, it must be assumed that Henry collected his five dollars from Grover Hicks and continues to call on him simply because he enjoys visiting him. But if *that's* assumed, why does he always go on Saturdays?

7.

Gussie Strickland's Individual Vacation

Gussie Strickland taught algebra at the high school. She wasn't the most outstanding teacher on the faculty, but neither was anybody else, and she didn't get criticized for that. Two things about her did cause some talk, however, her appearance being one, and her individual way of spending her vacations the other.

With a build as symmetrical as all those equations she taught, she walked with an interesting twist that caused one side of her to go up while the other was going down, and when she came to a halt, the two sides didn't stop at the same time. Gussie's halting was a production that men and boys enjoyed watching, and they were always dreaming up reasons to stop her on the street so they could look on. She was friendly and agreeable and didn't mind pausing a while if they wanted to ask about the workings of an algebra problem or to inquire into a loved one's progress in school.

Because of her friendly way of talking and interesting way of walking, not to mention her attractive shape, some people suspected that she had a wild streak in her. Others doubted it;

they thought she had the wrong kind of face to go with a wild streak, apparently forgetting that people's faces are not necessarily what they get wild with. Still, they might have had a point there, for Gussie's nose was too large. She had the biggest nose in the county, far more nose than she needed, so huge that no one else's nose was even in second place. It was long, high-bridged and stuck out like a beak, the kind of nose that would be conspicuous on anybody. On Gussie, however, it wasn't as noticeable as it might have been on a more conventional person—Marcella Overton, say—the competition from her other assets being so fierce and all.

Spectacular though they were, her other assets were in proper proportion, color, taste, and—above all—shape. From the top to the bottom of her five-foot-five configuration, she was streamlined. From her shoulders to her heels, there was not a corner, angle or straight line to separate one dazzling curve from the next. With brown eyes that were warm and friendly, brown hair that was soft and wavy, and a smooth complexion that was fair and creamy, she wore her clothes with a flair that made her look dressed up when she was not and not necessarily dressed up when she was. Of course, the frame over which she draped those clothes might have had something to do with that.

Yet, with all her assets, she had a genteel quality about her, a ladylike manner that restrained onlookers when they felt a long, low whistle coming on. They merely looked and marvelled instead. Possibly, she was the only woman alive with a shape that could be disguised with nothing less than a pyramidal tent who could evoke such a disciplined reaction from the bleachers. All of which made Gussie a more interesting topic of conversation than the average schoolteacher. Indeed, certain people around town analyzed her in much the same manner as they would study a set of blueprints.

Despite the talk, however, nobody could find anything to

talk about, for Gussie's reputation was spotless. Otherwise, Mrs. Maxwell, a fine, Christian lady who felt responsible for the morals as well as the comforts of her roomers, would never have rented her a furnished bedroom with kitchen privileges. Gussie didn't go out with strange men; she didn't smoke; nobody ever saw her take a drink; she didn't use swearwords; and she never missed a PTA meeting, which was more than most parents could lay claim to. What's more, she played classical music on the piano, listened to operas on the radio, read books that weighed three pounds each, and gave slim volumes of poetry that didn't rhyme for birthdays and anniversaries.

She was not a churchgoer, but she was so stylish, so cultured, and so refined that people tended to excuse if not forgive her. They polished off her dereliction with a simple explanation, "Gussie's not the churchgoing type."

She taught first-aid classes in her spare time and gave life-saving courses at the Municipal Swimming Pool when it had any water in it. She was never known to lose her head in a crisis, not even during the Big Sneeze—a trying period for teachers when their students induced sneezing by sticking crystals of Melo, the water softener, up their noses. With approximately 73.2 percent of her pupils sneezing as if competing for prizes, she went on teaching algebra, outshouting the kerchoos and sometimes saying, "Bless you!" after a particularly vigorous round.

Nobody really understood Gussie, but, giving her the benefit of the doubt, they did admire her—with a wee touch of awe. But trust her? That was another matter. Yet, when you came right down to it, she didn't give them anything not to trust except her appearance, which was remarkable, and her individual way of spending her vacations, which was puzzling.

Aside from the odd and somewhat perverse fact that she went on trips without visiting anybody, she went alone, and she went to places other people wouldn't have thought about. She stayed three weeks on a dude ranch in Wyoming, ignoring all the dude ranches in New Mexico, which were one third the distance. She spent an entire month on the beach at Biloxi, Mississippi, as though the beach at Galveston were not good enough. She went to Seattle, Washington, when most people went no further than Colorado Springs. She took a sight-seeing trip to Boston and Philadelphia without stopping in New York, where most people would have gone instead. Once she took a boat trip to Central America, which would certainly have been harmless enough had she not gone alone. Rumors got started about it, but she brought back so many souvenirs and other evidences of a wholesome vacation that she ended up with a clean bill of health, however hard-won.

It was not that anybody thought she should take vacations with other teachers, such as Miss Weathersby, say, who never went anywhere but to Eastern Star meetings and conventions, but it did strike them as standoffish for her to go chasing around by herself. She went to Tucson, Arizona, one Christmas and to Kansas City, Missouri, at Easter—by herself. Then in the summer, she fooled everybody and stayed home to teach summer school. Predicting where Gussie Strickland would spend her next vacation was a game people played but never won. She outfoxed them every time.

It was small wonder, then, that one summer several years ago, no one thought to predict that Gussie would get herself a job at the Dallas Fair. At the same time, who but Gussie would ever come up with an idea like that? And what kind of job was it?

"Maybe she's working a cash register," said some.

"Or clerking in a booth," opined others.

"That doesn't sound like Gussie," they all agreed.

"But I wouldn't put it past her," they said.

"Neither would I—but *clerking? Gussie?*"

It did seem rather ordinary and, for Gussie, dull. Somebody heard she had hired on as a guide in an exhibit hall, and that one caught on for a while. It was just offbeat enough to catch her eye and interest. Then, considering her friendly way of talking and interesting way of walking, the job would have suited her to a tee.

But as usual, they were wrong. Gussie had outfoxed them again.

She was appearing in a stage show on the midway!

In person.

That one grabbed everybody. In the long history of the town, not one of its citizens, past or present, had ever been associated with the glamorous world of show business, except Leo Gasser, who, years earlier, had left town with Harley Sadler's Comedians, and as soon as the show pitched its tent in Vernon, the next stop, twenty-nine miles away, got fired. Leo, then, didn't count. So that left Gussie, and she had really outdone herself this time.

"Now if that doesn't beat all!" said some.

"You can leave it to Gussie every time," said others.

"There's only one Gussie Strickland," they all agreed.

They shook their heads, chuckled and said maybe that was the only thing left that she had not tried.

But the story got better.

"Have you heard the latest from Dallas?"

"No—but I'm ready."

"Gussie's a *dancer* in that show."

"But Gussie's not a dancer!"

"She is now."

"You mean she's a chorus girl?"

"I don't know about that, but she's a dancer."

"But she's the high-school algebra teacher!"

"That don't mean anything! Clara Baker was a bricklayer before she started curling hair at the Marvella Beauty Shop."

At first, they didn't believe it, and who could blame them? Although Gussie was blessed with many talents, dancing was not one of them. At least, no one had ever seen her dance except at the Elks Club on the second Friday of each month when she went with J. D. Gribble, and that didn't mean anything. Even big fat Marcella Overton showed up at the Elks Club dances every now and then. Anyway, schoolteaching and chorus-girling just didn't match.

On the other hand, believing it was more fun than not, so without too much strain, they managed to convince themselves that the town's most spectacular schoolteacher was running true to form. She hadn't let them down, after all.

Gussie's vacation became Topic A that summer. People had a veritable picnic talking about her new job and wondering how her talents stacked up against the few chorus girls they knew anything about—Ruby Keeler, Toby Wing and the like. They could only speculate, though, until the first on-the-scene reports filtered back to town. Then they discovered that her talents stacked up very well indeed, and that she was showing them off better than they had thought to predict.

The message from Dallas was that Gussie was dancing in that show wearing nothing but a pair of shoes!

The fire whistle never attracted more attention than that message.

"Aw, come on now! You *know* that's not true! Gussie *Strickland?*"

"Nobody else's but!"

"You mean to stand there with your bare face hanging out and tell me that Gussie Strickland is prancing around on a stage nekkid as a jay bird?"

"Not a stitch."

"I'll be real frank with you—Gussie has done some peculiar things, but nothing that's downright indecent like this."

"Well—you can believe it or not."

[*236*]

Whether they did or didn't depended on how you looked at it.

People all over town began packing up and going to Dallas to see for themselves. They went on business or to buy a new fall coat or to visit kinfolk they were worried about, and as long as they were there, it seemed like a shame not to take in the fair. Sam Abernathy and his family went on vacation to Albuquerque and stopped off in Dallas, which was in the opposite direction. Mr. Hightower, the high-school principal, went to Dallas to visit an aunt he hadn't seen since he was eleven years old. Delsey Jacobs made an extra buying trip to Dallas; he claimed his stock was too low to last out the summer.

"Most expensive trip I ever made," he said when he returned and toted up the damage. "When I mentioned going to Dallas, eyebrows went up all over town. To get them down again, I had to take Rose and all six kids with me."

Some people went to Dallas for the first time in their lives. Others who hated big cities, especially Dallas, and had sworn off tall buildings and heavy traffic, went to Dallas to see if the congestion had been relieved. The only conspicuous holdout was Reverend McWhorter. He was scheduled to attend a church convention in Dallas, but for fear his attendance would cause too much talk, he canceled out and stayed home. Had the Fort Worth & Denver Railway been on the ball, it could have run a Gussie Strickland Excursion Special to Dallas and made a killing.

It took a while for everybody to get their stories straight, and some never did. You couldn't tell who had been to the fair and who hadn't, for those who hadn't seemed to know more about Gussie's dancing than those who had. Mrs. Purdy Robinson gave her neighbors the details of Gussie's dancing, making it sound as though she had seen it with her own eyes, but she didn't fool anybody. They knew for a fact that she and Purdy had gone no further than Bowie to visit their married daughter, and Bowie was a hundred miles this side of Dallas. Even so, the main features of Gussie's dancing became common knowledge, and all versions agreed on the most important points.

The Beaux Arts Ball was the name of the midway show, in which chorus girls wore colored face masks covered with sequins, jewels and fringe. Some of them wore wigs decorated with flowers and precious stones. Others wore feather head-dresses that spread wide and towered high. A few scraps of flimsy gauze here and there completed their costumes. And shoes, of course.

While the orchestra played French music, the girls danced in and out among white columns, up and down white stairs, under a white arch, and through clouds of white mist. Colored lights bathed them in blue, then pink, green, purple and orange. Toward the end of the number, the girls turned rosy red and started truckin'. Just before they left the stage, each girl ran out to the footlights, turned her rear end toward the audience, did a short little shake and ran behind a column or up the stairs or disappeared into the clouds of white mist.

That was all there was to the show except for a comedian, a juggler, a team of acrobats, a singer, a few trained dogs, a pair of adagio dancers, and a magician who made a girl vanish into thin air. But everyone agreed that it was a big seventy-five cents' worth, anyway.

People rolled their eyes, smacked their lips, nudged one another and whistled. They took a kind of backhanded pride in having a firsthand acquaintance with a real live chorus girl in a real live stage show; nevertheless, Gussie Strickland's prancing around in her altogether became the town scandal. Beyond question, she furnished the town with the best gossip it had enjoyed since Grandma Ledbetter went off to Texarkana to visit her niece and married a nineteen-year-old boy.

People clucked their tongues, shook their heads and said what else could you expect from a person who went off on trips by herself and didn't even go to church on Sundays? They wondered what kind of parents she had down in Kilgore and what kind of upbringing they had given their daughter. There was an explanation there somewhere, and they set out to find it. They worked hard and late trying to figure it all out.

They reviewed her past—what they knew of it—digging for a clue, a tip-off, an explanation for her indecent public exposure. They uncovered nothing. They recalled the clothes she wore, the cosmetics she used, the books she read, the music she listened to, and the picture shows she attended. Louisa May Alcott could have invented her.

They remembered how she danced at the Elks Club, how she walked down the street, how she talked to people, how she smiled at young and old, girls and women, men and boys. They could have been describing Shirley Temple.

They examined her previous vacations, where she went, what she did, how long she stayed, whom she wrote post cards to, and what she said when she came back. They could have been detailing a Girl Scout cookout.

They quizzed her children about her teaching qualifications, how she acted in the classroom, what she said, whom she liked, whom she disliked, what she taught and how she taught it. Any Sunday school in town would have been fortunate to add her to its faculty.

Gussie Strickland was without fault or weakness. Driven snow was never purer.

It was frustrating.

Meanwhile, nobody but the stupid and underprivileged missed out on a trip to Dallas. Some went the second time. Some became regulars. As tourist attractions, the Alamo, the San Jacinto Monument and Palo Duro Canyon combined ran a poor second to Dallas.

As the summer wore on, discussing Gussie became a habit people couldn't shake off, like cussing the government. Her role in the Beaux Arts Ball grew with the telling. She wore the prettiest and most elaborate headdress. She was the most skillful trucker in the show. She led the chorus line up and down the stairs. She was the last offstage. The spotlight followed her to the exclusion of the others. She drew the most applause. Make no mistake about it, Gussie Strickland was the star of the Beaux Arts Ball—and in a costume no bigger than a pocket handkerchief.

But for all the buildup, in many, many people's eyes, Gussie's name was mud.

"At least she has the decency to hide her face behind a mask," they said.

"I hope she's got enough decency to keep it hidden forever—"

"—and never show it around this town again."

"Yes. When I think of all the young minds she influences. . . ."

"Isn't it the worst thing you ever heard in your life?"

"It certainly is, and I certainly hope Mr. Hightower knows his duty and does the right thing."

"The only right thing he can do is get rid of her."

"I don't see how he can possibly do anything else."

"When I think of all the young minds. . . ."

On and on and on and on. . . .

Then J. D. Gribble, the telephone repairman, had to go and louse up a good thing. At least, the evidence points to him as the maker of the first wave. He started it one day in the City Drug Store, where he often whiled away the time between repair jobs and sometimes during.

"Now just stop and think a minute," he said to the loungers at large. "How can you be sure that's Gussie up there on that stage?"

"Well, it ain't Gussie's grandpaw!" somebody replied.

"But you're not sure it's Gussie," J.D. countered.

"You're just taking up for her because you took her to the dances a few times," somebody else offered.

J.D. rolled his eyes.

"Why wouldn't it be Gussie?" still somebody else asked.

"Because she's got on a mask," said J.D. "The bright green one with the upswept edges and gold beads hanging from the bottom—"

"—the third one from the right end," a mature algebra student finished helpfully.

"But with that mask on, you can't *really* tell if it's Gussie or not, can you?" J.D. went on.

"If it ain't, who is it?"

"I don't know personally, you understand," said J.D. "But look at it this way. Do you know anybody who's talked to her in person since she's been in that show?"

They didn't.

"Do you know anyone who's received any letters from her?"

They didn't.

"Do you know anyone who's visited her backstage?"

They didn't.

"Has anybody *seen* her put that mask on?"

They had to say no again.

"Has anybody seen her take it off?"

Still no.

"Then how do you know that's Gussie?"

They didn't. Not when he put it that way.

It's surprising that J. D. Gribble wasn't tarred and feathered on the spot or at least ridden out of town on a rail. He took one of the juiciest scandals in the history of the town and threw it in doubt. Many people still hold it against him. And why not? He forced them to admit that they didn't know what they were talking about. No one could take an ironclad oath that Gussie was in the Beaux Arts Ball at all. The outward evidence indicated that she was, but it wasn't strong enough to bet money on.

With that kind of rabble-rousing going on, the scandal took on a new complexion. It got watered down, and it changed into one great dispute. Arguments started up everywhere, but proof that Gussie was dancing in the show was hard to come by. You couldn't identify her by her hair, not if she wore a wig, and the last thing in the world you could identify her by were her clothes. A few men hinted that they recognized the way her two sides went up and down and stopped separately, but they had to be careful who they hinted it to, and their suggestions did not carry much weight. The nearest thing to proof that anyone could offer was her nose.

"I'd know that big nose anywhere," they argued.

"Me too—if I could see it. But it's covered with a mask."

"But her mask sticks out further than the others because of her long, big nose."

"Now look here—with all those other things sticking out all over the stage, who in the hell is gonna notice whose *nose* is sticking out the furthest?"

So they squabbled, and they speculated, trying to remove the doubts from their otherwise spicy accounts of Gussie's dancing in the Beaux Arts Ball. Those with front-row seats tried to prove their case by pointing to a small, barely perceptible mole on her left hip. Considering its location, though, they certainly couldn't claim to have seen the same mole on the same hip while Gussie was teaching algebra or walking down the street. Some offered no other proof than the fact that nobody in the whole wide world had a shape like Gussie Strickland's. Their detractors, however, argued that there were thirteen other shapes on that stage so similar in construction and design that selecting one with more glorious qualities than all the others would be as difficult as selecting the most perfect orange in a citrus grove. The summer was a lively one, even for people who did not go anywhere, but as it neared its end, the autumn promised to be even livelier. Something had to be done about the algebra teacher at the high school.

Parents and teachers put the pressure on Marvin Cross, president of the school board that year, to terminate Miss Strickland's contract. He took the problem to Mr. Hightower. Mr. Hightower felt that they were on shaky ground unless they had absolute proof that Gussie was actually the person in the bright green mask.

"Lord-a-mercy!" said Marvin. "Everybody in town saw her with their own eyes!"

"Maybe so," said Mr. Hightower, "but before we can terminate her contract, we'll have to confront her with the charge and give her a chance to refute it. And we can't confront her without proof. That's one thing. The other thing is that I've been over her contract with a fine-tooth comb, and I can't find anything in it that prohibits teachers from dancing in shows so long as it doesn't interfere with their school-teaching. Personally, I don't see how truckin' in the summer will necessarily interfere with teaching algebra in the fall."

"Even if she's not wearing any clothes?"

"Even if. Of course, I'd expect her to wear her clothes to algebra class—naturally."

"Your position won't be very easy to explain to all the mothers, fathers, preachers and Mrs. Purdy Robinson."

Marvin's prediction was an underestimation. Mothers, fathers, preachers and Mrs. Purdy Robinson raised holy Cain.

"Hmpff!" snorted Mrs. Robinson. "I'm not surprised. Mr. Hightower is certainly an unusual person, and he is a *most* unusual principal if he can't see how Gussie has damaged her reputation and character, which is *bound* to influence her students' morals, and if *that* doesn't interfere with teaching

[243]

algebra, I don't know what does. Why, when I think of. . . ."

Mrs. Robinson spoke the sentiments of more people than Marvin was equipped to cope with.

"That has yet to be proven and demonstrated," said Mr. Hightower, when Marvin reported back to him and tried to resign his position as president of the school board. "We'll just have to wait and see whether or not Gussie's dancing interferes with her algebra teaching."

The way he stood up for Gussie got some people to wondering how much time he actually spent at his aunt's house in Dallas; that is, if he had a Dallas aunt in the first place. While some factions said surely Gussie would do the decent thing and tender her resignation of her own accord, other factions were scared to death that she would.

July passed with no word from Gussie. As the end of August approached and she still had not resigned, the suspense became all but unmanageable. Would she or wouldn't she? Did she or did she not have the nerve to come back and face the music?

She did.

September and Gussie Strickland arrived on the same day.

She returned to town the day before school started and went directly to Mrs. Maxwell's, unpacked her things and settled down as innocently as a cherub. Mrs. Purdy Robinson was aghast.

"I could hardly believe my ears, Georgia!" she said to Mrs. Maxwell. "Why, when I found out that you took that girl back into this house, I told Purdy that surely Georgia Maxwell has taken leave of her senses! I just feel like I ought to tell you how I feel about it—not only as your good friend but as your neighbor."

The Purdy Robinsons lived two streets over and six blocks down.

"Well, Eula, what else could I do?" wailed Mrs. Maxwell. "She paid her first month's rent before she left in June. Anyway, it's too late to rent the room to any of the other teachers."

Mrs. Maxwell's other neighbors—those who lived in the same neighborhood, that is—were as horrified as Mrs. Robinson, and at closer range. They watched Gussie come and go and compared notes frequently. Yet none of them mentioned the Beaux Arts Ball to her. Not even Mrs. Maxwell said the first word about it.

On the first day of school, Mr. Hightower's telephone jumped all over the desk with one mother after the other calling to say that no child of hers was going to sit in that woman's classroom and study algebra. Mr. Hightower shut them up one at a time and in sequence by pointing out that no child of hers would graduate from high school unless he *did* sit in that woman's classroom and study algebra, for algebra was a prerequisite for graduation, and Miss Strickland was the only algebra teacher in the school. The children themselves did not seem appalled in the least. They stampeded the office. Those who had not yet taken algebra wanted to take it as an elective, and those who had already completed the course wanted to take it as a refresher. He refused them all.

The semester got under way, and everybody stood back from Gussie as though she might ignite. They watched her every move, interpreted her every action, gauged her every motive. Still, no one asked her about her part, if any, in the Beaux Arts Ball. A few edged up to the question, but they wasted their time.

"Did you have a nice vacation this summer, Gussie?" asked Calvin Turnbough one evening when Gussie was having supper in the Little Gem.

"Fine, thank you," she replied graciously. "How about you? I heard that you and Letty took a trip to New Orleans."

"New Orleans!" Calvin said. "You don't know the half of it! You ought to see that French Quarter!"

Whereupon he launched into so detailed a description of

Bourbon Street by night that when he came up for air, Gussie had paid her check and was departing without having dropped the first clue to her own summer vacation.

Mrs. Maxwell stopped her on the front porch one day as Gussie came in from school. Yielding to the pressure of her neighbors, and thinking she might do the town a service once and for all, she said, "I haven't had a chance to talk to you since you got back, Gussie, but there's been an awful lot of talk this summer while you were away."

"Yes, and it's too bad," Gussie responded, properly concerned. "Some of the other teachers were telling me about poor Aggie Lee Chism having that baby."

Mrs. Maxwell groaned. "Did you ever hear the likes?" she exclaimed. "I just don't know what got into Aggie Lee. Why that girl had as good a Christian upbringing as anybody in this town. . . ."

By the time she had finished with Aggie Lee's downfall, it was time to start cooking supper. Gussie went on upstairs and to her room. Her summer vacation had not been mentioned.

Miss Craig, the English teacher, stopped Gussie in the hall one morning between classes.

"It does seem strange that you've never told anybody about your vacation, Gussie," she said.

"Nobody has asked me," Gussie said.

"Oh, well—"

Miss Craig could think of no suitable follow-on. As she explained later, she felt that Gussie's attitude and manner didn't invite further questioning. But it was not a wasted exercise. On the following morning, Miss Weathersby, the history teacher, took courage from her colleague's ice-breaking and dropped into a chair next to Gussie's in the lounge.

"I understand you haven't mentioned your vacation because nobody has asked you," she said.

"That's right," said Gussie pleasantly. "And you know, that makes two of us. You haven't said one word about your own vacation either. Didn't you go to an Eastern Star convention in—where was it—Waco?"

"Yes, it was," said the history teacher. "And there was this drill team from Mineola that did the most beautiful floor work you ever saw in your life!"

She described it in detail until the bell rang; then she trooped off down the hall to teach history, knowing no more of Gussie's vacation than she did when she got out of bed that morning.

When Mrs. Purdy Robinson heard of so many vain efforts, she blew up at all the pussyfooting. *She* knew how to handle these matters.

She stopped Gussie one afternoon on the sidewalk in front of the City Hospital. She was coming out. Gussie was going in.

"*Well*, Gussie! How is everything in Dallas?" she said accusingly.

"Just fine, I suppose," Gussie replied. She glanced toward the entrance to the hospital. "Is somebody sick in your family?"

"Oh—no. I just took a little gift to Mabel Fuller. She's got gallstones as big as the end of your thumb." She held up her thumb to demonstrate. She sighed. "I just don't know why she won't let them operate, but you know, Mabel Fuller has always been the biggest 'fraidy cat in town. Why I said to her, 'Mabel, why in heaven's name. . . .'"

Gussie stood on one foot then the other and from time to time glanced at her watch. Once or twice she murmured something about visiting hours being over. Eventually, Mrs. Robinson interrupted her own marathon narrative when Miss Addie Barker pulled up to the curb and honked.

"Good heavens! What happened to the time?" she exclaimed. "There's Addie Barker already. I told her to pick me up at. . . ."

She turned and fled.

The pressure on Marvin Cross increased so that in self-defense he stayed in his office more than on the sidewalk at the foot of the stairs. Geneva Caldwell, his stenographer, was not accustomed to having him underfoot, and she grew tired of it.

"Looks like you could at least answer the telephone when it rings sometimes, Mr. Cross," she said irritably. "It's always for you, and it's always about Gussie Strickland."

And it was. The preachers were calling to state their position on "the Miss Strickland matter"; parents were calling to demand that something be done and quick; other people were calling—people who had no children—merely to see what was going on. Marvin relayed all complaints to Mr. Hightower.

"If you don't hurry and confront her," he said, "you're going to have to find yourself another school-board president."

"Confront her yourself, if you want her confronted," Mr. Hightower replied.

"You hired her," said Marvin. "All I did was approve her contract—a rubber-stamp process."

"You see, Marv, Gussie doesn't have to prove that she was not in that show," he explained. "We've got to prove that she *was*. It's in the Constitution. A person is presumed innocent until proven guilty."

"Well, good lord-a-mercy! Plenty of eyewitnesses saw her with their own eyes!"

"Round them up, then, and get them to swear to it, and we'll go on from there. But I don't know what good it will do. She's teaching algebra just fine. As a matter of fact, I was by her room the other day when the bell rang. The kids came pouring out of all the other classrooms like a big belch, but

Gussie's algebra class just kept sitting there staring at Gussie without moving a muscle. Personally, I didn't know algebra was all that interesting."

"It's not, but Gussie is."

"You know, Marv, I don't have the heart for this kind of thing. I hate to try to scare up witnesses against her."

"You don't need to worry—not yet. I haven't got any witnesses, and I don't know where I'll find any."

But duty called, and off he went, nevertheless, to round up those he might find.

Then a strange thing happened. No one would admit seeing Gussie with his own eyes. All of them seemed to know plenty of others who had, though. Marvin said he wished to goodness he could find one. Just one.

A few people admitted privately and informally that they had seen her, but when it came to swearing to it, they could not be positive. Not with that mask and all.

"Why don't you ask her?" Sam Abernathy suggested.

"Why don't *you?*" Marvin countered.

"Because I'm not the president of the school board."

"You've got kids in school."

"Yeah—and one of them makes A's in algebra."

The truth was that Marvin was reluctant to ask Gussie for fear she would admit to the whole thing.

"And I remember seeing you in the audience one night," she might add.

Half the town shared Marvin's predicament. It was the other half, however, that was causing the ruckus. The half who thought they had the goods on Gussie were too discreet to admit it to the half who didn't. The town's most famous schoolteacher had them over a barrel, and they knew it.

Meanwhile, Gussie went right on teaching algebra and walking down the street after school with her interesting twist. She continued to be as friendly and agreeable as ever.

No more and no less. She didn't mind pausing a minute or two if someone wanted to ask about the intricacies of an algebra problem, and for some reason algebra seemed to bother more people that fall than ever before. A few mothers snubbed her, but most of them hung onto her every word, hoping for a clue, a hint or a quotable slip of the lip to liven their over-the-fence chatter. They got nothing.

After school when Gussie went to the City Drug Store for a soda or to the Marvella Beauty Shop for a finger wave, she attracted more attention than the fire engine with siren blowing and lights flashing. In the evenings she went downstairs and played Mrs. Maxwell's piano as she had always done. The neighbors sat on their porches and listened to "The Moonlight Sonata" and Schubert's "Serenade" and said it beat all how that girl could do the things she had done and still play such highbrow music.

Before school had been in session a full week, Miss Strickland had become the most popular teacher in the history of the town, public or private, hands down and running. By comparison, every other teacher was frumpy, dowdy and a thousand years old. Her pupils regarded her with fresh awe each time she entered the room. They watched her closely, always hoping she might forget herself and cross the room in one of her show walks instead of in her regular way, which was pretty good in itself if only they had had sense enough to realize it. Only once did things threaten to get out of hand. She instructed Fatty Huffman to erase an equation from the blackboard.

"You mean *take it off?*" Fatty asked with small voice and large significance.

His classmates tittered and held their breaths.

"Yes," said Gussie, calm, ladylike and full of decorum. "Take it *all* off."

The poise with which she handled the situation sent her

stock soaring higher than a kite. Poise was one of Gussie Strickland's strong points, and her students admired her for it. Only once did her equilibrium seem to go off center and glaze her eyes with shock. That was the day the Winbury sisters—Winnie, Etta Nell and Olive—appeared in her algebra classes, one each period, with identical hairdos in unmistakable imitation of Miss Strickland, the apple of their collective eye.

In the third week of school, the seniors elected her their class sponsor and set off a wrangle with the juniors, who claimed to have elected her first. Mr. Hightower settled the dispute by changing the rules, making class sponsors appointive rather than elective positions. He gave Miss Strickland to the 4-H Club. That choice, however, had its unfortunate aspects. The 4-H Club's project for that year was a Jersey that gave twelve quarts of milk a day, and the connotation was uncomfortable.

Not long before Armistice Day, the principal got into a squabble with the yearbook staff when, fearful of parents' overreaction, he persuaded them not to dedicate the year's volume to Miss Strickland. It was an achievement roughly similar to walking on eggs. Fortunately, Miss Weathersby was scheduled to retire at the end of the year, and he moved the staff to real tears over the prospects of her ending forty years of faithful service without one yearbook dedication to her credit. They capitulated and wrote her a prayerlike dedication that got their principal off the hook and convinced Miss Weathersby that she deserved it.

The days grew shorter and colder, and the parents got angrier. The angriest were those who had been ringleaders in trying to terminate Miss Strickland's contract but couldn't complain about how much algebra their children were learning. Actually, they were learning more algebra than economics, history, civics and English literature combined. Purdy Robinson said he'd never understand how his boy could learn to multiply all those x's and y's and still not know how to make change from a dollar bill.

At Thanksgiving, Gussie went to visit her grandmother in Dalhart.

School continued, and the angry parents waited for Gussie to take a misstep, to make a false move, to drop a careless remark that would give her away. They waited in vain. Gussie was wearing them out.

At Christmastime, she went home to visit her parents in Kilgore.

The New Year got under way and still no one had confronted Gussie to accuse her of overexposure in Dallas. She still had not volunteered a single word about the Dallas Fair and her individual role in making it such a huge success. If a poll had been taken, it might have revealed that Gussie Strickland was the only person within the city limits who was never heard to utter one syllable about the Dallas Fair. The people felt cheated.

At Eastertime, Gussie went to visit a sorority sister in Corsicana.

The Dallas Fair began to make some people sick at their stomachs.

As school reconvened and went into its final stretch, people reviewed the extraordinary events of the year. Among the items to come under scrutiny was Gussie Strickland's new and revised pattern of vacations. At Thanksgiving, Christmas and Easter she had done this unusual thing of visiting family, relatives and friends. What had changed her? Why had she stopped chasing around alone?

They chewed on that one for a while but not with much heart. After much sifting and weighing of evidence, they concluded that she had turned over a new leaf. Reluctantly and with an acute sense of loss, they settled back and tried to adjust to the new drabness in algebra teachers. They would have made the adjustment in fine shape, too, but summer rolled around and Gussie threw them another curve.

She went on *a hiking tour of Europe!*

In a manner of speaking, it was good to have Gussie back in form again. It revived some sagging interest in the Beaux Arts Ball, but not much. The people discovered that the horse had died, and beating it was no fun. Besides, other events engaged their attention. The Texan Theatre burned to the ground. The Wilhoit sisters swapped husbands. Rhoda Fryer reformed (temporarily). A truck spilled forty-two crates of fresh eggs on Main Street. Wallis Simpson married the King. A tornado blew the roof off the Fort Worth & Denver depot. Christmas Tree Johnson married a Holy Roller preacher. Bank Night went up to $515. And Calvin Turnbough got ptomaine poisoning in his own cafe.

At the end of the summer, Gussie returned from her European hiking trip and told everyone all about her adventures. A few suspicions were aroused at her frequent mention of a young Yugoslavian cello player, but they didn't amount to much. The Beaux Arts Ball as a conversational topic was dead.

Gussie left town at the end of that school year to marry a wholesale distributor from Houston. Nobody knew anything about him, and it was never clear what he distributed. It was assumed that he distributed something peculiar, else Gussie wouldn't have given him a second glance. They heard that he was twenty-five, fifty-five, and seventy-five years old; that he was a millionaire, a billionaire, a pauper on relief; that he had been married once, twice and three times. Gussie never brought him to town, so no one had an opportunity to interview him and confirm or deny anything.

As far as any one knows, she never pursued her dancing career any further, at the Dallas Fair or elsewhere. Her admirers—and despite the talk, they outnumbered her detractors

—did not really expect her to become another Sally Rand or Ginger Rogers. After all, dancing in the Beaux Arts Ball had been just another of her individual ways of spending her vacation. There was no more reason for her to repeat the experience than for her to go back to Central America or Seattle or any of those places where nobody else had ever been.

To this good day, it's easy to set off an argument about whether or not that was Gussie Strickland in the bright green mask with the upswept edges and gold beads hanging from the bottom. The town is still divided. Some think it was she and some think it was not. But they are doomed to live out their days uncertain and wondering, which when they get to thinking about it makes them so mad they nearly bust. But you can't tell if they're mad because she was in the Beaux Arts Ball and wouldn't admit it, or because she was not in the Beaux Arts Ball and let them think she was.

8.

꘎

Ben Hodges' Last Trip

For thirty-one years, Ben Hodges had been a rural mail carrier, and in all that time, his routine had varied no more than his route. Each morning he parked his automobile behind the post office, went inside to sort his mail, trade small talk with the other employees and bring himself up to date on new regulations or changes that might affect his work. Outside again, he arranged the letters in tidy bundles on the front seat of his car and spread the papers, magazines and packages across the seat in the rear. After a final look around to make certain he had forgotten nothing, he pulled out from behind the post office onto Third Street and drove two blocks east, turned right on Court House Square, drove south on Main Street past Walter Tully's place, the last house on the street, turned right on Old Loop Road, and drove two miles to where the road split and formed a big Y. His route lay over the right fork, nine miles to the west, six miles south, eight miles east, then back into town on Main Street again.

During the entire thirty-one years, Ben lived in the same house (on Ninth Street), went to the same church (First

Baptist), carried the same watch (an Elgin), had his hair cut at the same barbershop (the Bon-Ton), took his car to the same mechanic at the same garage (the Model Garage), and visited the same friends on the same streets in front of the same stores on Saturday afternoons and nights. Purdy Robinson, who had lived next door to the Hodgeses for twenty-seven of those years, could not understand why Ben didn't go crazy doing the same things day in and day out.

"For one thing, I've got two married daughters and two married sons and nine grandchildren living right here in this town," Ben explained again and again. "You can't get bored raising four kids, and even if you did, I'll guarantee you that you won't get bored watching them raise *their* kids. Anyway, don't forget, Purdy, I've got a traveling job. I don't have to stay in the same place all day every day like you do."

"That's what I'm talking about," said Purdy, who had owned and operated Robinson's Hardware Store in the same location on Main Street for twenty-three years. "You go out on the same route, drive over the same roads, pass the same farms, and if the truth was known, put mail in the same mailboxes. Why, I'll bet some of the farmers have still got the same mailboxes they had when you started on that route."

Ben laughed. "As a matter of fact, one of them does," he said. "Clay Quisenberry, out past Shradersburg schoolhouse, has been patching up that same mailbox ever since I can remember. He solders up the holes and wires the door back on when the wind tears it off. The thing you got to remember, Purdy, is that driving over the same roads all the time, you get to see the land change from season to season and from year to year. Why, there's a stand of scrub oak on top of a low ridge on my south leg that's just as nice and pretty as any stand of trees around here, I guess. And do you know, I can remember when the top of that ridge was as bald as Booby Duckworth's head. It's kind of interesting to watch a whole section of mesquite get cleared off for planting and put into feed or cotton. And it's just as interesting to see one of the farmers turn a patch of land back to grazing. I'll bet you don't have any idea how long it takes to turn a cultivated field back into a pasture. A lot longer than the other way round, believe me."

"Maybe so," said Purdy with resignation. "But personally, I don't see how you can stand it."

"Well, now, if you want to put it that way, staying in one place like you do every day, year in and year out—that would drive me crazy."

"But I'm always seeing different people, Ben. You might not realize it, but people don't go to a hardware store as often as they go to a grocery store or drug store. People might go two or three weeks or two months without coming in the store at all. But you deliver mail to the same people all the time."

"No, I don't," Ben said. "They get old and die and grow up and get married and move away. Some of them stay put, though. I've got couples on my route right now with three and four kids, and I can remember when *their* parents got married. The names on the mailbox might be the same, but the people are different. It's kind of interesting to watch how some of them fix up the old family place and how some of them let the places run down. The Clark boy built himself a new house in front of his daddy's old one. He's busy tearing down the old place right now. He was down at the mailbox the other day. 'When are you coming up and inspect my new place, Mr. Hodges?' he asked me, and I said, 'Oh, I've been intending to for a long time now, but it looks like I've been running behind ever since you got it finished.' I've got to do that before long."

Purdy said he guessed Ben could go over every mile of his route with his eyes closed, and Ben said he guessed he could at that. Unless there was another washout on Miley's Creek, like once before when he had to go back to the highway and come up on the route from the other side. He didn't get home until dark that day. He got lost in a dust storm once, too, but not for long. Only long enough to end up in Wilmer Thatcher's front yard. He never mentioned it to anyone; it was too embarrassing.

Not Purdy Robinson nor anyone else could ever persuade Ben Hodges into becoming bored or dissatisfied with his rural mail route. He held to the idea that he was the link that connected farm to farm along his twenty-three miles, even though a family toward one end of the route might feel no connection whatsoever with a family on the other. Even so, there had been a time when he was a dependable communication cable that ran from farm to farm. He had delivered messages and invitations, relayed questions and answers and passed on information and gossip, but those days had passed. Everybody drove automobiles nowadays; the roads had been paved or blacktopped; and the telephone connected the people with a closeness that Ben's services could never equal. But he continued to perform little personal services for them, nevertheless.

Sometimes he picked up a child who had loitered too long and caught him up with the school bus at its next stop. He never refused a ride to a housewife who might be waiting at the mailbox on the chance that she might catch a lift to the next farm. He had never served as midwife, but he came close to it when he fetched the doctor from a nearby farm that had no telephone. In his day, he had delivered preachers to funerals, grooms to their weddings, teachers to their classes, baby chicks to their mothers, and once he even took a man to jail. Ben's wife thought he was running things into the ground, however, the day he overtook Joe Cranston's old bird dog trotting alongside the road and gave him a ride home, three miles away.

"That dog was *hot!*" Ben said. "If you could of seen how he stopped and turned around when he heard the car—just like a hitchhiker—the durndest thing you ever saw!"

When rationed out over a space of thirty-one years, you could not say that such events made mail-carrying an exciting job, but that didn't mean that nothing exciting had ever happened. He would never forget the problem of old Mrs. Elmdorf.

Her place lay just beyond the Y, over a gentle rise in the land that crossed the horizon like a crumpled bed sheet. It was the first stop on Ben's route. As he turned onto the right fork of the Y, he always looked ahead expectantly, waiting for the top of her windmill to peep up at him over the ridge, to be followed by the tip of her roof; then, as he climbed the gentle slope, he watched the house rise from the ground, first the eaves, then the top of her windows, then the faded shutters, until he reached the low summit, and there it was, a full-grown house, complete with sun-baked yard, scraggly trees, a wire fence, and the outbuildings beyond. At the bottom of the slope on the other side of the ridge, he pulled over to Mrs. Elmdorf's mailbox, and his workday had begun.

Mrs. Elmdorf lived alone, renting her farm on shares to an endless succession of down-and-out itinerants who occupied a two-room shack back of the barn. They stayed for as long as they could tolerate their landlady's crotchety ways and impossible fits of temper; then they moved on to be replaced by others. She was the one person on the route whom Ben disliked. He disliked her waiting at the mailbox to complain about an overdue package, or to hand him a letter with the money but no stamps and strict instructions to bring her the change the next day. With scrawny hands that resembled buzzard's claws and a face as pinched and dried up as the land she lived on, she wasn't much bigger than a fence post, and she was certainly as weatherbeaten. But what she lacked in size, she made up for in unpleasantness. She never smiled; her eyes were never bright nor happy; she never had a kind word for anybody. She was especially cantankerous with Ben, whom she treated as her personal body servant.

"Where's my Montgomery Ward catalogue?" she demanded of him one morning in Ben's twenty-sixth year on the route.

"Hasn't come in yet, Mrs. Elmdorf," he said pleasantly.

"Bring it tomorrow," she snapped. She turned abruptly and hopped like a bantam hen back up the road toward her house.

The next morning she was waiting.

"I thought I told you to bring me my catalogue," she cackled.

"The Wards still haven't come in," he explained. "Sears came in last week, but no Wards—and I can't bring it if I haven't got it."

By the following morning she had worked herself into a temper, and on the fourth day she was angry enough for a stroke. She handed him a letter.

"This letter is gonna git you fired," she said, "and I better not hear of you not mailing it, either!"

He looked at the envelope. It was addressed to President Hoover, Austin, Texas.

On the fifth day, she was waiting again. "Did you mail my letter?" she asked.

"Sure did. It'd be against the law not to."

"Did you bring my catalogue?"

"Still hasn't come in yet, Mrs. Elmdorf. You've got to be patient. I'll bring it as soon as I get it."

"I'm giving you one last chance, Ben Hodges," she said. "If you don't bring my catalogue tomorrow, me and you's gonna have trouble. I'm a-warning you!"

Bright and early on the sixth day, Ben drove over the ridge to find her waiting at the mailbox, this time with a 20-gauge shotgun in her hand.

Ben pulled to a stop, fighting off an impulse to throw the car into gear and move on.

"Where's my catalogue?" she demanded. Her eyes were blazing.

"I'm real sorry, Mrs. Elmdorf, but it didn't come in today." He was trying to control his excitement.

She raised the shotgun to her shoulder and leveled it at him.

"I tole you yestiddy that me and you was gonna have trouble," she mumbled into the stock of the gun. "This thing is loaded, and I aim to use it."

"Now wait a minute—"

She squinted one eye. "I been listenin' to your alibis long enough," she said. She fumbled with the safety catch.

"Now you look here, Mrs. Elmdorf!" Ben shouted. He opened the door and fell out onto the ground. He banged the door shut and crouched low out of sight. "Don't you know you can get put in jail for aiming a gun at people?" he called out. "Now you put that gun down and go on back up to the house and behave yourself!"

He peeped around the front of the car.

Mrs. Elmdorf was winking into the sight, correcting her aim. Ben drew back.

"Mrs. Elmdorf!"

She fired.

Ben hugged the side of the car, his heart racing. He waited for a second shot. It never came. Instead, he heard a low groan. Again he peeped around the front end of the car. The old lady lay sprawled out on the hard ground, the shotgun off to one side in the dust. Ben stood up and came around the car. He hurried to her side.

"Are you hurt?" he asked, bending over her.

"The durned thing kicked me in the shoulder," she muttered.

She struggled to her feet. Ben helped her; then he took the gun from the ground and put it in the back seat of his car.

"Do you want a ride up to the house?" he inquired, turning back to her. She was brushing herself off.

"I don't want no ride up to no house!" she said savagely. "I got down here by myself, and I reckon I can get back the same way!"

"I've got a good mind to turn you in to Artie Whelan! You haven't got any business out here with a gun pointing it at people. Don't you know you could've killed me?"

She searched the ground for the gun. "What did you think I was trying to do?" she asked.

"Don't you know you would've gone to jail if you'd of shot me?"

"You're the one that belongs in jail!" she raged. Whereupon she turned and darted up the dirt road toward her house, rubbing her skinny shoulder as she went.

Ben gave the gun to Artie and urged him to go out and see about the old lady, her being so dangerous with that gun and all. But he didn't want to press charges against her. He merely thought she should not be allowed to keep a gun in the house.

Artie spent two hours at Mrs. Elmdorf's; the first trying to get inside, and the second searching the house without letting her know what he was doing. He reported to Ben afterwards.

"I'm pretty sure she doesn't have another gun on the place," he said. "But if I was you, Mr. Hodges, I'd dig up a Ward's catalogue from somewhere and take it to her. It might cool her down."

Ben took his own catalogue down to Riley's Grocery & Market for Dice Riley to wrap in brown paper. Jack Goodnight at the Post Office typed a label and pasted it on. You couldn't tell unless you looked at the date on the cover or noticed that an order blank had been torn out of the back that it was not a new issue.

The problem of Mrs. Elmdorf was an exception. For the most part, there was nothing distinctive about Ben's job. Anyone could have done it and probably as well. He drove the route day after day, year after year, with little to mark one day as opposed to another. So automatically and unthinkingly did he move from mailbox to mailbox that frequently he would cover two thirds of the route with no conscious recollection of having done it. He sang, talked to himself, yelled at dogs that wandered out into the road, dodged chickens, carried on imaginary dialogues with farmers along the way, and rehearsed benedictions when he figured it was about time for Brother Wallace to call on him at Sunday night services again. He installed a radio in his car, but after the novelty wore off, he seldom turned it on. He was accustomed to silence. When it happened, as it sometimes did, that no one along the twenty-three miles was waiting at his mailbox, he completed the entire circuit without opening his mouth. But silent or not, he had no more trouble passing the time on that mail route than he did in his own house when it was spilling over with children and grandchildren. Ben and his rural mail route were parts of each other. He was a happy man.

That was why, when time caught up with him, he balked at the idea of retirement.

"I don't need to retire," he complained. "I can still see. I can still drive the car. I've never had an accident in the whole time I've been on the route, except that one time when I slid into a ditch—and even that didn't hurt anything. Just scared me a little. As long as I'm fit and healthy and can read the addresses on the mail, I don't see why I've got to quit. I just want to keep on doing what I'm doing."

The Civil Service rules and regulations, however, allowed

for no exceptions that would fit Ben's situation.

"Looks to me like you'd enjoy being retired," Purdy Robinson consoled him. "You can sleep late, work in the yard, spend a lot of time with your grandchildren, go fishing—just about anything you want to do. I wish I could retire like you're doing. The things I wouldn't do!"

"You don't understand, Purdy!" Ben answered. "You never have. I don't like to sleep late. I'm an early riser—always have been, and I always will be. I work in the yard already. I go fishing when I feel like it. I get home at two-thirty and three o'clock every day, with Sundays and Federal holidays off, and I probably spend more time with my grandchildren than most people get to do. Mail carriers' hours are the best in the world for leading your own life. I do everything I want to do and when I want to do it. Now I don't need full time off to do what I've been doing all my life, do I?"

Mrs. Hodges tried to pacify her husband and reconcile him to what lay ahead. She had small success.

"It'll work itself out," she said. "But you've got to give it a chance. Naturally, it will take some adjusting on your part. Mine, too, for that matter, because to tell the truth, I'm as used to your being gone all day as you are. But I'm looking forward to having you around, and I don't see why you can't take the same attitude."

He tried, but with little enthusiasm. Before retirement day, they made minor repairs on the house, replaced the living-room rug, bought a new kitchen range, repapered the bedrooms and put new screen on the back porch. They traded their automobile for a new one, which they figured would last them for the rest of their lives.

"What do you want to do by way of celebration?" asked his wife as the day drew nearer.

"I don't feel much like celebrating," he replied.

"But we've got to do something. This is a milestone, and

we can't let it go by without marking it with some kind of celebration."

"I don't know. I hadn't thought much about that part of it. I guess about the best thing is to have all the kids come for dinner, but we do that all the time anyway. I don't know what would be so special about that."

"We'll make it special," said she, seizing on the idea. "We'll have a regular retirement celebration when you come in off the route for the last time. We'll have dinner in the middle of the afternoon the same as if it was Christmas or Thanksgiving."

"But the boys have to work! They can't be taking off in the middle of the day like that—all on my account!"

"Yes, they can. This is a special occasion, and they can make arrangements to take off like people do for special occasions. That will make it more like a celebration than ever to have all of them here in the middle of the afternoon in the middle of the week."

"Won't that look kind of funny?"

"It's supposed to look different, Ben! It's not supposed to be like any other day. Now here's what we'll do. . . ."

She outlined a plan which took shape as she talked about it. Dinner would be at four o'clock. That would allow Ben the time to visit along the route and also extra time back in the post office for a special good-bye. As she saw it, the celebration would lose some of its flavor and miss its point unless the dinner was on retirement day itself, not the day before nor the day after. What's more, it would be doubly important that the dinner take place when Ben came in off the route, at the end of that last trip when he hung up his mailbag forever.

Ben agreed, and she went to the telephone to call the children. They fell in eagerly with her plans.

Came the last day, and the sky was as murky as Ben's own gray mood. Mrs. Hodges walked out the back door with her husband, anxiously examining the sky as they crossed the yard.

"Oh, dear! I was hoping the sun would shine!" she exclaimed. "But it doesn't look like it will." She followed Ben through the gate and out onto the driveway. "Well—I hope it doesn't rain anyway," she went on. "Not on your last day! I was hoping you'd have a pretty day—bright, clear and real nice for your last trip."

"It's not going to rain," Ben reassured her, opening the garage door. He stepped back and looked out across the top of Purdy Robinson's back fence. "This is just an overcast—it's too high for rain. See all that haze?" He pointed to the distance where the earth and sky came together. "When it's like that, it won't rain. It'll be like this all day, though. You won't be able to see the sun. But it won't rain."

She waited by the driveway as he backed the new automobile out of the garage. When he came abreast of her, he stopped and leaned out the window to kiss her good-bye. As he put the car in motion again, she reminded him of the schedule.

"Be sure and watch the time." she said. "Don't get to visiting too long and too much. You can go back out next week and the next and visit as long as you like, but today we're having dinner at four o'clock sharp when you finish your last run. The children will all be here by then, and the boys will have to go back to work afterwards. So don't be late."

She waved at him as he drove off on that last day, just as she had waved at him on the first, thirty-one years earlier. Then she went back inside to attend to the dinner that she had started to prepare early that morning.

At the post office, Jack Goodnight and the others neglected their own work to watch Ben sort his mail and to give him a big send-off. He had taken the new carrier over the route earlier in the week so he could have the last few days to himself. Except for the elaborate preparations at home and the special farewells at the post office, his last day on the job started like any other.

He pulled out of the alley behind the post office and onto Third Street. He drove two blocks east, turned right on Court House Square, drove south on Main Street past Walter Tully's place, turned right on Old Loop Road, and drove two miles to where the road split into a big Y.

Then a strange thing happened

After thirty-one years on the same mail route, Ben Hodges forgot the way.

Nothing had changed. Nothing had been added nor taken away from the landscape since the day before. The triangle formed by the intersection and framed by the barbed-wire fence was as familiar as the whiskers on his face. Beyond lay the rise in the land, stretching across the horizon like a crumpled bed sheet. More than six thousand times he had approached this same intersection, each time taking the right fork as automatically and unthinkingly as he drew air into his lungs, but now the mechanism that had operated him had somehow ceased to function. Abruptly, as though he had flipped a switch, everything inside him stopped running.

He had no idea which fork to take.

His mind played tricks on him. He knew that over and beyond that gentle rise, Mrs. Elmdorf's place sat unchanged from yesterday and the week and the month before. He could see her mailbox atop its lean cedar post at the edge of the shallow ditch alongside the road; he could see the rutted, hard dirt lane hemmed in by barbed wire running up to her gaunt house, the scraggly trees and pitiful swatches of lank shrubbery in her yard, the wire fence that tied it all together. He could see the windmill facing into the stiff breeze, the shabby two-room shack down behind the unpainted barn, the blacktopped road stretching on past her farm and out of sight over the next low rise in the distance. He saw it all, but what he could not see was which fork of the road, the right or the left, could lead him to it.

He could see each house and mailbox along the route. He saw every turn, every twist, every jog in the road. He knew exactly where the road was worn, where it was rough, where it had been patched, and where it needed smoothing over. He could even count the telephone poles between that short, stumpy one two miles past the Shradersburg schoolhouse and the one that leaned at a forty-five-degree angle just this side of Miley's Creek. There was nothing along that route that he could not see as clearly as he saw the windshield in front of his face.

But he didn't know how to get to it.

The low ridge stretched across the land, from right to left, from left to right, as far as he could see, and he sat there studying it without even the sun to give it shadows or him a clue. If only he could drive part of the way to the top of the ridge, far enough to see the tip of old Mrs. Elmdorf's windmill peeping up at him, then everything would fall into place. But which fork of the road should he take for that one tiny peek? He sat for a few minutes stunned into inaction, bewildered and frightened. At that moment, he would have given all he possessed for that one tiny glimpse of the top of Mrs. Elmdorf's windmill.

Collecting himself and thinking to remedy the strange malfunction, he turned around and drove back into town, this time not to the post office, but around Court House Square, from where he started anew. He drove south on Main Street, searching carefully for signs of change along the way to justify or at least explain his curious loss of memory. Past Walter Tully's on Main Street, he turned right on Old Loop Road, trying not to think, trying not to figure it out, hoping that by not bringing it into focus, he could bring it in sharp and clear.

The Y came into view, and he did his best to shut out all that had happened the first time. He approached the intersection with a burst of speed, but as he drew near, he lifted his foot from the accelerator and coasted to a halt.

Again he did not know which way to go.

Reason told him to take either fork, and if it should be the wrong choice, to turn around, come back to the Y and take the other. But he was unwilling to risk being wrong. For reasons that edged close to his consciousness but not close enough to crystallize, nothing terrified him more than the prospect of driving to the top of that ridge and not finding Mrs. Elmdorf's farm on the other side.

He stared at the barbed-wire fences and the tangle of tumbleweeds that framed the fork of the Y, unable to think. Then he turned the car around and headed back into town once more, this time with no purpose, no plan, no goal, no reason for going back. He went back only because he didn't know how to go ahead. He knew that he could return tomorrow or the next day or the next week and drive the entire route to figure it out and to reassure himself. But he also knew with a sickening awareness that he could never alter the circumstance that after six thousand trips, the last one had defeated him; the one trip he had not wanted to make but which would crown thirty-one years of honorable service, nevertheless, had somehow been denied him.

He drove in on south Main Street, crushed by a sense of failure, gnawed at by the guilt of a job unfinished, sad that he didn't even get the chance to tell all the people good-bye.

With his mind a turmoil of shock, confusion and bewilderment, he stumbled through the rear door of the post office and tossed his mailbag onto the sorting table, too dazed to notice how Jack Goodnight stared at him, then at the clock on the wall and the bag of undelivered mail. He felt old, and feeling old wore him down with a strange sadness.

"You feeling bad, Mr. Hodges?" Jack asked.

"No—not really," Ben said softly, not looking at him. "I'm not sure how I feel—I'm not sure at all. . . ."

Then without another word, he walked out of the post office, got into his car and drove home, his life's work completed.

Mrs. Hodges was bending into the open oven basting the turkey when her husband came through the kitchen door. Alarmed as well as surprised, she rushed to meet him, thinking he might be ill. Something on his face, however, stayed her tongue, and she asked him nothing. On his face, she saw hurt, defeat and a kind of wistfulness. She saw him look at her with a childlike pleading for understanding.

"I forgot the way," he said simply.

He stepped around her and on through the house into the bedroom, where he emptied his pockets onto the chest of drawers and lay down across the bed. Mrs. Hodges followed him as far as the door and stood silently until he had stretched out and settled himself.

"Ben, can I get you something?"

He shook his head.

"Do you think maybe I ought to call Dr. Beasley?"

"No—I'm not sick," he replied. He stared at the ceiling. "I just couldn't remember. . . ."

She stood in the doorway for a moment. She opened her mouth to ask him more; then thinking better of it left the room and closed the door softly behind her.

Ben continued to stare at the ceiling, trying to rearrange the pieces of his mind to cover that awful nothingness. He tried to rethink the morning step by step, but the images flitted in and out haphazardly, refusing to follow one another in sensible sequence. Time stood still, or it jumped ahead. It rushed forward, then fell backwards with crazy abandon. He threw an arm across his face and tried to shut out the morning and all that he could not remember. And he tried to shut out the coming celebration. He didn't know how he could face it. On the other hand, he didn't know how he could wait three or fours hours for it either. . . . Maybe he dozed. Maybe he dreamed. Maybe he fell into a sound, deep sleep. Maybe he remained awake. He didn't know. . . .

Later—and he had no idea how much later—his wife came to the door and called him to dinner.

"Golly! I didn't know it was *that* time," he said, swinging his feet onto the floor. "You ought not to have let me lay here all day like this."

"Well, it hasn't been exactly all day."

"Are all the kids here?" He rubbed his eyes and reached for his shoes.

"Yes, they're all here, and they're waiting for you."

He started a yawn and stopped in the middle of it. "Listen. Don't tell them I didn't make the trip," he said.

"Oh," she said, with a questioning—and then an understanding—look. "All right."

"I didn't hear them come in."

"I told them to be quiet so they wouldn't bother you."

He got to his feet and smiled. "That was nice," he said. "For some reason, I don't feel hungry," he added.

"You will when you see the dinner," she said brightly. "Freshen up and come on." She watched him for a moment, returned his smile and left the room. In the bathroom, he washed his face with cold water, patted his thinning hair into place and straightened his clothes. Then he went into the dining room.

His sons and daughters, their husbands and wives, and his own wife were standing behind their chairs at the table, smiling and waiting for the guest of honor to take his place at the head. The card tables had been set up in the living room for the children, who were dancing in and out of the dining room watching their grandfather with an excitement they could not hide. Mrs. Hodges stepped away from her chair and took her husband by the hand to lead him to the big armchair at the other end of the table.

"What's all this?" he exclaimed, throwing up his hands in a gesture of surprise and helplessness. The children's giggles broke into snickers then exploded into laughter, full and loud.

Heaped high by his plate was a mountain of happily wrapped packages, all shapes and all sizes.

"Do you mean you all brought me *presents?*" His eyes widened. The children's squeals grew louder.

"How in the world can anybody get Christmas presents in September?" he asked. He winked at the children. "I'll bet you thought it was my birthday!" he added.

"They're your retirement presents, Granddaddy!" they shouted. "Open them! You've got to open every one of them before you can have any turkey!"

The adults sat down. The children crowded around their grandfather with cries of "Open this one first!" One at a time, he removed the paper and ribbons from the packages. There were socks, neckties, cuff links, a comb and brush set, house slippers, and the most unexpected gift of all, a desk barometer framed in silver and set in polished walnut the color of chocolate candy. Enclosed was a card signed by every family along his twenty-three mile mail route.

"Even old Mrs. Elmdorf!" he exclaimed in disbelief, too overcome to say more.

"It's been in the house for a week," said Mrs. Hodges. "That Clark boy's wife brought it in. They thought about waylaying you at the Shradersburg schoolhouse and having some kind of coffee-and-cake party, but they couldn't get everybody together at the same time, so this seemed like the best idea."

Some little thing flitted into his mind and out again before he could ever form the thought that he never would have reached the Shradersburg schoolhouse. . . . He opened the remaining packages, surprised and delighted with each card, each gift, while his grandchildren whooped and hollered and their parents echoed appreciatively. By the time the girls had cleared away the paper and ribbons and Mrs. Hodges had brought in the turkey, the disturbing event out at the Y had faded into nothing worth remembering, and Ben lost himself in the spirit of his retirement celebration.

The dinner was as successful as Mrs. Hodges had determined it would be. It was an occasion that none of them would ever forget. With the turkey roasted to a burnished gold, there was chestnut dressing, giblet gravy, creamed corn, butter beans, apple and nut salad, cranberry sauce, hot biscuits dripping with sweet butter, and mincemeat pie topped with great globs of whipped cream.

Afterwards, Ben leaned back in his chair and sighed happily. "I don't remember ever eating so much at one time in my life," he said.

"Why don't you go lie down and take a nap, Papa?" one of his daughters suggested.

"I've been lying down long enough," he said. "Anyway, I can't very well run out on my own retirement celebration, can I?"

"Sure you can," said one of his sons. "I don't see any reason to retire if you can't do what you want to do, and taking a nap strikes me as just about the best kind of celebration there is—after all this dinner Mama served us."

"You might be right," he said. "And I am kind of drowsy —too much to eat, I guess." He loosened his belt a notch and pushed back from the table. "But before I go lay down, let me tell all of you that this is just about the best retirement celebration anybody ever had. All you boys taking off from work just so you could come eat dinner like this in my honor, and all you girls coming over here to help your mother fix this regular Christmas dinner here in the middle of September."

He turned to his wife.

"Of all the dinners you ever cooked," he said, "I guess this one was the best of all. And I *know* that was the best turkey you ever put on this table. I don't see how you got it so tender and so much flavor in it."

Mrs. Hodges smiled. "Thank goodness, I put it in the oven last night before we went to bed, and when I got up this morning, all I had to do was baste it a little and brown the outside."

"There wasn't much for us to do when we got here," said a daughter. "About all that was left to do was make the salad and whip the cream and set the table."

"Mama must have been up all night cooking," said another.

"Well, I did try to get a head start, so I wouldn't have to stay in the kitchen all day," Mrs. Hodges admitted. "I made the corn bread for the dressing yesterday—like I always do at Christmas and Thanksgiving. I put the beans on as soon as I got out of bed so the time wouldn't slip up on me. I intended to cook them regular, but I ended up using the pressure cooker, because it's faster, and I needed the burners. Everything else just seemed to fall into place."

Ben winked at the children. "All those presents you brought me is what *really* made it seem like Christmas. I don't know what in the world I can ever ask Santa Claus to bring me now!"

While the children laughed and everybody talked at once, Ben went off into the bedroom, took off his shoes and stretched out on the bed for the second time that day, grateful that no member of his family had been ungracious enough to question why he had come home early and the retirement celebration had been rescheduled. His mind wandered out to Old Loop Road and the intersection at the Y, and quite unconsciously he saw himself taking the right fork over the ridge and down the other side to Mrs. Elmdorf's mailbox. So natural and familiar was the vision that he did not realize that a correction had been made.

Ben Hodges was the most fortunate man alive.

As he felt himself getting drowsy, he turned toward the bed table to see what time it was. The clock was gone.

"I guess one of the kids has been playing with it again," he mumbled half aloud.

He could see the thin edge of his Elgin watch with the gold chain crumpled around it on the chest of drawers. For an instant, he had an impulse to get up and check the time, but he let it pass. It was too easy not to move . . . the pillow was so soft . . . he felt warm . . . drowsy . . . happy. . . . He straightened himself out on the bed and fell asleep.

And it was just as well that he did, for had Ben Hodges looked at his watch, he would have seen that it said two o'clock and would have been reminded that his retirement celebration was over and done with all of two hours earlier than his wife had originally planned to start it. He didn't feel quite right about upsetting her carefully planned schedule, but Mrs. Hodges didn't mind.

"I knew your daddy would never sleep until four o'clock," she explained to the children after their father had left the room, "so I moved the dinner ahead, thinking it would be good for him to get caught up in the celebration as soon as possible instead of wandering around the house brooding and worrying about not making his last trip. Something went wrong with your daddy out there today, and I don't know what it was. I didn't bother him about it when he came in, and I never intend to ask him about it, for whatever it was is all right now. The main thing is that your daddy had his retirement celebration, and none of us would have missed it for the world. He can go back tomorrow and tell everyone good-bye."

But Ben didn't do that. He did not go back out on the route the next day nor the next to tell anyone good-bye. He waited two or three weeks and drove over the entire twenty-three miles to tell everyone hello. It was more pleasant that way.